# CROSSING THE RIVER CALLED SUFFERING

Patricia Engelking

This book was a cathartic experience of the caterpillar to the butterfly. My journey was hard and painful for a very long time. Through my choices, life events and priorities, change had to happen for my survival. Like a caged wild animal released into a world that was plentiful, bounteous, and exciting, I ventured into an exploration of my sexuality and ultimately my value as a woman.

Given the nature of sexual exploration, it is to be expected that you will encounter many explicit tales as I navigate fetishes, BDSM, swinging, and more. My story was about experimentation and reflection, not making the same mistakes, and understanding the power exchange between people.

Dedicated to

Queenbee70 and MNJohnny24/7
and the Twenty-Year Plan

*Some people survive and talk about it. Some people survive and go silent. Some people survive and create. Everyone deals with unimaginable pain in their own way, and everyone is entitled to that without judgment. So, the next time you look at someone's life covetously, remember…you may not want to endure what they are enduring right now, at this moment, whilst they sit so quietly before you, looking like a calm ocean on a sunny day. Remember how vast the ocean's boundaries are. Whilst somewhere the water is calm, in another place in the very same ocean, there is a colossal storm.*

*~ Nikita Gill*

# Chapter 1

"I need to go to my sister's." I said frantically. I needed to leave. I couldn't stay one more day, I needed to run far away. I didn't even consider the heat. June was an odd time to want to visit Florida. I'd have to tell her why I wanted, no, needed to come down. This was so out of nowhere. I started packing before I even talked to her. If she said no I would use her as an excuse to leave and just drive and drive and drive until I ran out of resources. It made me think...what was I going to do when I got there? What happens next?

My sister lives in Florida, I had been there once before for her wedding. That was a happy time for her, the dress, the beach, the heat, our father in his navy-blue Hawaiian shirt walking her down the aisle. I was not happy. I hadn't been for a very long time. Decades in fact. Katie had no idea how unhappy I was today when I called her. I was desperate.

Katie and I had never been close, we grew up at odds. Our fractured sibling bond was facilitated by my parents and their faltering marriage. We were split like property, like assets in mediation. I naturally gravitated to my father, the "son" he never had in a little girl's body. I was fascinated by nature and learning and doing. My sister was not as easy for my father to entertain at the time of their union's demise, four years younger than me and a handful as most second born are, my sister was assigned to my mom.

When our parents fought, we were often sources of contention, opposing magnetic fields drawn together yet forced apart. The tension between my mother and father was palpable and came out sideways between my sister and me.

I needed my sister, the woman that I was genetically linked to and hardly liked. I only knew bits and pieces of what her life was like these days. Our Mom would fill me in from time to time, but it was a no ask no tell situation. My sister was opinionated and out spoken about her feelings, especially about my situation.

We didn't talk much, randomly at best. No checking in, no happy holidays, we kind of existed without real thought or care of one another. She lived her life and I lived mine. She was an irritant to me with her seemingly perfect life. I was an irritant to her with my pathetic existence, she wouldn't say that *to me*, just my mom.

I joke about us being opposites, but it is truth. She lived South and I was North, she was thin and a runner I was heavy since I was thirteen and walking caused chaffing. I had four children and she didn't have any. She is more of an introvert and deals with people on her terms, I am an extrovert and love to experience people and places in the moment.

She went to college and became a teacher after many years of school, fun and traveling. She married a man that was interesting and intelligent and had the patience of a saint, he had to being married to her. She lived up and down the East Coast but settled in the Everglades Basin and went to the beach all the time. She went to warmth, ironic because I believed she was a very cold person. She needed the sun, it made her happy. Maybe I needed the sun in Florida too. Was the sun different South of the Border than the sun in New Jersey in June?

I anticipated that Katie would ask why I wasn't asking Maggie for help. For the longest time now, she referred to our mother by her first name. It was very disrespectful in my opinion and in some weird way I felt like it was an antagonistic move. My bratty sister was equalizing herself to the level of a friend or neighbor, elevating herself from being below the woman that bore her in hierarchy.

I was sure this was a coping skill for her ego, she was still very mad at my mother for the challenges put on her as a child. Katie was greatly affected by our father during her younger years. He had a booming voice and was very no nonsense. Katie was like a submissive puppy trying to please but was hiding behind my mom's legs, wetting her bed, and developed a stutter.

Twenty-seven years later, I had settled close to my mother, only twenty minutes away, not far enough for me to get the space I needed now. He would follow me. I had gone to her before, never overnight. Going to your Mom about issues with a controlling boyfriend or husband is a dangerous trail to walk. A mother's natural tendencies are to pace and protect. I didn't want that for her. I was supposed to be strong enough.

I needed her to understand that there are things that she doesn't know about this charming fool that fixes her VCR for her, which elevated him to a knight in shining armor. I think she felt out of place trying to empower me. It was too late.

"Mom help me!" my eyes would cry out while making excuses for his behavior. She didn't see it. I learned not to share too much over time. I'd try to defend him to save an interrogation from either side. He was constantly concerned with people conspiring about him and he would tell me it was my fault for painting such a shitty picture of him as a person.

When I did share with my mom I'd often get lectures about money. Money affected her most, she felt obligated to bail us out for the grandkid's sake. It was embarrassing. I wonder if she had regretted leaving my Dad because she seemed determined for me to make things work with my worse half. I didn't want to worry her any more than I already had. She knew nothing of my thought life these days. This wasn't her problem.

From the age eighteen, I was diagnosed with depression. From the age fifteen, my mother was worried about it. Strongly hereditary, the black cloud loomed over my mother's side of the family. It was commonplace to be depressed in the 90's. I ate my cares away. Depression was a constant. Antidepressants were sediment in my blood.

I had trouble with my weight since my parents split at age thirteen. I found comfort in food. Tastykake Krimpets or cupcakes didn't yell or scream. I had eaten myself into a body that wasn't me many times over. I was hiding from facing what I had become.

I often decided, on my own, to go off the various pharmaceutical agents in a hope for clarity. I lost twenty years of my kids childhood to drug clouds over my brain. Unfortunately, my situation never changed so the stressors and triggers continued, and food continued to be my outlet. I was underneath all the layers of fat trying to not suffocate.

I wore my fat like a Teflon suit, not allowing hurt too deep. My captor wouldn't let me out of his sight. You would think I was a slut, that's how I was treated. So many times, I thought to myself I should just do what he is accusing me of. At least I'd deserve the torment and consequences. My loyalty and my weight kept me small. My life might have been easier had I been more impulsive back then.

I refer to my husband as a capture because I was like a bird in a cage. We only had one car. We could never afford a second. For a short time, we did, it was a huge source of mistrust because it gave me autonomy. We didn't have cell phones then to be tracking my actions, or he would have. I was always with him because it wasn't worth the hassle and questioning of my every minute that he didn't have eyes on me. Depression was where I lived. It consumed me.

Was Florida far away enough from New Jersey? I didn't care, I wanted out, NOW. I was not proud of myself in this moment I wasn't thinking, really, I was reacting and doing. I had to verb my way out of this, you know, an action was necessary. I was embarrassed to ask my little sister to visit, let's be honest intrude, but had no choice. Doing, I had done all I could. I was empty, worn out, depleted. That is why the last few weeks happened. A few weeks that showed me that my life isn't in my control and that there had to be another way out. What I had been doing wasn't working any longer.

My current job was demanding. Every morning I would be up at 4:30-5am and ready to take on the world; making the coffee and breakfast sandwiches for super entitled, self-absorbed people floating through existence. Working 60-70 hours a week on and off the clock for a convenience store chain was like a vow to a cult. You had to be all in to be successful.

There was no work and home balance. They were an economic machine, cranking through individuals. Immersion is like cultivating an addiction or reliance. I needed my job to support my family. The challenge was good for me at times, lots of small goals and achievable positions. It was a time passer. I focused on the next rung of the ladder instead of the issues at hand at home. Every morning, time to make the coffee like a drone. Keeping my mind busy and focused on my job helped me survive.

The company had sent me back to school. I was thankful because I would need a degree if I ever wanted to leave the company. I had worked my way up through the organization. I put my life on hold to achieve success. I'd have to be all in to get to the sweet spot where I could make the money I needed. I knew when I "joined" that I would only allow them to have seven years of my life. I figured any more than that and I would get hard and bitter or dependent on the money and unable to leave.

The accelerated college classes were filled with my peers. Fast paced and stressful, a continuation of my day of fast paced and stressful workplace and home. I was a manager after all, and that's what they do. I manage things, tasks, people, issues, machinery, bills, pets, children, and him. Him. He was the most difficult because he was always there; selfish, demanding, unsatisfied and unreliable. I needed away from all of it but especially him.

I was tired, so very, very tired of everything. One morning I just couldn't get out of bed, a prisoner of sorts restrained by my sheets. My limbs were lead filled, heavy and taking extreme effort to move. My brain was stagnant and yet very determined to be somewhere, anywhere but there. I called out of work for a day, then two, then a week. Only left the room to relieve myself. I could hold it for hours, I didn't want to see anyone.

A mother of four, my kids were busy at ages 8-16. Chances of bumping into one of them was high. I didn't want to explain myself to them or him. He told them I was sick with the flu. Occasionally my littlest would sneak in the room and come around the bed quietly and just stand there peering at me. Her little loving eyes, worried about her Mommy, maybe she really knew what I was struggling with. Would she be okay without me? Yes, I convinced myself that all my children would be better off if I was gone rather than live with the conditions that I enabled all these years. They just might break free too.

It had been two weeks since I left my room for more than a few minutes to use the bathroom. I stayed in bed all day and night watching the light change as the dust particles floated aimlessly through my space. My room, olive green with bright white glossy trim. There was one wall that had old, dark paneling from the 70's which I covered with brown paper bags torn into abstract pieces and pasted to the wall overlapping edge over edge looking like weathered leather.

My room reminded me of my parent's room as a child, I used similar colors and had some of their old furniture that had been divvied off as needed over time. The only thing missing from my room and theirs was the large fern print wallpaper making it look like a jungle canopy. I had their dresser with the mirror, the one I spilled nail polish remover on as a child and then tried to sop it up with a tissue. I destroyed the top of that beautiful furniture. My sister told on me and I got punished for hiding it, I got better at hiding things as the years went on.

I'd returned to my journal while I laid helpless in my bed. An entry from a few weeks earlier reads

"I spoke to Pastor about my sleeplessness. He recommended Tylenol PM every other night to get myself back in a sleep pattern. While I was out at Walgreens I picked up the economy size Benadryl. I read on the internet that this or Dramamine in large doses with a bottle of wine will do it. That is, IT. I am ready now, I will go off my antidepressants and wait." I had a plan.

It was exactly that; a waiting game. I gave up a long time ago. He beat me, not physically, though mentally and emotionally, which I allowed. I didn't respect him. I couldn't. All my life I have been running away from something. I ran to him because I mistook his control and jealousy for love. The last few weeks, years, decades had made me hard, bitter and resentful and that wasn't me. A product of my environment; as my children would be if there wasn't a change.

My escape was planned. My sister and her husband welcomed me to come and they were surprised that I would arrive the next day. I planned to leave now and drive straight through. Twenty-four hours to get to the Sunshine State from Cherry Hill, NJ. I was packed in minutes and loading the van. I had money in the account oddly as I had just got paid the night before. Enough resources to get me there and I wasn't worried about coming back, if I'd be back or I'd be alive.

I had tried to go to sleep and not wake up…but I failed. I had to figure out what next. Dying was my only hope of getting away from him. I couldn't divorce him because I didn't have the money or autonomy to be able to breathe without him knowing every move. I had already been suffocated years ago, the death of my spirit had already happened. I wanted to die so I could find freedom; instead road tripped to Florida; a beautiful detour. It was a hiccup in my plans that undoubtedly drew my sister and I closer together.

I left the driveway in Cherry Hill in the afternoon and drove following my TomTom. All I remember is driving through Georgia and seeing animal crossing signs that moved. I was hallucinating jack rabbits hopping up and down. The drugs from my initial suicide attempt were still wearing off. Miles and miles of blacktop with ominous haunted trees lining the path with no place to stop for sleep. I think back now, what was I afraid of? I had no music on for the entire trip, alone, me and my thoughts. When I did have thoughts, it was about how I wouldn't fail next time. Next time I wouldn't run, I would be free.

# Chapter 2

I had a purpose to get to Naples, a safer place to be, no judgement or anger. I was driving with a determination and nothing would stop me. I still had no plan yet for what would happen next. My supervisor was calling after me wondering what was going on. I had to finally admit that I was falling apart. My strong exterior and resolve had cracked and exposed huge fault lines that had been under the surface, that no one was aware of, so there was no concern. Funny thing is that I had been falling apart for years by this point. This was it; the point where the tide had turned.

Have you ever wondered when exactly that is and where the edge of a tide lies? The place where the swelling and swirling waters mix together, the coming and going. In my mind, I had reached a tipping point about a decade before while I was pregnant with my son. By that time, I was tired of the life I was living. I was in limbo, between what I had always thought I'd be and who I was being defined by.

When I was a little girl I didn't tell myself that I would be this. I didn't know what I wanted but I knew it was not this. My relationship with my husband was unhealthy from the very beginning but I have officially declared that the Summer of '99 my wtf moment had penetrated my brain and set roots of change in motion. Looking back, I was so proud and stubborn that I was suffering unnecessarily at my own doing. I felt so stuck that I had no idea how to drag myself out of the quicksand. I needed help, perspective, a voice that was heard, validation, appreciation, but mostly love.

I had two girls by that Summer and was pregnant with a boy, the boy that my husband really wanted. The baby would be the pride of the family, the only boy to carry on the family name. This was finally going to make him happy, I thought, in some weird way.

My girls were six and seven and becoming little females, busy and talkative. They were learning that two together could be stronger than each apart. I know they didn't devise a plan but the idea of divide and conquer seemed to work well for them. Girls can be quite manipulative and sneaky individually but put two together and they could take over the world.

They were smart and funny, but their father didn't find their creativity amusing. I tried to keep them busy and tire them out, so they would nap. Managing their sleep and keeping them on a schedule was common sense. I found any free activities I could for them to plug into. I wanted to enrich them and teach them great things. Every moment was teachable, and church was a natural extension of that.

I don't remember the details of how my spiritual journey had happened. Maybe it was the result of taking the girls to Vacation Bible School? Wait, it was a lady by the name of Carol that stopped at a yard sale we were having, yes, I do remember now. We would set up yard sales frequently to make some money to pay bills. At this time, we had the two girls and no car, but God came to us in the form of an unassuming woman with a mixed-race child that I assumed was her grandchild, but I was wrong.

Carol and Roy were a gentle older couple in their sixties. They had raised their children and had a heart for the Lord, so they adopted a crack addicted baby to challenge them and keep them mindful of their mission in life. They called her Rachel and she was a behavior nightmare. I wondered if it was because of her birth mom's drug use or the fact that this lovely old couple couldn't keep up with her demanding nature.

Carol had a real love for animals. Her ministry was visiting schools, nursing homes, and churches sharing the story of Noah. We had some aquariums for sale and a pair of sugar gliders that needed a new home, I think the fact that there were two clinched the sale. Carol invited us to her home for a meal and to see all her pets.

Of course, they modeled the ideal Christian home, complete with grace and a plea for our souls before dinner. The invitation to church and Vacation Bible School, and Ladies Prayer Meetings came shortly after dessert. The girls were drawn to Carol and the animals. I was drawn to her peaceful nature and calmness in all things.

She drove a big white conversion van with aquamarine pinstripes and swirls with plenty of room to pick up the girls and me for church. Childcare was always provided where they would learn about God's Love. My husband welcomed Carol, at the time, because he saw her as cash cow and he didn't seem to mind me hanging out with the old church lady, so I did. A freedom that I savored.

Don't stop reading now. I am not a Bible Thumper; this was a chapter of my life with profound impact or perhaps it was a stalling tactic from the Universe. As I am sitting here writing this, I look to my right and see a stack of books anchored by my well used Life Study Bible.

My Bible is something that I will cherish for the rest of my life and hopefully pass on to one of my children when they are ready to seek God full in the face. It is written in, highlighted, underlined in pen and pew pencil. Tear stains have crumpled spots and blurred print. There are notes from my children and pictures they drew while waiting patiently for the service to be over. The cover and spine are falling apart and held together with duct and packing tape. You would think I was a zealot for the Lord based on its appearance. All I wanted to know was, "Why am I struggling so much?"

# Chapter 3

I was excited to go meet new people, be around some positivity, and feel genuinely cared for. Each time we went I felt nourished, yet hungry. I felt like God was speaking to me every day, just to me and helping me make sense of all my disappointments of life. I was learning and doing, plugged into a community that was focused out instead of focused on self.

I attended as often as I could, I took the kids because I wanted them to see love and kindness and that there was another way to be. A place for the kids on Sundays during football season was appealing, it was a reason for my husband to be okay with me going. He didn't want to come, he didn't have to yet. I was supposed to have faith and follow the lead of my husband regardless of his faith or lack thereof.

I was weary of talking with the women of the church in their prayer circles. Living in New Jersey, you have a certain cynicism that is part of your nature. Women's prayer groups were just a permission slip for gossip under the guise of mentoring or prayer. I had always related better with guys than females, probably because I was raised as a buddy to my dad until the divorce.

I never felt like I fit in with the stay at home moms that were supported by their husbands and that homeschooled their super obedient children while ministering and being prayer warriors full time.

Discovering your spirituality later in life is like taking a tiger out of the wild and training it to do tricks. I was unruly in my thoughts, defeated in my attempts, and miserable in my life. I sought out some counseling with the Pastor of the church. I had so many questions about marriage and having a meek spirit, how to break free of my depression. I needed to learn how to mitigate my husband's words and actions to my children who were seeing very different behavior at their church friend's houses.

I tried not to be judgmental and just live with Jesus in my heart and this didn't go over well. My husband was angry and annoyed, conflicted with his own behavior while I worked on mine. He was a passive aggressive personality with sarcasm that flung out like thunder but was jagged and precise like a bolt of lightning. This was how he had always communicated with me. It was like we spoke two different languages. He was fluent in hate and anger, sounding hard and cold like Russian or Czech. I would try to understand, reading his body language, responding to his every mood while living in this foreign place called home.

I was frustrated that he wouldn't hear me. At times, I would lash out in return sometimes in a struggle for him to just understand me. I made no sense to him. I was stuck but resourceful and hardworking. I had a drive to be better someday never knowing when that day would be. I spoke a language of heartache, disappointment, concern, stress, and hopelessness and he never tried to learn my language or understand me.

It got old, yet I was determined, loyal, and dedicated to my family and making it work.

I was pulled in the perpetual limbo line, bending back over end, dancing to his tune, a slave to the pressure to take each pass under the bar. I married him back in '92, my consequence, my sufferance, my cross to bear for my choice, that is what church taught me. This was all a part of a bigger picture meant to shape and mold me into God's image.

I was a shadow, following Scott through life. I felt like a resource. I was merely good enough. What we had was good enough according to him. I needed to figure out how to put a voice to my individuality and speak my needs, wants and dreams. This, I feel, was my utilitarian portion of my story. A phase where I was not in control but used for all I was worth. With the guidance of the church, I found myself trusting God's plan for me. I was right where I was supposed to be. I devoted myself to Jesus, I was saved.

I drank the Kool-Aid. I was a very sad person even then. The only reason I had my last two children was because I was focused on God. In school, I learned psychological development. Looking back, that is exactly what I was doing. Following the course of natural growth through a lifetime. I was looking for purpose and meaning to pass on to my kids. I tried to make sense of all the good and bad in the world, and in my own life. This was my lifeline, my hope.

What my church life taught me was that I was a sinner deserving of nothing and that being alive and persecuted was a gift. This limbo decade of my life was necessary as a life experience. I have struggled with the balance of humility and self-worth ever since. When my life was falling apart I learned to cope, settle, and serve. I was not important, like the dirt that I came from. Happiness was a farce. It helped to stop looking for it.

# Chapter 4

As was a common theme in our history, rent didn't get paid. It wasn't long until we were evicted from our apartment, we had to move. Our income afforded us an apartment owned by a slum lord much farther away from Carol and her Magical Ministry Van. I felt that I was being tested. Everything was planned by God, so why this? Why now?

It was necessary for me to go to work if we were ever going to get above water. I got a job at Toys R Us as a stock associate climbing thirty-foot ladders while pregnant and filling and fronting the store for the next day.

I would come home from working all night, to bill collectors calling all day. Collection agencies were relentless, and I couldn't give them any answers because there weren't any to have. Scott was adamant about overseeing the money, always. I attempted to stay calm and pray through the crisis, the church helped occasionally with bills, but always came through with support for me and the kids.

I was sure that God was trying to get a hold of my husband's heart and the rest of us were along for the ride. It was the only sensible reason. Beyond embarrassing, beyond stressful, beyond my wildest dreams my husband had his first affair.

On Palm Sunday, in the middle of the night, I hear a pounding on our front door. I was seven and a half months along at this point and sleeping was difficult at times. This was a night that I was sleeping well so the noise startled me from my deep sleep in a panic. I see the dancing red and blue lights out the window of our illegal, converted third floor attic bedroom. I hurried down the creaking wooden dangerously pitched attic steps to see my husband at the door talking to police officers.

I was in a fog, what was going on? My husband tells me to go to bed, he is sweating profusely. The television is on and WebTV is on the screen. A conversation with a female user name is there. I shake my head in awe as I hear him explain that he called 911 for a woman he was talking to in Iowa. Even then I knew, that this isn't the way things work.

He explains to the police that this woman is in an abusive relationship with her husband and that she stopped chatting with Scott abruptly, so she must be in danger. He knew her phone number but not her address. The police tell him there is nothing they can do from here and that he needs to keep trying to reach her or let it go. Things are adding up rather quickly in my mind and there was a real problem.

"I love her", "feel like I know her", "while you are at work we talk all night", I hear him say in response to me questioning why he is so involved in this woman's life. I had his son growing in my stomach and he was having an emotional affair with a chick on WebTV in Iowa. Is this really happening? I sobbed, cried, ached, bled. Yes, bled. I started spotting immediately, as my body went into shock before my soul could even grasp the betrayal.

His answer was that he knew it was wrong and that he wanted to end it with her, but he had to do it in person, "I owe her that much." He said. I was furious, but a strange sense of what will be will be came over me. Maybe God was talking to me? Maybe I felt like I had no options or will to fight? I think back now and realize that this is when I was finally done.

I bought him the bus ticket to go with the last money in the account. Was I crazy sending him into another woman's arms? I knew he was going to fuck her. I was hurt but I sort of rationalized that men cheat, at least I knew what he was doing. Did that make me feel less betrayed? No, just more in control. I felt used, bewildered, numb. I married him, my choice, my fault this is my thinking over and over. I expect people to own their mistakes and wrong doings, this was mine.

He went and came home five days later after screwing her and proclaiming that it wasn't over, he still loved her, and he intended to take our son to Iowa and be with Jasmine and her 1-year old son after she was divorced. He didn't want the girls, just the baby boy I was still carrying.

He was calling her whenever he thought I wasn't paying attention and now he had made love to her. More rationalizing, I couldn't be mad, I had sent him right into her vagina. I was pregnant and fat. I was tired from working overnights. I wasn't there for him.

I was numb, conditioned by his verbal assaults, accepting all the blame. I took the high road and prayed for him, and that I would have the grace to deal with him. I prayed for Jasmine too. It wasn't was her fault, he didn't have to get on the bus.

It was during this time when my spirit died, and I started thinking about life after. Was it a sin to pray that your husband would die so you could be free? He had a family curse; no man had lived past sixty-three at the time. I knew he would be the fucker that would live to be ninety.

After a couple weeks of him wanting his cake and eating it too, I had enough. He had to decide. I wasn't going to sit around and wait like a turkey on Thanksgiving for my belly button to pop and him pretend to be supportive all while they were devising a plan to take my baby. My ultimatum worked, and he chose her.

I didn't buy him a ticket this time, instead I threw all his belongings down the steps of our apartment where the police had stood exposing this Jerry Springer story. He grabbed a duffle bag and packed up his stuff and started walking down the road. He was headed to a bus station to catch a greyhound bus to Iowa, to Jasmine. I cried because things were so badly broken, including me.

I was scared and alone, ready to have baby number three in weeks, unable to work due to stress and spotting. My girls were in school oblivious to the bullshit that was going on. I got in the car and drove to the only place my car would go, the church. I don't remember driving there, maybe it was God or the Holy Spirit, I don't know but that's where I ended up.

"Is Pastor Browning in?" I sobbed.

The church was in transition, the pastor serving was an Interim. He was a Professor from a bible college and I was captivated by his teaching and preaching. I trusted him as a Pastor, the fact that he was filling in made me trust him even more. He had nothing to gain or lose by being invested in my life. I just needed some serious help navigating my rough seas.

Visibly shaken, and obviously pregnant the church Secretary told me to have a seat. I had counseled here before, my tears told the story, urgency was implied. He came out a minute later, "Follow me." I did. I walked down the narrow, dimly lit hallway to his outdated office. Dark wood mismatched furniture with books filling the shelves from bottom to top that surrounded me like Stonehenge. A couch faced with the back to the door and two arm chairs looking out of the office were positioned in the middle of the room.

The Pastor's desk was large and strangely ornate, a gift from a church member that made it by hand. I noticed all the little knick knacks around the room from various mission fields as well as strategically placed tissue boxes and waste baskets. This man was well traveled and experienced, he had seen much worse situations than mine. He directed me to have a seat. His face looked tired, lots of deep wrinkles like that of a sharpei. He took his glasses off and set them on the coffee table,

“Why don’t you tell me what’s going on?” he softly asked. The dam broke way, there was no stopping the flood of tears and despair that followed. I needed help, direction really. What do I do next? I couldn’t focus on myself and the baby because I wasn’t prepared for this. I was completely out of control, maybe that was the point. I had tried, I let my husband be the leader for the past several months and it walked him right out the door into another woman’s arms.

“What now?”, I asked after I shared all that had happened.

I was right, this wasn’t new, different or even shocking to Pastor. He had done this before many times. Should that make me feel better, or worse?

He responded, “I will meet with the Elder Board, we will help you however we can.”

He calmed me down talking about The Lord’s Will and all kinds of verses of comfort from the Bible to get my brain thinking on something other than my desperation. We made a follow up appointment for the next day. I was to bring in my bills that were outstanding. The Elders would sort through and prioritize my finances and help me with a plan and some monetary help. I could at least breathe without sniveling like a child.

“Shall we pray before you go?” Pastor recommended in that leading way that you know isn’t really a question but what is happening next.

He starts, “Lord, we come to you with heavy hearts. We know that you are in control of all things that happen in our lives.” The tears start again.

“Please Lord, help this dear woman to deal with these events happening in her life right now. Mold her and grow her through these experiences that she will be able to minister and help others through your grace in her life.” He continues for what seems like forever then he said the oddest thing.

“Lord, you know Scott’s heart, Lord. (like repeating Lord twice in a sentence added meaning or filled space) Prick his heart Lord. Show him what he needs to do. Lord, we know that if it is your will, you could have him call here on this phone” He lifts the rotary phone up off his desk and plants it firmly back down on the elaborately carved desktop that was covered with a thick sheet of glass and the phone tings like a typewriter from the impact.

“On this phone right now, Lord!” raising his voice.

I think to myself, yeah right. With all due respect, he doesn’t know this man like I do. Just a week before he had referred to himself as The Father, the television as The Son, and the remote as The Holy Spirit just to offend me. It was almost comical to think about as I was leaving. I was coming to terms with the fact that Scott walking out on me was my way out.

I walk out of the church office and into the foyer of the Baptist High School. The bell had rung so classes were changing, and the hallway was busy with youth dressed in uniform. Some of the teenagers looked at me in passing with pity on their face. They would pray for me their eyes said, as they met mine inadvertently. I went out the heavy double doors, if they want people to come in they should make these doors easier to handle I thought to myself.

I walked down the handicap accessible ramp to avoid a crowd of women coming up the steps, they looked like they were touring. I didn't want my red face, puffy eyes and handfuls of used tissues to distract them. Why didn't I throw those tissues away? I was parked along the building directly below the room where I had sat for two hours divulging my misfortune and lot. I take a deep breath and open the door of the Toyota Rav and slide into my seat. As I start the car, something catches my eye.

"He's on the phone!", "Scott called, and he is on the phone!" The Pastor is hanging out of his office window, waving enthusiastically.

Moments like that must be what keeps a Pastor going. Can you imagine the awe and surprise on my face? My disbelief turned belief as I ran back to his office.

"He is at the bus station and he is hoping you pick him up and work this out." Pastor conveys the message with inspired eyes.

What was I supposed to say to the Pastor, no? This was sermon material or a Hallmark movie script. What the heck God, you've got my attention? What am I supposed to do with this new revelation? I had just left at peace with my marriage being over and my husband moving to Iowa. Scott didn't know that I went to the church after he walked down Chapel Ave. I'm sure he knew there wouldn't be many other places I'd go, but still. He knew I had been attending there. He knew I was trying out some of my new-found Christian directives from the Bible in our marriage. He knew that I had asked him to come to church over and over. He knew he had fucked up too.

I went to pick him up. We went back to the apartment. I was soft after being infused with scripture and purged of my tears in that office. I sensed that I was right where God wanted me. "God Moments", as I call them, happen all the time but often people aren't paying attention to catch them. This was a case where I was smacked with a 2X4 straight up. It was hard to be mad at Scott when I felt like God had hand delivered him back to me in the span of hours like a stork delivering a bundle.

I took charge of the next few weeks and we went to some counseling sessions together. The ultimate humbling vetting of Scott and his deplorable financial budgeting and follow through was a hard pill for him to swallow. Scott's pride was still very much intact, and it wasn't going anywhere fast. He was buddied up with a couple men of the church that excelled in finance and they tried to teach him principles to get us on track. It was very difficult, but we did workbooks and budget envelopes. He had a bad money management gene that wouldn't allow him to commit, oh wait, or was that the fuck other women while my wife is pregnant gene. Could I forgive him? I thought I had to.

While he was being mentored he tried to act the part but whenever something challenging would pop up old habits would rear their head. I knew a transformation wasn't going to happen overnight, time was the yeast and he was the dough. He would be focused on me or the kids and all the things that were going wrong. Picking us to pieces.

Audrey is our second daughter. She is a free spirit and saw things through different glasses than everyone else did. She had an analytical mind, and she could find a loop hole in any discussion or situation. I would tell her she should go to law school. Her non-conformist thinking was a direct irritant to her father's controlling ways. I defended her and protected her all the time. I wish I had taught her to be strong instead of weak. Interceding for her or anything against what he wanted meant I was on the firing line.

I wished I was a fad. I wished he'd get tired of me and put me aside, so I could move on. Through all this I tried to justify his behavior, upbringing, Mommy/family issues, immaturity, and birth order. I also tried to justify my behavior, upbringing, Daddy/family issues, immaturity, and birth order.

# Chapter 5

The power was shut off by the power company while I was sleeping after work one day. I woke up, groggy and exhausted, my sleep interrupted by the white noise of the fan stopping. Nothing new here, the utilities being shut off happened often because bills weren't paid even with counseling from the church.

Thankfully, the girls were in school. It was summer and hot. We lived in an old Victorian home on the second floor. We had window air conditioners in every room that were second hand and froze up often, so we would alternate running them, so they could defrost and hopefully work another day. This day of course was one of the hottest so far. The groceries that were bought the day before were going to go bad in the fridge.

"Can you call your Mom?" he said when I called him with the news.

I was tired of going to my mother to bail us out of these situations. He had become reliant on it, my mom's sympathy for her only grandchildren and the squalor they were living in. She didn't visit much. I think it broke her heart. She hurt for me, she knew I wanted more. I was hurting her because I knew she expected more. I didn't know what to do.

This is the rest of Scott's story with church, humble only if he was getting something out of it. After our marriage was shook by his physical and emotional infidelity, we started counseling together. We gathered all our bills and brought them to the church for help exposing us to scrutiny and judgement with him as the shitty leader of our family. While being patient with a new soul to save, they paid the electric bill from an emergency fund, but it wouldn't be until the next day that we would have power.

My innocent girls came home to a dark house. Ironically, after leaving the church we lied and said a car crash had interrupted our power and we should pray for them. We tell our children things to keep them from what they don't fully understand. I tried to protect them from the harsh reality that their father was an opportunistic narcissist with no ability to handle money, who lied and cheated and would always put himself first.

Utilities being shut off, car being repossessed, being macaroni and cheese poor and being at church whenever the doors were open was the norm. I studied the Bible and took notes feverishly during studies, sermons and revivals trying to stay focused on God instead of my circumstances.

We were the white trash family that everyone felt pity on. We were recipients of books, retreat registrations, ladies group trips, and men's fellowship events. Scott sat begrudgingly at any church event with a scowl, resting bitchy face to the max, making him unapproachable and then would condemn the church people for not engaging with him. Always someone else's fault, blame shifting was his specialty. They call it Gaslighting now.

Scott never leapt in with both feet. He was a hypocrite to the highest degree but as far as he was concerned so was everybody else. He proclaimed to be saved. It was not for me to worry about, it was God's business. I'm not going to be looking for him when I die.

Doing a spiritual inventory is like a personality test or skills assessment. All the parishioners sat in the auditorium and filled out a four-page survey of multiple-choice questions that contained mind-probing queries. It was a mental Taco Bell, nine questions that could be interpreted a thousand different ways. My husband's result was something like this "Your Burrito is ready Sir...You are a Prophet, with the fixings of an asshole wrapped in God's Tortilla of Love."

This merely gave Scott the fuel to hold up in his righteousness and judge. Better yet, he was the judge and jury, right and wrong, black and white and he was one of two people in the whole congregation that scored out like this. Can you imagine a church full of people like that? It wouldn't work, ever, in any scenario.

My gifts were encouragement and administration. It helped me to focus my intentions in places that I excelled I helped in the Ladies Bible Studies, organize outreach events, and became a youth leader. It was important for me to be giving my time and skills because I had nothing else to offer. This is when I realized the power of my struggles. Ladies in the church could feel bad for me but not relate to me.

Their problems were slightly different than mine, for example instead of them working outside of the home and producing income for the family for example, they worked all day sewing pillowcases into dresses for little girls in Africa while their supportive, loving, Godly husbands worked. While I shared about my husband having an emotional affair with a woman over the internet they would complain about how much time their spouse spent being a good steward taking care of the car. While I struggled to bring to light that the church was demographically dying, and it wouldn't exist if we didn't reach out and touch people's lives they would be steeped in traditions and gatherings like they were rituals.

Hey, the struggle is real, whatever it is I guess. In my experience, a lot of the Born Againers I met were generational, meaning they were born into a "culture" of beliefs. Church was made up of many large families, that then produced more large families that were having kids. For a long while, a couple of decades, the Baby Boomers held it together. The biproducts of their grandparents, these baby Christian fools are led around by their subconscious, repressing feelings or labeling themselves as sinners that got saved because they got wet in a pool at six years old and gave their precious little hearts to Jesus. A lot of the judgement and hate we see today starts here, with these people who have no experience outside of the bubble of familial expectations and protection. Sad really, and also made them unrelatable.

Generational Born-Again Believers have been born into the Bible business, it consumes all they do. Prayed for in the womb, dunked in church life, right up to immersion at Baptism, the age of accountability, the scriptures are taught with devotions and sermons.

Bible songs and Veggie Tails, felt boards and Fire and Brimstone Preachers, Missionaries and Vacation Bible School are huge influences as well as being at the church whenever the doors are open, being constantly busy doing something for the Lord. I never had all that in my life. I struggled with being good enough.

The little kids sitting in the pews through church playing quietly with a picture to color from Sunday School aren't quiet because they want to be, it's the expectation. From the time they can understand, many children are taught to accept their sinful nature as a bad thing and be constantly asking forgiveness because those are the words Mommy and Daddy use. Through prayer and "teachable moments" the groundwork of positive and negative reinforcements is laid. The angels and demons are constantly at work, tipping scales from time to time.

These kids are held to ridiculously high standards that set them up for failure in most cases. As teenagers, these little angels find their individuality, voice and freedom. Some realize that what they did at six had meant nothing and they rededicate themselves to Christ. While others go for broke and become love children, smoking weed, drawing sexy pictures of nude women, following astrology and rebuking their parent's judgmental hypocrisy. Yes, I know that one and I applaud her awareness and individuality. Someday I hope she finds peace by reconciling all her experiences and achieving balance.

I remember thinking how lucky the little zombies for Jesus kids were for having such structure and direction at such an early age. I wished that as a child my parents had found Jesus and possibly rewrote history, staying together because they put God first in everything. I thought of how different things would have been for my own kids if Scott and I had met at a Bible Camp instead of at a party and did things differently.

My older girls were old enough to see a change, and old enough to resent it. These little fragile girls that hadn't been raised in a Christian home were now expected to mesh with the likes of angels. I was prompted to get rid of all the Barbie dolls. We stopped watching tv and changed the music from Rock and Pop to contemporary Christian. We started spanking because we love them instead of in frustration or anger.

Eventually, I started homeschooling because the other children at school were hateful and mean and lacked good parenting or, so I was told. I thought I was doing the right thing and with hard work and due diligence our family would be different, functional, and maybe even Godly. My mother thought what we were doing was extreme and even abusive.

We are all born with a will, a drive, a personality and we are all self-centered. Survival requires it, my children taught me that. Children are resilient because survival requires that too. Even the most submissive people in the world have the will or drive to serve. A person always chooses, I will, or I won't, to do or not to do something. Consequences are the great leveler. Free will is what tests our character on a conscience and subconscious level. The idea of Higher Power has always been around.

It was a couple of months before the pressure of making good and right choices proved to be too much for Scott. He wouldn't go to church, and he would blow off bible studies. He would go to a social "fun" event and then criticize it relentlessly with no concern for little ears or how confusing his words would be to the minds of our kids still developing their core beliefs that were exemplified by actions.

I always taught my kids about the consequences of their actions. If you do "X" then "Y" will happen ultimately resulting in "Z". "Z" was usually the outcome of ending up in hell in some form or sense. This is the dribble that I allowed to filter through me because it was the only thing that made sense. The endless sermon of consequences of our actions played out, repeatedly.

My children gave their hearts to Jesus and have struggled with low self-esteem and fear of everything still today exhibited by high anxiety and panic attacks, poor social skills, and being highly judgmental. Will they forgive me someday? Survival doesn't require that.

Our life was what I settled for. I allowed the mediocrity. This was the path that my choices had manifested through my will. I was not satisfied at all. These are the mantras that I told myself daily. I was always wanting more. I wanted more, still so much more. I wanted more stability, structure, trust, love but above all intimacy. Then it hit me. I was discontent with what I had, why would God bless me with more? I do believe we need to take responsibility for our parts in things good and bad however this was a deep undertow of despair from which escape was futile.

It could have been the Koran or Buddhism, it didn't matter. I love learning, so I was a sponge. My time at church without my husband was a mini-vacation where I could recharge. It was my balancing scale. I forgave him repeatedly for things because he was blind to his sin or didn't really care. My husband was my mission field.

Staying in the bubble of protection kept me reflecting and self-deprecating. I had been diagnosed with depression since I went to the doctor as a teen with my Mom. I had been medicated and numb off and on for a long time. I decided to try going off my medicine and letting Jesus be my physician. Devotions and prayer kept me centered daily but overall sad, very sad, still depressed. Scott stopped trying, so our marriage counselling stopped in its tracks. I continued alone.

I cried a lot. The more things changed, the more they stayed the same. I was stuck and depressed, discontent enough to try ending my life. I was showing signs for more than three years in a pastor's office that I was ready to quit, unable to conquer this insurmountable mountain of hurt, disappointment and pain. The man listening to me had more faith in me than I had for myself. He thought they were just words, they weren't.

I wasn't as strong as I needed to be. I wasn't making my marriage work. I was not able to shake my depression even through prayer and fasting. I wasn't a good enough Christian, or I would have worked through all that muck and mire. I was changed by The Word, enlightened to the joy that was saved for other people. A decade of my life was poured into changing who I was fundamentally, and not changing the external factor that kept me unhappy, Scott.

I know that all things happen for a reason and not in my time, this is where I found rest.

# Chapter 6

Change is the very last thing that is recommended during therapy. I was at a fork in the road. My brain was foggy from the heavy meds after my commitment, my survival depended on the choices made now. It was life or death, this isn't drama. I had been on disability for a long time and had to decide to return to work immediately or sever my employment.

I couldn't go back yet. My instability had been rumored in refrigerated coolers all over South Jersey. I would have panic attacks if I pulled into a location parking space none the less try to jump back into a full GM position in a new store. My previous store had been staffed by a Manager in Training now. If everything had stayed the same while I was away I think it would have been okay. If I was going to have change at this point, it had to be on my terms.

Between going to my Sister's and now approximately four and a half months had gone by. I was a different person after being committed. I had major anxiety just leaving my house. Living with mentally ill people for months has affects that linger. I wanted a fresh start.

We had discussed moving many times. We wanted out of New Jersey for very different reasons. He hated the congestion; road rage was an obvious problem. It was so fast paced, and people were very entitled and hard. I wanted to move because I like change and challenge. If I'm honest, the moving was a distraction from my shit marriage.

From when we met we moved twenty plus times mainly because of money because Scott couldn't keep a job, or roommate issues with him. I knew why it was happening and who was responsible for our instability. I went along with it because I was stupid, young, immature, full of pride, and loyal. The abuse had been there from the beginning and I didn't see it. It would be years until I could identify it for what it was.

I sat in front of my computer and typed in these nine words into the Google search bar, "Homes for sale with a hobby farm or kennel". Very vague, very open, no other parameters. When I typed in that phrase in my computer I was blankly throwing out a net. We had Newfoundland's and we wanted to breed our girl, Stella Cous Cous.

I was hoping for a place to present itself with space to put our dogs during the day while we were at work or to hold puppies safely. I was surprised when the very first search result was a beautiful large home with an actual kennel business on the property. I thought immediately this is something I could do. I always wanted to own my own business since high school but never knew what kind. Here it was on a computer screen; in front of me. Simply, a gift.

I was keeping an open mind and the search provoked a further look at other kennel businesses for sale. I then broadened the scope to bed and breakfasts, board dogs or board people, oddly interchangeable. There were many for sale but they all paled in comparison to the first. I had run a million-dollar location with 25-30 employees, a 24/7 operation focused on customer service in hard, cold NJ. Caring for dogs and talking to their owners for drop off and pick up in cold Minnesota would be a walk in the park.

I may have been star struck or had tunnel vision, but I kept coming back to the mom and pop kennel in the land of ten thousand lakes. There was five acres of land with the site which was a lot to take care of in my mind. We had a small yard in Cherry Hill, NJ, our house only separated from the neighbor by a driveway width. I could handle the house and the business, but the yard was huge. Funny that grass would be my concern.

I said casually to Scott, "What do you think of Minnesota?". When I asked him similar questions about other regions he would say no. I really wanted to be near water and sun. When I mentioned locations south of Maryland, like Virginia or North Carolina, he would claim that there were ordinances against him being shirtless.

"I'd love to live in Minnesota!" he spouted.

"Really!?!" was my reply.

I showed him the listing of the beautiful home and business in Wolf Lake. His reaction after that was typical.

"Huh, well, if you can make it happen we'll go. It isn't going to happen though." Typically, negative.

It was all I needed to hear, it was accepted as a challenge. I could make it happen and I had a new goal and aspiration.

The home was listed all over the internet. The owners had tried to sell the property privately and had posted private websites so there were many extra pictures and views. There was a phone number listed and I called. I spoke with a man that had a Midwestern accent that drew out his o's and he chuckled like Santa. Lenny was enthusiastic and cautiously optimistic since they had been trying to sell for three years. He claimed they were waiting for just the right owner. It was 2010, the middle of the economic downfall. It was a terrible time to sell or buy when you needed to have a contingency to make it happen.

We would be leaving a wonderful home that was in my Mother's name. After watching us bounce around so much, my Mom felt terrible that we had no home place for our children to grow up. She even suggested putting our oldest up for adoption because we weren't financially stable. She wanted to see me enjoying my life while she was still alive. She proposed giving me my inheritance in the form of a house before she passed. She helped me find the house and negotiated an amazing deal. The house stayed in her name to protect her intention. This was a constant thorn in Scott's side. He had no control of it.

When I was a girl, we lived on Feathertree Court in Howell, New Jersey. It was a new development that my parents bought into. There were phases of construction and floor plans, build to order. I loved visiting the sample houses, staged and clean, great light, and there were always cookies.

Our house was located on a cul-de-sac, backed up to a plot of woods. The trees were mainly pine and maple and graded steeply uphill. My sister and I would play in those woods all day creating play houses where the rooms were marked off from tree to tree like the sample houses.

From the top of the steep hill we could see everything like Mufasa surveying his land in The Lion King. A new phase of the development was being built below us. I saw it then, a beautiful colonial blue cape cod with white trim. That would be the house of my dreams, which I found with my realtor and my Mom twenty-three years later in a much different setting. It wasn't the same, but it was quaint and charming, and it was mine, thanks to my Mom.

As a married couple our credit was destroyed from my husband running up my student credit cards and not having a job to pay the bill, payments always being late, and having our furnishings repossessed from Rent-a-Center. We couldn't have qualified even with a co-signer. I was glad, it was in her name, a safety net for me, she knew. If anything had ever happened in my marriage the house was still mine and he couldn't have half. It was for the benefit of the children.

When we stumbled onto the cape cod in Cherry Hill, the sellers were a divorced couple dividing assets. The ex-wife had been court ordered that she could stay in the house with the children until the house sold. She made the house unsaleable. Mounds of stinky laundry in the family room three feet high, dog hair and dog poop in every room, magic markers on the walls and wood work, filthy dirty bathrooms, and piles of trash in the yard were the first things we saw. It didn't scare me away. I saw potential, a fault in my character. I had seen potential in Scott at one time too.

My Mom figured in some renovation funds to the house deal and we gutted the kitchen and rebuilt it from the floor up. We cleaned and painted everything. It was home, our home. There was plenty of space for everyone. The neighborhood was great and there were plenty of kids in the area for the girls to play with. All around it was a great place to raise kids in southern New Jersey; except in was in NJ.

I didn't recall the blue cape cod memory as a child until many years later while contemplating my blessings. We lived there for nine years, the longest residence we had ever maintained. Time had come for us to make a move, a fresh start, a needed change.

We were in regular contact with the owners of our future homestead, in Minnesota. Pictures were nice but not seeing the property raised some skepticism from the peanut gallery. I couldn't continue to press without a visual on the place and a real agreement. My mother, sister and anyone else I told of my interest thought I was flaking out.

It was January and I arranged to take a whirlwind visit to Wolf Lake, which is something I would never advise to anyone. We came into Minnesota in a blizzard counting seventy-three cars off the road, or in the ditch as the locals would say, on our trek up I35.

Even in the stress of the storm it was beautiful. The trees were mostly perfect pine trees like you see in a Bob Ross painting segment on PBS covered in snow. They were happy little trees all straight and pointy at the top covered in a flocking of snow set back off the highway fifteen feet or more.

Wide margins for error I figured as we passed all the cars stuck in the snow banks lining the corridor that traveled North and South through the state. I was amazed at the design for handling snow, very smart, they must know what to do with it because they must get a lot of it. I look ahead and there is a long line of yellow flashing lights ahead on the opposing side of the highway. A layered convoy of snow plows barreling down the snow-covered asphalt cleaning up one after another.

Cars would fall in behind them and ride their coat tails on the newest treated surface. Some drivers would blow past me in the right lane and not be phased by the accumulating slippery mess only to end up turned around and off the road ahead a mile. I drove slow and steady; my Jersey plates were my pass like a student driver car with a teen behind the wheel.

When we got to the hotel the trip had taken four hours longer than it should have. My knuckles were white, my hands were cramped, my neck was stiff, and I was exhausted, but this was just the beginning of the adventure. We slept and arranged to visit the house and business in the early afternoon.

As we drove to the house, we observed the area, small town America at its finest. The necessities were present, a grocery store, gas stations, laundromat, eye doctor, pizza place, etc. The houses were varying in style and appearance. Many homes were very small, and the garages were huge to house all the farm equipment and toys. Then there were actual farms with horses, beef and alpaca. It was the country, a town that had two stop lights and people we met were nice. One wrong turn and you were in the middle of nowhere within three miles of the main artery.

The lake, Wolf Lake, was large and shaped like a wolf head which was where it got its name. The water was frozen and there were ice houses for fishing positioned in carefully studied spots by the local fishermen guaranteeing lots of pole action between bottles of beer and shots of whiskey. Large pick-up trucks were parked in hubs around the little villages of ice fishing.

I remembered wondering if car insurance covered your vehicle if you were stupid enough to drive out to the middle of a lake and fall through because too many cars wanted a front spot to their ice house. The change of environment would be fun but culture shock to the kids. They will adapt I convinced myself, but will I?

We pulled onto the road that lead to the house, Military Road. My son would like that because he was into the service ever since an Airman gave him a patch from his uniform in the airport on our trip to Disney. Anything we could use to bring a positive spin to moving him half way across the country was good.

The house was half way down the road at the top of the hill, on the left just after the huge solitary pine tree that stood seventy-five feet in the air and leaning a little to the left. The snow covered the ground, a blanket of white leaving us to imagine what the yard would look like dressed in green or covered with autumn leaves. The property looked just like the photos, dirt driveway, and horse cut outs across the railings of the front porch in full gallop.

We approach the house first and we are met cordially by Lenny, a lumbering man with piercing blue eyes and a big smile. Invited inside, the house is inundated by shrunken versions of huskies, there were twelve in total. The pack was let outside barking and yipping creating quite a commotion. Lenny and Sue bred Alaskan Klee Kai as a supplement to the kennel business, a woodworking business, and his state prison job.

The house was dazzling because I was sold on the idea of the move already. There were no piles of laundry or magic markers on the walls. There were lots of details that caught my eye, but nothing was a deal breaker. We talked and talked, they answered many questions. There was excitement and promise for change. I could feel my stress level reduce as I looked at the beautiful nature that abounded.

You couldn't live in Wolf Lake and be like Snookie from Jersey Shore. That would be like a square peg in a round hole. This would be a great place for my kids to finish their childhood I fantasized. Two were teenagers and two were just in double digits. Maybe I could get them out before it was too late, before Jersey rooted in their soul?

New Jersey had been my home most of my life, but it was a different time, before cell phones, internet, computers; hell, microwaves weren't affordable for our family until my early teens. My parents moved us around as kids while my father advanced his education and career. In retrospect, I wonder if it was the generation that I grew up in or if it was the moving around and being forced to make new friends that contributed to my extrovert personality. I was convinced that kids are resilient and would adapt, like I did.

We packed the car for the trip home on a -22-degree cold blustery morning, Scott in shorts being a tough guy. We drove home early in the morning trying to get ahead of another storm which was normal for the area. I plotted out a plan of execution for getting the house on the market during the worst economic downturn in decades.

Our house had to sell at high end numbers for us to move, period. I needed to invest my retirement money into some upgrades to make the house stand apart. I had a friend who'd be my general contractor. If it fell through at least I'd have an upgraded bathroom, a practically new interior, a punch list of stupid things that were broken fixed, and that big garage in the backyard that was full of black mold would be gone forever.

I had severed my employment at just the right time to cash out my retirement fund. If I had waited even two weeks later, I would be waiting another six months to access that money. I ordered the pay out and waited for the check. My career ambitions changed after the visit to Minnesota. I knew that for the business to succeed I would have to learn to groom dogs.

Grooming was a third of the annual income and sales were already down for boarding because people heard of the kennel being for sale and had started looking elsewhere. I purchased a cd set and interactive course over the internet immediately. It was adequate, and I watched for hours and hours as this elderly couple passed on their knowledge of technique and helpful hints.

The lady instructor was annoying with her grating voice that sounded like she'd been smoking cigarettes since she was 10. Her hair was big, teased and sprayed. She was overweight, and the grooming jacket didn't help her hide any of it. I wondered if this was what I will look like after grooming for a while.

The husband, I found out through the credits at the end, was tall and had to hunch his shoulders to see certain angles of the various dog's anatomy. He was very gentle and the tone in his voice was calming and reassuring that yes, even I could do this. He wore a baby blue grooming coat that made me think of a prom in the 70's just missing the white carnation on the lapel.

The setting of the whole educational series was very dated. These two, dare I say forward thinking power couple, filmed this very early on in technology advances. It was probably a VHS set before being reformatted to CD. They probably make nursing home payments off my $600.00 purchase, I laugh.

As soon as I mentioned I was learning to groom people came out of the wood work with their dogs for me to "practice on" in NJ. Little did I know that "practice on" was code for my dog is not welcome back to any groomer in the tri state area because of how unruly it is. I needed to trim and shave various breeds and take pictures of my work to send into my video instructors for critique.

I really had a feeling that the man and woman in the videos were already long gone and someone else was cashing the checks and just making the consumer feel engaged, who knows? Maybe Shirley, I don't really remember her name, is still grooming? They say groomers never die their scissors just slow down.

I was angry at her and her husband, they lied. They must have picked the most well-behaved dogs on the planet for their video business, maybe they weren't even real. I was persistent and determined to slip into a groomer role. The biting, scratching and wrestling beast dogs was my new profession.

I kept in touch with the owners of the property in Minnesota regularly. They needed reassurance that we were doing everything we could to get there. We needed reassurance that they were committed to selling to us on a Contract for Deed and they wouldn't sell out from under us to someone else that was interested. Both parties had a lot on the line and we needed each other. This was the Universe interceding in my life showing me a path out. Who was I to question the Universe? What happened next was incredible.

I am talking to Sue and she mentions that she needs to have wrist surgery and that they might have to closeup the grooming side of the business until we arrive and take over. I was concerned, a third of the business revenue came from that skill set. The customers would find other groomers and maybe never return. The bank wouldn't finance a mortgage for us because of our credit, because we never owned a business before, and we didn't have employment arranged for when we moved.

We had to make enough money from the kennel to support the whole family until we found supplemental jobs. I needed grooming practice and she needed a groomer. I needed to learn the business and she was checking out. We talked about it and decided I would volunteer to come out and get the experience I needed, and they would provide room and board for the two months of her recovery. The decision was a no brainer for me.

I got a unique look at the business. I worked the kennel from morning until night every day and when there was grooming I did that too. I plotted out where all our furniture would go piece by piece in the house. The building was almost double in size from what we were used to. I also got to see all the things that needed attention around the property, house and business that got noted for negotiation later.

I wouldn't have been nearly as aware of all things big and small in Wolf Lake and on Military Road if I hadn't gone. Meanwhile, the house in Cherry Hill was being worked on in my absence. I was returning just in time to be nitpicky about all that had and hadn't been done while I was away. Scott was still in denial that we were moving forward with the plan and didn't push the contractor but when I got home I had a vision and I was making it happen.

The process of committing to the move, renovating the house, selling the house, and getting to Minnesota took eight months but everything happened at just the right times. While the house was being worked on we packed all non-essential items and purged anything that hadn't been used or needed in the last year to make room on the eighteen-wheeler. We labeled and marked everything with my new vision of right where to drop the box when it arrived.

We had Home and Garden TV on around the clock for months picking up tricks for staging the house to make it the most appealing for sale. I asked friends for recommendations for a realtor and was referred to a dynamic couple with whom I felt instantly kismet.

I picked up a part time job doing dog training at one of the big pet superstores and got accredited as an Obedience Trainer to add to my box of tricks. I continued to groom dogs on my gazebo in the back yard for practice.

I bought new furniture for staging to replace old pieces that had been used hard by our family of six. The house looked beautiful and we had to keep it that way to sell it. Clean, neat, organized, a little bland for my taste but the strangers walking through our home could picture themselves being there, move in ready!

Enter Bob and Bobbie, the real estate gurus I entered an arrangement with. Bob was the realtor, Bobbie was the brains behind the operation as it usually goes. Bob did marketing in magazines and newspapers, but Bobbie did the internet listing. She had a 360 camera and a great panache for selling points and what draws the eyes attention.

The house looked stellar on the MSL. There were forty homes for sale within one mile of our house. We had a number that we had to hit to make the move work. Our listing was the fifth highest priced house in the mile circle. We priced it slightly lower than it was worth to dangle the carrot for a quick sale and it worked.

Thirty days from listing, six showings, living out of totes and constantly nagging the kids or kicking them outside to play, our cute colonial blue cape cod with white trim and a barn red front door sold at asking price. It really happened, we were homeless. Being homeless became Scott's obsession.

"What if we get there and they changed their mind, or they don't follow through with our agreement?" he would argue.

He was right to be nervous I suppose. This move was all being done on sheer determination and faith. We signed nothing, just shook hands and drove away eight months earlier. My answer was that they had dreams too.

They were moving to Wyoming, getting off the grid, being real cowboys for the autumn season of their lives. Sue had left already with the twelve, yes twelve Klee Kai, in a little camper and was living on the land they purchased several years earlier. Just Sue and her Dad, and twelve dogs, that's brave.

She was patiently waiting for Lenny to arrive and start building their new home from the dusty soil up. Her husband had many things to wrap up here in Wolf Lake before he could leave town, some of which required the money from closing. They had a lot riding on our arrival. If we ended up homeless we would stay in a hotel until we could rent something and start with a new plan. I saw it all as a huge expedition.

The tractor trailer came and took our stuff on the last Friday morning of July, we cleaned any remnants of our existence for the walk through scheduled at 1pm. Closing was immediately after if all went well. It started to get late in the day before I got the call from my Mom that all the paperwork was done and filed, one problem.

"What is it?" I asked tentatively.

"Well, the proceeds from the house won't be credited to your account until Monday." Mom replied in an anxious tone.

She knew we had nothing, we had put all the chickens in the basket and needed that check available to take the next step.

"I'll loan you $500.00 to get you started, will that be enough?" Mom offered.

I knew that her offer would have been fine if it was just Scott and me but with the four kids and dogs the expenses would add up quickly and leave us stranded in another state somewhere along the turnpike.

# Chapter 7

We needed to stay in NJ although all our belongings were already careening along to MN scheduled to arrive in five to seven days. What if they got to the house before we did? Ok, here is where I had a few concerns but again I had to act in the moment. I am a consummate fixer, putting out fires is my forte. I called my best friend Gina and asked if our family of six could crash at their house completely unexpected, oh yeah and our two dogs. Her answer was yes without hesitation. I don't think she even asked her husband.

We descended upon their white traditional style two story home like a swat team securing a building. She had three in her brood, one was away at college. She displaced her two boys to the couches along with a few of my kids the rest of us found bedrooms upstairs.

My friend's house was an eclectic collaboration of yard sale finds. Her husband owned a landscaping business, so she changed the flower beds every time I'd visit. It was energizing and refreshing to see someone as bold as she was with her wall colors. Her home was very comfortable and fun. The kitchen was in the center of the mix where we would sit, she and I, pouring out our hearts to each other about life, husbands, work.

This visit felt like a going away party. We enjoyed spending time together food shopping for the hoard and then preparing meals, I sliced vegetables. She was in awe about how we were picking up and moving half way across the country. She was very attached to her home and the memories made there and never pictured herself leaving.

Gina is a spit fire full of scripture and motivational quotes and she lives by whatever floats her boat at the time. She tells it like it is and keeps going without missing a beat. I always appreciated her friendship because she knew Scott longer than any of my other friends and had experienced him over and over with his narcissistic tendencies. She had seen my struggles to keep things together and knew how hard he was to deal with.

She had her issues with her husband too, don't we all, but pot seemed to help her through the tough patches. She would dismiss herself and head upstairs coming back smelling of weed and perfume. Maybe if I had been a pothead I could have hazed over the past twenty plus years too. She has always been my go-to friend.

She had a pool which kept the kids occupied and entertained between squabbles and tattling. Gina loves carbs and can eat them like no one I have ever seen before so Scott's potato salad recipe from Lancaster, PA was a condition of our stay. He loved the attention and desire for his cooking from people, so he was very happy to make a huge bowl of it that she would shovel in by the spoonful every time she opened the fridge. It kept him busy and bitching passively about not having his bowls and his spatulas and blah blah blah.

Joe, her husband, had to work so that left Gina and me to kibitz to each other. We mostly talked about her recent affair and her marriage counseling with the Pastor from my church in Cherry Hill.

Neither of us had fond memories of Pastor Lee at this point. I had trusted him and found him very intelligent about the Bible, real life, well that was a different story. Gina had been referred to him from the Pastor of her church, however I had been in counselling with him for more than three years trying to keep my marriage intact and managing my depression.

Often, I left his office feeling worse about myself. I am a perfectionist. and I couldn't fix myself, my kids, my husband, my marriage. My counseling ended with PL when I drove to my sister's. Gina, on the other hand, was dismissed from counseling and told to change her attitude or not come back. We were very different gals but besties to the core.

Quickly the weekend passed. We decided to leave on Monday morning and see how far we would get with the cash loan from Mom. We said our goodbyes until next time. We were diverting through Connecticut to pick up a new Landseer Newfoundland puppy to start expanding our future breeding program which would help supplement our income if needed.

It was planned this way to drag out our trip, we had time to kill before our belongings met us that Thursday or Friday. It was yet another case where we leapt not sure of the outcome. I trusted the money would be in the bank and it was, just in time.

Once we got the puppy, Agnus Peppercorn Brisket, we were on our way to our new life. Money in the bank, two vehicles, four children, and three dogs along with all the accoutrements, a traveling show. Every stop was a mass exodus like clowns getting out of a car at the circus. It was a twenty-one-hour drive directly, plus six more for the puppy, so twenty-seven hours of drive time over three days. We tried to stop at times that would allow us to use the hotel pool and let the kids stretch and get exercise. We would stop at points of interest like murals or world's biggest whatever.

The natural split of our children happened for most of the trip. My oldest daughter and son gravitated toward their father because they were preferred. She was a carbon copy of him, attitude and demeanor and all. Our son was the only boy, our miracle child and a most easy-going kid on the planet. These two were often found with Dad because he found them less testing than the other two in our equation of four.

The donut shenanigan was a typical "have what we want now" scenario and neither of us driving wanted to cave for such a silly request since we had just stopped and fueled up 20 minutes earlier. The Dunkin Donuts in the Avenger needed to get to the minivan. Driving very carefully, at 70 plus miles an hour, my second oldest that wanted the donut, hung out the rear window reaching for the ultimate prize a Bavarian Crème pastry. My son reached out the other vehicle held by the ankles and pants by his older sister, puppy sleeping through the whole thing. I had no idea how close the two vehicles would really have to be to accomplish the task without compromising the delicate treat. The kids thought we were the coolest parents around, we were just stubborn about not stopping. Perspective is everything I guess.

When checking in with Allied, the moving company, our belongings weren't going to arrive until Friday. We pulled into Wolf Lake Wednesday night, stopped at the kennel and checked our dogs overnight so we could then check into a hotel. It was a quick exchange and we would be back early the next morning. Our entourage entered the hotel with our luggage and Jersey accents. We'd arrived in Wolf Lake!

We woke excited for the day. We stopped at Mel Café for breakfast, a run-down local favorite judging by the crowded parking lot. There was a group of old redneck men that gathered there 7am, 2pm, and 7pm for coffee every day and to talk local gossip worse than women I supposed. Their little man club was the oxygen keeping them alive, a purpose to get through the day to the next cup of joe. The average age was 70, I would find out later that this was the average age of most of the ideology of the area too.

I had met the men during my stay in the Spring. I was bold then, pulled a chair right up to the circle of testosterone and started introducing myself to the gentlemen that were there asking all the silly new to the area typical questions. They would chuckle at my questions and answer cordially, often pulling my leg. I was nicknamed Jersey, which was obviously fitting and endearing.

This day the crowd that was there consisted of mostly tourists and at 9:30am the Brotherhood had already come and gone. Wolf Lake is a hub of activity in the summer and August was prime time. People from the cities come up North and people from the Northland go south to this crossroad area of ATV trails, lakes and boating, bike trails, camping, etc. Growing up at the Shore, I was very good at identifying "Benny's", out of towners, the shoe was on the other foot now. There were eyes glaring as we entered and spoke to each other with our notable Jersey twangs. We were very different. Breakfast was passable, nothing extraordinary which we would find to be the norm in midwestern fare.

The older girls were not impressed with the two traffic lights on the main road through town. Our little metropolis had all the necessities. I encouraged pointing out the grocery store, gas stations, hospital, two automotive supply stores, coffee shop, hair salons and Dairy Queen. They felt like we were moving to middle of nowhere. In comparison to where we lived it was very different, but on the map.

The little ones were like owls, head's spinning looking around at everything and taking it all in. When the kids saw the movie theater they were in shock, they had been to Multiplex's all their lives. The Lake Theater shows one movie at a time and in an old run-down building that had seen much better days.

As we pass through the light at town square the blinker in the van clicks to a rhythm of anticipation. Up the hill, one mile out of the hustle and bustle of downtown, we turn right onto Military Road. We pass a few houses on the road and Scott toys with the kids.

"We're here," he proclaims as he pulls into a rundown uninhabitable shack.

They were terrified for a split second however they were used to Dad's jokes and pranks and quickly disregarded the notion. We had shared enough pictures with them to have an idea of what our new abode looked like from all angles. Proceeding down the road, looking for the tall thin singular pine tree with a split top that became my landmark, we arrive finally and forever, or so we thought.

We pull in the dirt driveway trying to avert the mud potholes staggered like an obstacle course. We park the vehicle and unload from the clown car once again. The kids want to see our dogs, I want to inspect the house, my husband is worried about the trash in the car, then we find Lenny in the garage with table saws running.

All his cabinetry and wood working tools are still in the garage, red flag one. He is building something, a bunch of somethings, looked like a full kitchen worth of cabinets in mid project. The snow is all gone, it is August now, and there is trash piled up all over the property. I wonder if it had all been there when we visited eight months earlier and the blanket of snow just covered over everything making it look virginal and pristine, red flag two. Lenny invites us in the house, red flags three, four, five, six through ten, hit all at once. He hasn't moved out, hadn't cleaned, and had serious ADHD.

It was Wednesday afternoon. We had made good time coming across on our trip even with stops. He was supposed to be gone on Thursday giving us time to do any painting or fixing or fussing before the truck arrived Friday. I was nervous that he was going to really leave. I am thinking this guy didn't think I was really going to show up with his check. He bit off way too much for him to chew. His wife was gone, and it was just him living the bachelor life for the last four weeks. Left to his own agenda he kept the business running and was wrapping up favors he promised people before he skipped town. He has no arrangements for help to move furniture, and only a long horse trailer to haul everything to WY. Lenny now has no choice but to start packing and getting ready to leave. I stress that we have a big truck with lots of stuff barreling down a highway headed for this house in less than two days.

We had to check back into the hotel and extend our stay until Friday, it would take that long for him to move out. We took over the kennel operations on Thursday morning, so he could concentrate on moving. During down hours we would help him by taking things out of the house and placing them under the tree on the East side near the trailer. Once a room was clear, I would attempt to get the hair of the dozen dogs captured and discarded and clean with bleach to cut the smells. The couple had stopped caring after I left.

While I visited, the house was lived in but clean, now, not so much. This was an eleventh-hour cram of everything from appliances to junk drawer contents, nooks and crannies filled in the trailer packed with a delicate balance of I hope nothing breaks and I don't really give a shit.

He did what he could I guess. We signed papers and handed him a significant check, the purchase of the business outright and a down payment on our contract. We went inside the house and the next thing we see is the dust from the driveway billowing in the air as he pulls out the driveway with trailer in tow. Left behind was a large pile of household items that didn't make the cut, not important enough to make space for the trip.

They had tried to negotiate more money for the washer and dryer, the beat-up Ford pickup that had been rolled in a ditch, and a John Deer tractor with a bucket. All those items were left for us simply because he had no way to handle or transport them for free. Also, for free, we had adopted two horses that also didn't make the cut to go to Wyoming.

The horses were a blessing and a curse. Chief was an older soured pony that had walked in circles for too many years. He was black and white splotched and had ice blue eyes. I am a sucker for animals and the previous owners had me pegged. "He will be a great starter horse for your daughter." they exclaimed, "He just needs to trust you and you need to bond with him.". Chance on the other hand, was a beautiful stallion, uncut and rowdy. Chance was 16 hands, standing tall over Chief and was every bit a wild overpowering beast. "He just needs training, you can send him away for that and he'll come back a great riding horse." I was told. My kids loved visiting them and doing chores was entertaining at first, it helped with the transition. I was out of my league. They were ours now, guess we were country folk officially, horses, five acres, a tractor, and a two tone F150 with confederate flag decals on the back windows.

We worked late into the night cleaning, and cleaning, and doing more cleaning. I was sure that it was only as bad as it was because they wanted to be gone so bad to their next chapter, just like me. The bright orange truck glided noisily down Military Road Friday just before Noon just as it started to rain.

Despite many attempts the road and driveway were too narrow to support the angle the truck needed to take to enter or exit the property. You could tell that the driver was disgusted even though he tried to keep a good attitude. Every bit of the truck had to be unloaded at the end of our football field length drive and carried or carted in the house where I waited to direct traffic minus the bright yellow vest. Every piece went right where it belonged, just as I had envisioned while I was back in NJ or sleeping in the basement of this very house as Lenny and Sue's guest.

I was thrilled to have a new life, new people, new adventures. No one here knew how bad things the year before had been. No one knew Scott yet, so I had a chance to make friends. We needed each other in this new foreign land, much better decision than having another baby. The newness was inviting and exciting and the kid's exposure to an existence outside of New Jersey was happening, a totally different way of life.

We felt relief and awe that it really happened. Yes, it did, I did it, willed it, wished it, prayed for it, paid for it, planned it. It was an incredible connect the dots to achieve this final picture. It was meant to happen just how it did to set up my exit from my marriage.

# Chapter 8

We pulled in the driveway of the white house on West Pine Branch Drive. It was Lynda's house, the third wife of my father. A large colonial style set back on a lot that backed up to a small patch of woods, yet plenty of grass to manicure and a nice plot of garden for Dad's tomatoes. My dad's lifeblood comes from the outdoors. He has a Master of Environmental Science Degree. He made a name for himself while working for the Health Department adding a fleet of boats for oceanic Red Tide monitoring, closing beaches because of hypodermic needles washing up on shore, and closing Chinese Food restaurants with hanging dog and cat carcasses in the basement.

A hardworking man when it came to things he was passionate about. My mother was one of those things at one time. They met while my Dad was in college. My father was an officer in the Army when I was born and was sent to Vietnam when I was only days old.

I was his Barnacle, or Barny for short. I was not the son he always hoped for, but I was Daddy's Little Girl. From the military, Lester returned to school. He graduated from Rutgers before the war and his master's degree was earned at Tulane University. My mother worked very hard putting him through his education in hopes of a better life for all of us down the road. His education and career goals were the priority for the first several years.

We moved a lot, forcing me to adapt and embrace change or at least think of it as normal. I look at it now as a huge bonus in my upbringing because I am very openminded and accepting. I had some poor me moments thinking of how I was robbed my childhood not living in my childhood home and having friends since kindergarten but overall, I liked the excitement of a move.

My father joined clubs and organizations to network. He liked to rub elbows with the right people in his areas of interest. His circles of influence would result in campaigns for office. "Get more with Les" was the slogan I remember the most. He had an artist friend do a pen and ink drawing of Cher in her shear beaded Mackie dress using sex as a marketing tool. He won of course.

He was charismatic and charming and handsome with a male porn star mustache that was common in the late seventies. He was young, vibrant and dynamic so it was no wonder he was offered Health Officer title at a very young age. This is where he made a name for himself.

He was working hard on his personal career while my mother crept up the ladder of corporate entities without a post high school education. She worked hard the whole time behind the scenes in dark dingy warehouses and closet sized offices. My mother was a Buyer, a career that suited her natural gifts. She was savvy and smart about all her purchases even the clothes she would hide under the bed from my father that she'd buy while he'd been watching football.

She started working in hospitals purchasing medical supplies, later moving to the rope industry, then military parts and computer components. A self-made woman completely. As her position elevated she was required to travel but most of her time was spent dealing with misogynist salesmen. She knew how to use sex to her advantage too. She always dressed very classy, but her tops were very shear. She wore sexy bras and satin camisoles that were visible and left men wanting more. If she was going to be paid like a woman, why not distract like a woman.

She was beautiful with her brownish-red flowing and wavy hair. She has striking blue eyes and held people's attention as she peered into their soul with intent and a smile. Pencil skirts and high heels even in the factory were worn by her every day, never dressed down, ever. She was given a lot of promotions, and I knew her sex appeal and provocative dress helped from a young age, and it was good.

"You need to dress the way you want to be perceived." This was advice I'd return to during my post-divorce shenanigans.

My parents were very focused on their own career paths. Although, as my mother grew in confidence and self-worth my father still had expectations of dinner on the table every night when he came home. He was stuck on his morals of how he should be treated with no regard or appreciation for my mother's work, stress level, or need to relax. He started having affairs and accused her of the same.

The eighties were an empowering decade for women as they started finding their value in the world as individuals, sexual beings and a race all their own. She had built my father to what he was, a prominent public figure, and she would tear him down too. They were married for fourteen years. It was very hard on my sister and me. My mother had to work even harder now to prove to herself that she didn't need a man. The following years of visitation issues and child support battles were brutal from our perspective.

My mother was a man hater now and for a long time after the split. She would only ask her father to do things for her. When he passed, she was forced to look beyond him. She dated married men, intentionally. She like the attention without the commitment and she could always send them packing pack to their pitiful wives. It was a control game.

As time went by, she fell into an adulteress long-term relationship with a man that was sexually unfulfilled in his marriage because his wife was dying of Cancer. Sixteen years later, at age sixty-four, she remarried this man one year after his wife died. I was shocked when she a called and asked for my blessing. She had said she would never get married again and I had believed her.

I knew she was getting lonely and feeling the pressure of her years coming down on her. She wanted security and someone to grow old with, someone to hold at night and to watch the neighborhood with. I understood, I always knew I wasn't made to be alone either.

Dad, on the other hand, loved women and sex. He moved into a bachelor pad when they separated, then in with his secretary Joyce who I think was the affair that broke the camel's back. He was living with a lady that had a mean goose as a guard dog at one time. He loved the blondes with legs. Maybe that's why his second marriage, to Diane, didn't last very long. She was a 5'2" brunette. Born of pure Italian descent, she was a force to be reckoned with. She was my Dad's match, toe for toe. They married and were divorced after Dad cheated on her with a blonde bimbo, with legs, after only two years. Diane didn't have patience for that and he found his belongings on the front yard after she found out.

Enter Lynda. A short time after the failed marriage with Diane, Dad announced he was getting married again. Apparently, he wasn't meant to be alone either. Lynda was a blonde, with legs, and a peculiar resemblance to my mother. She was Orthodox Russian and had a very cold demeanor that fit her genealogical roots.

She was fifteen years younger than my Dad. My sister and I figure she tricked him into marrying her with a pregnancy. The clock was ticking, and he was a good catch. And along came T, our half-sister arrived the same year Dad's first grandchild was born. Dad being a grandfather appalled Lynda and reminded her of his life before her.

As she was running out of eggs, Dad was running out of marbles, little did she know. When Lynda came on the scene, my grandmother on my father's side was dealing with dementia on steroids. She was packing up her grocery bags every night and leaving for Blue Anchor, her childhood home. Her boyfriend, Walt, kept her safe the best he could until she had to be admitted to a nursing facility where she stayed until she died. She had a sister Glenda that suffered the same affliction and behavior patterns. Alzheimer's was the post mortem cause of death and a strong familial lineage on the Bate's genepool.

My sister and I can trace our father's mental demise back to about age fifty-five. We weren't regular visitors because of where we lived, so when we did see him the changes were bothersome. Somewhere around fifty-eight he was forced to retire early because he wasn't functioning with predictability in his leadership role.

He was a great story teller and his stories got better and better every time I heard them. Then I started hearing the same story multiple times in the same visit. He couldn't remember his grandchildren's names but would light up like a Christmas tree when he saw their faces.

He started getting belligerent during visits and his moods would flare and wain in a second. Lynda started screening phone calls and limiting his conversations on the phone until phone calls went right to voicemail and were never returned.

Katie had more of a positive rapport with Lynda than I did. I am not sure what I did except have the four grandchildren. Katie would call and talk directly to Lynda if she could catch her picking up the phone. His wife shared that Dad wasn't himself and that she was struggling to care for him but wouldn't accept that he was following the path of his mother and aunt.

I would call during the day while she was a work if I wanted to talk to him. Infrequently he would hold a conversation, most of the time it was a one-sided myriad of racist slurs, or about chores. I struggled with his ability to do tasks like chopping wood alone, but I wasn't close enough to do anything about it and Lynda would accost me about my opinions. She was right, I had no idea what living with him was like.

I would try to plan visits by leaving messages on the answering machine that we were in town and the possible times we might be passing through. Those calls were not returned with acknowledgment or anticipation, they weren't returned at all. It was never really passing through though, going past Dad's exit on 295 meant driving a half hour out of the way creating a huge loop on the way to someplace else.

So, we pulled in the driveway and the house had aged and tired since the last time I saw it a year before. Her SUV was in the driveway, but his Jeep wasn't around, it could be in the garage I thought. I wonder if he can remember how to drive since he can chop wood, but where would he go? I imagined he stopped driving a long time ago because otherwise he would get as far from his witch of a wife as possible.

The grass hadn't been mowed or trimmed, the deck hadn't been stained, the garden was full of past peak plants and looked abandoned, never touched from the year before. I knew Dad was deteriorating and this was a big house with lots to maintain. They had the greenbacks to hire a landscaper for sure, I was confused. Scott waited in the car and I'd see if they were home. It wasn't unusual to find them not there.

I knocked on the door. I knocked again. I knocked again. The door they used to enter the house was into a laundry room. I figured it may be hard to hear a visitor if clothes were in the washer or dryer. We had come out of the way to visit via a loop that got us to the airport for our flight back to Minnesota. I was unsure if we would see them or not, so I allotted two hours that could be used to visit without rushing.

I start walking back to the VW bug convertible rental car and hear the door lock mechanism disengage and out steps Lynda.

She is dressed in black from head to toe and has been crying. I say hello and asked to see Dad.

"He's not here." Putting all the pieces together I start to think that my Dad may be dead.

I have had a looming fear of this scenario and had taken measures to reach out to my aunts and uncles to please call me if they heard anything about his condition.

"Where is he?" knowing full well that he doesn't leave the house without her anymore.

"He's not here. Go home and get off my property" she snarks.

"Please Lynda, just tell me where he is? Is he okay?" I plead.

> "Your Father is in the hospital. You have a lot of nerve whisking in and acting like you care after your Father has been taken away by ambulance." She's ready to blow.

"Ambulance? What? Is he okay?" "Where is he?" "I have to catch a flight back home, please." I beg.

"I don't have to tell you that, he is stable and in professional hands and that's all you need to know." She says as cold as Smirnoff on ice.

This Russian bitch is keeping information from me and won't even tell me where he is.

Scott had music playing but was waiting for my signal to either come inside or for me to return to the vehicle disappointed. At this point, her voice was raised, and she was cursing and yelling and pointing very aggressively and moving me toward the car. Scott caught on to what was happening, and he called the police. I called my sister. I was hysterical. I wanted my Dad.

We explained to the 911 operator that we wanted to verify that my Dad was not home and to find out where he was. Lynda was in the health care profession and knew what she was doing. She had obviously researched this herself because she told the officer that she didn't have to disclose his location just his condition and that he was getting professional help. The officer politely expressed how sorry he was to deliver the news that she was correct. I was in shock that this woman could be so heartless for no reason.

Here I am, in NJ, getting ready to fly back home with no idea when I'd be able to return, knowing my Dad is in the hospital, not knowing which hospital, having a panic attack. I can't breathe. It was one of the most helpless times of my life.

Scott and I start driving toward the airport. We have now eaten up our hundred and twenty minutes of "visit time" and had to get to TSA to make the flight home.

I'm talking to my sister realizing the only way we will have resolution and answers is if I stay and find him. This was a pivotal moment in my life where I had to make a choice. Scott pulled off an exit and I got out. It took about twenty minutes to go through our two suitcases that had gotten tremendously comingled over our ten-day trip and make sure I had enough clothes and toiletries to get me by for a while.

I called my Mom and she and her husband got in the car and drove 45 minutes to find me at a Valero sitting on my purple suitcase.

Scott supported my decision to stay. He had to get back to the kids and the kennel. He immediately started a Facebook campaign of support for this horrific travesty I was going through asking for prayers. This is ironic and humorous based on his past. He glorified himself in the fact that he was this amazing husband that LET me stay to find my father.

The kids were informed of what was going on and started sleuthing. I asked my oldest back in Minnesota, to look up all the hospitals and Memory Care facilities in NJ. My phone was dying, and I couldn't charge it until I got back to my mother's house and went through the luggage to find my charging cord. My sister, in Florida, was looking too. I was there in NJ looking for a needle in a haystack.

It's 1 AM, Scott has landed in Minneapolis and is driving home.

"I found Pop Pop, I found him!" My daughter exclaimed.

She had called over forty facilities asking if my Dad was a patient. The third shift people tend to be more relaxed with information. She had found a chatty Cathy that was very informative.

I had a ninety-minute drive to the hospital in the morning and I would check into a hotel room close by and stay until I was satisfied that he was okay. I arrived at 7:55am. I wanted to get there before Lynda and I had no clue when that might be. I didn't let her know that I stayed or that we had found him.

I approached his room number and there was a male attendant outside his door like a prison guard holding a clip board. His name was Eman.

# Chapter 9

Eman was a large and burly fellow. He was of African descent and had an accent that was thick like syrup dripping out of his mouth. I found that I hung on his every word because he was interesting to listen to, I had to work to understand some of what he was trying to convey, mostly though he would talk to me about my father. He had kind eyes that smiled when he did. I would put him in his mid to late thirties for an age, but I suck at the age guessing game. His laugh was deep and wide and echoed through the hallways. I introduced myself and didn't have to finish, "Lester's daughter?" he asked. "You look like a female version of him. He looks great as a woman." he cajoled

I asked lots of questions. Eman was helpful in a way the nurses wouldn't be. The attendants were dealing with Lester's wife and were on the front line for her ballistic missiles of nastiness. My step mother had made no friends and I was a breath of fresh air to all the staff. My father's dark friend was giving me insight into his condition and hers. I was not authorized according to HIPPA to have any details from the doctor, nurses, physical therapists, or social workers. No one would talk to me except Eman. At least, I had Dad in front of me to hug and hold.

He was very thin, that was the first thing I noticed as I looked at him sleeping in his bed. He had apparently been up all night which is not uncommon for Alzheimer patients. He laid there breathing nice long deep breaths. When I touched, him he was pleasantly warm but not hot. His skin was thin like tissue paper and bruised from all the IV ports he had experienced. You see, my dad had been in this hospital for a month and the bitch never called and told me or my sister, or any of his brothers or sister.

He stirred in his bed, raised at the head and under the knees. Was this position necessary for his treatment? I still didn't know why he was there, no one would tell me. I stepped out and called my sister and my family, then my mom. I was with him and I wasn't going anywhere until I had the answers I needed. They were relieved, even my mom in a weird way. The universe interceded for her in their divorce. She would never have been able to handle where he was today with his illness and she knew it too, but she was still concerned for him and her girls.

When I stepped back in the room my Dad was sitting up with his back to me, looking out the window at the people walking six stories below. I approached slowly as not to startle him. He looked at me with his piercing blue eyes and wiry out of control eyebrows, he smiled like he'd laid eyes on a long-lost friend. Did he recognize me? Even for a split second? I hoped. He motioned for me to come sit next to him on his bed. He smelled like shit. I used the controls on the side rail to lower the bed to flat. He stood up and put his hands behind his back and watched me very closely making sure my actions were acceptable.

His conversation with me was jumbled and mixed up but every now and then a sentence of clarity would come out. Please say my name. Please. He would obsess over the blankets on the bed being straight and that the corners were done right, I assume flashes back to his days in the Army. He would talk a lot about water rising and buckets and buckets and more buckets. He was already very afflicted with this terrible disease when Hurricane Sandy had hit the Jersey Shore. She had impacted his affected brain.

He had a house in Mystic Island on a lagoon inside the bay. It was destroyed by the storm and he was there during it all mechanically reacting to the water rising like muscle memory. I'm sure his wife was doling out instructions to bale water, hence the buckets. Like chopping wood, I supposed. He loved the water and always had a boat so flooding protocol must have been tucked away in a cavern of his brain unaffected yet by this dementia.

He told captivating ramblings of how the water was rushing in with sound effects whoosh, or about his time in Vietnam with Pa pa pa pa ttttttt gun fire noises. His eyes would get wide and bright like the old days when he would tell about the biggest buck he saw and chose not to shoot or whale of a fish that gave him the fight of his life and he saw it eye to eye off the side of the boat before the line broke. I liked those stories much better.

He seemed okay on his feet, walking around the room. He was looking all around on the floor and walking in circles until he found a trash can and whipped out his penis and started to pee. I trained dog owners to watch for this behavior in their puppies to house break them, funny how things come around. I corralled him to the bathroom and once there he seemed to know what to do. This was the first time I ever saw my father's junk and his ass as I removed a turd from between his ass cheeks that was the source of his stench.

I was prepared for this. I had worked with Alzheimer's patients when I was a Certified Nursing Assistant while I attended nursing school. It was a unit that specialized in memory care. 60 patients and all of them were challenged with dementia at different levels. Our job was never routine, and we knew many diversion and redirection tools that minimized agitation. My skills kicked right back in like I had never left. Working with what I was given, reducing choices and stimuli, asking leading questions to a result, giving tasks to do like sorting condiment packages were quick easy tactics to use to pass time and get results.

I got him cleaned up. I got him dressed. He didn't look like I remembered. I got a pair of scissors and trimmed his hair, I am a groomer and I had cut my husband's hair for 25 plus years. I trimmed his crazy eyebrows which I inherited and need to tame and shape almost daily. We went back in the bathroom and I let him shave himself. I watched like a little girl fascinated at her father's precision and ease with a razor on his face. Dad made all the same faces he used to when I watched him forty years ago. It made me smile and feel warm deep inside that he was still in there somewhere. He looked great, a lady killer, he resembled the man I knew as Dad.

We walked the hallway loop around the nursing station endlessly. I would have to speed up or distract him when we approached and exit door because he wanted to leave. He walked with his hands behind his back like he was assessing the situation and everyone's work ethic. He would wave or salute or hug almost every person that we would pass. Now, remember that we were walking a loop, so the people didn't change from lap to lap. Dad made new friends or new enemies every 10 minutes. He especially liked the blondes.

He referred to me as his beautiful lady. He would look in my eyes and it would seem like he was going to spit out my name, but he didn't. He played with my hair and touched my face adoringly. He was a gentleman still, making sure I had somewhere to sit when we would take a break. At first Eman escorted us round and round but Dad started to get paranoid that he was following us, so I promised Eman we wouldn't leave the floor and we would check in every lap.

When Dad got tired we returned to his room where he would fidget with everything. He wanted to stash things in his pocket. I found spoons, sugar packets, a comb which made sense, a toothbrush, food and various other items. If he couldn't find his pocket, he would shove the items in his underwear. I had a moment of awareness, therefore children are born, to take care of our parents when they revert to be a child. I had heard that many times before, I was living it now. I cherished every moment I got the privilege to care for this incredibly intelligent and proud man.

In floats Lynda, shocked at the sight of me sitting in the room.

"Oh, Hello. I see that you've made yourself comfortable. How are you today Les?" as she leans in and gives him a kiss on the head.

"Uh oh, the Boss is here." Dad says. He calls her the Boss and the Manager at different times.

Roles of authority over him, which he respected as a military officer. She rifles through a bag bringing out toiletries and fruit. She admonishes me for bringing him a blueberry tastykake. I want to shove it where the sun doesn't shine.

She pulls me aside and asks how long I'm staying and I respond with undefined parameters. She is bothered by my very existence and excuses herself from the room. As I look down the hall, I see her chewing out the nursing staff for not calling her and letting her know I was with him. I snicker to myself at what a fool she is making of herself and how riled I have made her for a change. She gave reaffirmed directions to not give me any information, nothing new there. She couldn't keep me from spending time with him while he was here and that infuriated her.

The first day was down, he was safe and cared for. I passed on reports to my sister regularly. I posted some pics of my Dad and me on Facebook, so everyone could see he was okay. My cousin on my Dad's side reached out and filled me in on the dissolved relationship between Lynda and my Uncles' and Aunt. None of them knew he had been hospitalized. My back up plan had been obliterated.

The story of his admittance went something like this. There was a huge storm that had branches down all over and lightening had struck a tree in Dad's neighbor's yard. The storm and the lightning strike had my father reverting to the jungles of Vietnam in heavy artillery strikes. He started reacting as though a bomb had just exploded and was up all night.

The next day, the neighbor hired a landscaping company to come remove the fallen tree and the branches. A van of Mexican workers showed up and scattered to work. Dad thought they were the Vietnamese and that he was under attack. He left the house and attacked the neighbor for trying to calm him down resulting in the police and ambulance taking him away.

When he got to the hospital it was traumatic because many strange people were trying to do things to him. He was heavily medicated and that is when they found his big toe swollen and angry, full of puss. A serious infection from an ingrown nail that had started to travel into his foot and ankle was the culprit. He had a high fever.

The hospital was not a Memory Care facility and he needed care multiple times a day, so he was admitted. At first, they sedated him heavily to get the infection under control, but he couldn't stay there, and he couldn't stay in a near coma. The social worker came up with the attendant idea because Dad was too much for the regular nursing staff to handle especially overnight. A month later, they need him to go somewhere else because his infection is healed.

Lynda refuses to bring him home because he is a danger to her and her neighbors. Insurance is hitting the limit. She is considering nursing homes but wouldn't put her dog in any of them. I appreciated her diligence for a clean place with some privacy, but they cost more. The money, here is where it all falls into place.

Lynda was losing ground. She had two homes, she will have to sell one. She has two cars, she will have to sell one. She is being supported by his pension and a nursing home would take all of that. Dad was so young to be existing in a nursing home until he dies. She would lose everything.

He was very strong, apparently playing tennis with T the day before he went to the hospital. This would be a long, expensive, draining process. Here is where Lynda would pay literally and figuratively.

She looked at VA hospitals, but Dad didn't spend enough time in the service to get all the benefits. Some that he would qualify for had waiting lists for months. She had to settle on something fast, her time was running out. She will never admit it, but my being there allowed her the time to regroup and go visit facilities.

She didn't spend near the time at the hospital that she had been. She didn't ask me when I was coming either. She knew, I would spend as much time with him as I could. I stayed for meals and meds. He was so smart we had to hide his pills, in blueberry tastykakes, to get him to take them and he'd only take them for me.

I checked out of the hotel after the first night and stayed with my Mom. I would stay until he was moved; and I knew where he was being placed. Scott was supportive but wanted me home. Our anniversary happened while I was away, and I sent him a card out of obligation. He was getting mad that I was choosing my dad over him.

I had started researching and thinking. Early Onset Alzheimer's Disease (EOAD) is a genetic disorder passed by the parent to the children with 50/50 odds. Katie and I both needed to think about the future. If we would start losing our memories at 55 would we have a plan?

Would I have a plan? What would happen to me? What would Scott do with me? What funds were in place to care for me? Which of my children would be burdened with caring for me? Was my life memorable? Did I do things that made me happy and was I happy right now? Answer Key: No, No Clue, lock me in the basement, none because he'd spend them all, one of them had to, no, no and I was Not.

These questions rolled around in my brain. There was a blood test I could take to the tune of $1500.00 to find out if I had the gene. If I found out that I in fact had the gene, then what would I do? I knew myself better than that, I'd freak out.

I called the University of Minnesota Research Department and offered myself to them for regular screenings and to be a candidate for experimental drugs if I did start to lose it. I hoped to be part of helping someone else through research. They never called me back.

I got home two weeks later than I originally thought I would. I was torn. I was sad. I was missing my Dad. I was contemplating life, my life. I immediately made plans to go back.

I worked down the back log of put off grooming appointments. Groomers live their lives in eight-week cycles until a Shiatzu's hair grows back.

It was at this time that I wanted, no needed out of the marriage *now*. Dad's illness made it necessary for me to act and not just go through the motions. If I was only going to live another ten years with my memories then for God's sake they would be good ones, happy ones, fun ones alone or with a mate I didn't care. Scott was immediately offended. How could I? After he had covered things for me to stay in NJ? Who did I fuck while I was there? That was the question that put the nail in the coffin.

I wanted to have no regrets, he was my biggest. I immediately felt the weight lifted off me and I had a calm resolve, unshakeable really. All the yelling, and emotional torture that happened thereafter was predictable.

It was horrific to see my children being used as pawns and lied to. He claimed I was sick again and needed to go to the hospital. He knew he reached the end of his mooch train and there would be a price to pay for it.

I was free in five weeks. I filed divorce papers myself. He wanted nothing, except everything. Nothing to do with the kids but everything I had financially and that had value. It was all stuff and it was worth it to be rid of him. Take all the negativity with you, I will rise.

He stripped my house of everything he wanted while I was visiting my father again and locked valuables away in a storage container. I still look for things today that coward took.

People here are Minnesota Nice. They don't file for divorce over Christmas, but I was a Jersey Girl. I didn't have much money. I filed on my own, handwritten on 56 sheets of paper downloaded off the county courthouse website.

Our hearing was scheduled very quickly and was very cut and dry. I had full custody of both underage children. He played the martyr yet didn't pay a dime of child support and tried to destroy my business through social media and bad mouthing me all over this small town.

It all happened the way it was supposed to, not in my time, this is where I find rest.

# Chapter 10

Toward the end of my marriage I had found an occasional break from the company of my spouse. Every once and a while, after my older girls had turned 21, they wouldn't have any friends to go out with, and they would ask me. The girls really didn't want to spend time with me, they were bored or broke and they knew I'd pay and be entertaining.

When Scott agreed that I could go, I would be hesitant to take him at his word but grabbed on to a favorite phrase, "Let your yes be yes, and your no be no." He said yes, I was going. I knew it meant being on pins and needles, harassed by text, and having it held over my head for weeks. I would meet my friend Zin to loosen me up. A few glasses would do, a few bottles and I was free for a while.

I would get myself gussied up, taking pride in my appearance as if I was still going to a bar in New Jersey where people tried. The place we would go was called The Rabbit Cage. The little bar and grill, situated in a town along the Moose Horn River, was three exits away on the interstate. The girls didn't like the local municipals and the chances of running into their friends out in Willow River was slim with distance.

I would hit the ATM for cash, we would designate a driver, it was never me because I would pay the bar tab, an unspoken rule. My girls knew I needed to get out and dance and interact with people without the menacing gargoyle peering and judging my every move and those of anyone else around.

After having bypass surgery, alcohol metabolized differently and fast. I couldn't eat more than three ounces of food in a meal or eat anything with more than fifteen grams of sugar. But wine, I could put away. The more wine, the freer and funnier I became. The girls seemed to like my outgoing personality and free speech when I was intoxicated. I was always respectful, quick witted, and craving attention which I would get.

By this time, I had lost ninety pounds and was feeling a lot more confident about myself. I knew that I wasn't hidden by fat anymore. I knew how to dress that I was attractive and not slutty, so my husband would approve. I did wear plaid flannels a lot with cammies underneath so that when I'd be drenched in sweat from dancing I could shed layers and reveal more skin.

My husband would let me go so for a reason. Scott and our son would slink to the basement playing with RC cars for hours on end and if I wasn't home there was no feeling guilty about it. Better yet, I wouldn't see them spending hundreds of dollars on orders from hobby shops and eBay. Scott would see money and spend it; a dangerous habit that put me in a constant place of angst.

If I complained about his spending I would be torn down, accused of not valuing him and controlling him. Conversely, letting Scott spend was a defensive move for me allowing peace in the house. Ultimately, I was enabling further behavior through his spending and emotional hijacking. Don't do this or he'll do that, was the chess game I had to play moment by moment. My home was a cage, his presence was a cage, our marriage was a cage, my mind was a cage, but The Rabbit Cage was a catch and release.

I never had trouble meeting people and making friends so the bartenders where easy. Ash and Matt were the usual fellas to be working the L shaped bar. I felt like I was entering "Cheers" in Boston every time I went there. As I approached the bar Ash would put two bottles of white zinfandel in the cooler and break out the goblets instead of the little flute glasses they usually used for wine customers.

Ash was a tall young man in his twenties and a jokester with all the inappropriate innuendos a bartender should know. Matt was shorter and older, around my age so not older, with a bald spot surrounded with a halo of dark hair.

Matt was personable but more mature and business focused, this was a second job for him. During the day Matt worked at the prison like a large majority of people in the area, the rest of the time he was caring for his parents in their advanced years and health conditions. I think The Cage was an escape for him too.

It was usually tame until midnight. I would call it networking and advertising to my girls. I would always promote the kennel because that was my identity. People in this area of the Midwest are generally judged and defined by their employment. Dogs will judge and define people by association, this is really, no different. You own your own business, means you must be rich with endless resources. You work as a waitress or bartender, you must be a slut. You're a Doctor, you are an honorable person and you have probably given birth to so and so's cousin's baby. You teach Yoga, you are strange stay away.

Most men out in this area were "Loggers" which meant they were horny and not used to seeing a woman from NJ getting drunk on wine with her two beautiful daughters. We were mesmerizing like sirens and had a lot of harmless fun dancing, playing pool, having conversations about all things East and West.

After Midnight the younger crowd seemed to migrate from Sturgeon Lake over to Willow. There was a well-known stretch of the rules that would happen Friday and Saturday nights depending on the crowd. At eleven the kitchen closed, and they would be gone by twelve. At one in the morning Matt would be done working, sometimes he left and sometimes he stayed. But at 2am the doors would be locked, and the lights turned down and whomever was there, the chosen crowd was able to stay hours later.

This possibility drew party people from all over, driving considerable distances drunk to get to The Cage before the doors were locked. While I was married we never stayed that late, we all wanted to avoid dad being pissed so we would try to get home at a reasonable hour. I'd be drunk, but home. My girls could account for my every moment, my every move.

At the end of every Girl Time Outing, I would pay the tab and tip the boys behind the bar handsomely because they certainly weren't handsome, but they took great care to top off my glass all night long. Some fellas would be sweet on us and buy a round and I let them. I was naïve thinking it was just what the good old boys do out here.

I found most people to be kind, fun, and generous as was I. It wasn't until later that I realized I was a source of entertainment, different, and unique to these parts. Let me be clear, there was no impropriety just harmless flirtation while I was with my daughter posse. However, it's all fun and games until there's a divorce!

After I announced that I wanted a divorce I started frequenting The Cage alone. My posse wasn't there to back me up any more. I was being accused of having affairs for the last twenty plus years what the hell did I care anymore? I was being screamed at, harassed, and stalked while at home.

I retreated to my bedroom, the second floor of the house had everything I needed except food, but I was so nervous I that I wouldn't eat. I was incredibly calm, relieved, non-emotional, at peace and there was no U-turn this time. It had been our room and there was no lock that would keep him out or from invading my space if I wasn't there. I stayed in my room trying to avoid him, worried about my mental safety. My kids were his next target. If he couldn't make me cry or scream directly he would sacrifice our children to hurt me.

He paced the house continuously, slamming things, having horrid discussions with our children loud enough for me to hear. He would accentuate trigger words to try to infuriate me and get me to engage with him. He was trying to provoke me every chance he could. He wanted to call the police on me, prove me unfit, have our children see me losing my mind *again*.

I would pass out from trying to stay awake protecting myself, again never physically, instead waiting until I woke up sitting at my bedside glaring at me, pushing his fingers in my face, threatening to turn my family against me including my mother.

He kept telling me how mentally ill I was and that I should just kill myself for real this time. “Oh no, you tried that multiple times back then, you are here for a purpose and he isn’t it” that was my inner spirit talking. I didn’t know her until much later, I am glad she was with me then.

He spun stories to our children to make them think I was unstable, reminding them of how sick I had been, giving my older girls things to look up on the internet to support his case. He labeled me with Borderline Personality Disorder and told anyone with an ear he could prove it. BPD was the only other diagnosis they came up with at the hospital besides Severe Depression.

If you look up BPD it is a loose blanket diagnosis that eighty-five percent of Generation X are labeled with and even more of the Millennials. Childhood traumas and familial dysfunction leads to some insecurities that show up in the coping mechanisms of an individual. There are like ten qualifiers and a person needs to exhibit more than half of them.

As I researched the condition given to me at The Time Out Resort, my husband exemplified to the extremes eight of the ten points. I felt like I was walking on eggshells all the time around his episodes. The doctors called that blame shifting. They would consider me recovering when I wanted to go back to the toxic relationship where my fears were rooted.

My husband knew I had stuffed all my anger and hate away since my breakdown. If he didn't know, like he claims, this master Machiavellian was stupid to really think I still had one speck of respect for him or dignity of my own to keep pretending after all he had put me through. Yeah, I said I loved him over and over, I would insist on holding his hand. It was a filler for the silence and tension, it was like keeping an attack dog at bay by throwing him a bone or flesh.

We were in a small community and I was acting the part of the nice family from Jersey, so people would trust leaving their dogs with me. Appearances were everything. This was a life lesson learned hard. I had been putting on the appearance of being okay, satisfied, happy and healthy so long that my lines blurred somewhere.

I was existing, surviving as best I could with the skill sets I had in my toolbox. Like an exotic animal in an enclosure way too small I was unable to grow and thrive, but this was all I knew so I adapted the best I could for as long as possible until insisting on my freedom.

I have thought back to our marriage trying to discern if there was anything that would have made our relationship tolerable. The area that I struggled with most as a woman was his total lack of desire for me. Yes, we had kids, four of them, so we had sex. Sex is not desire. I have been a sexually engaged partner since the very beginning.

This was yet another area of emotional abuse, purposely withholding affection when he knew how badly I wanted and needed it. Most guys would like a partner to participate and get excited to try new things in the bed, not my husband. It felt like sex was dirty to him, too much effort to have to clean up afterward. I had to initiate ninety-nine percent of the time by blowing him and I was often rejected. I did what a lot of women do; took responsibility. I'm too fat, I've had kids, I'm nagging, I'm being impatient.

The problem with all of that is that he took no responsibility for his part of anything, selfish bastard. I worked hard to dress nice, tease and flirt, be accessible, work around his moods, not bother him and let it happen. There was so much time that went by that this was a major issue in our marriage that there is no way that all these factors could be attributed to all the seasons of our relationship. I resolved in my heart and head, after all the rejection, that he is probably a closet homosexual, but he is such a coward he will never own it to be happy.

I didn't cheat on him with my body during these weeks of hell in my own home. I did know my marriage was coming to an end and so did he. I had chatted with some men from the bar to pass time, entertain myself, and feel desired or sexy. In my mind, I think I was proving to myself that I what I didn't have in my marriage was something wrong with him. Not that he was emotionally manipulative or mentally mean and abusive which I already knew, but that he didn't show up to care for me as his woman. I was sure that this scenario could be why so many women and men cheat on each other, they feel unappreciated and expendable in a significant area that holds their value.

I flirted with texts, never phone calls. I would look for eyes looking at me, so I could stare back and flash my untethered passion at them as an ultimate cock tease. Men sent me dick pics and I responded with art, I'll explain. I hate dick pics. I don't find the penis very attractive to look at, a vulva either for that matter. I find it vile for a man to send a photo of their nether regions unsolicited, there is a time and place for that. My response would be laughter at first, shake my head at what the world was coming to second, then insecurely attach a photo of myself. I didn't think I was pretty, I just knew I didn't get hit with an ugly stick. I knew someone would find me attractive and want to fuck me eventually. I wasn't even thinking about a relationship, I just wanted some sexual chemistry.

The picture I would include was a beautiful shot taken by a very close friend. It wasn't beautiful because I was the subject, it was beautiful because it was candid. Gina knew me a long time and knew my struggles. She was inspired by my return to the living after my breakdown and my weight loss. She had done shoots with a heavier me in the past, I don't recognize that woman anymore. She is very talented with the camera and has an ease about her that gets to the root of a mood in a picture without you even knowing it.

While visiting my dad, I had announced to her that I was planning to leave my husband when I returned to Minnesota. I was feeling more in touch with my body and always loved the female shape in tasteful pictures. She took portrait shots and boudoir pics, sexy and sassy. We scheduled an impromptu shoot and the mood she caught in the pics where far off, sullen, and detached.

As a last-ditch effort, I'd send one of these pics a day to my husband hoping he'd respond coveting me, longing my return, wishing he had his hands on my body. Nope, nope, and no. Instead the response was "Who the hell are those pictures for?", "What am I supposed to do with that?".

My favorite from that shoot was an accidental catch. I was in beautiful morning light in a gorgeous decorated home of a friend of my sister that graciously let me stay for free while they were in Dubai. I was shy about my body, so my back was turned to my friend as I repositioned the stiff white men's shirt I found in my host's closet.

Gina asked me a question about leaving Scott and I looked at her joylessly over my left shoulder and she snapped the shot. My nipple was in the picture, not my whole boob, just the tip. She converted the pic to black and white and sent it. That mistake turned me into art.

# Chapter 11

I had realized what I wasn't, and who I didn't want to be. I had reached many goals that I had set for myself. I was at a place in my life where I had options; I had made options. My marriage was over and, scratch that, I was a new beginning. I was no longer defined by the prick I was married to. My kids were old enough to be on the road to be their own people. I had moved away from my mom and dad; therefore, I was no longer on the path to be their caregiver until death.

I wasn't all the horrible things my ex had said about me. I wasn't the insecurities of my childhood, or adulthood for that matter. I wasn't heavy, like I had been. I wasn't a Baptist, a GM, a college student, those were labels of no significance anyway. I wasn't a disappointment to my parents, hell my Dad doesn't even know who I am, literally. I wasn't boring, unattractive, unsuccessful, angry, or mentally ill.

My morphing pain was confusing my identity. I began to wonder if butterflies experience pain in the cocoon? I couldn't see past it and I had been stuck for about seventeen years. I was relieved, that's what I was, like a pressure cooker releasing steam. I was free of the binding that held me; I was supposed to be something else. It was time to change.

I was so over our marriage years ago, so making the final decision to dissolve it was hard because of the twenty-eight-year time investment but moving on wasn't difficult. I wanted the attention I hadn't gotten for so long. I wanted to be treated like a woman and not a bro. I wanted to have fun and try new things. I had lost myself and needed to get back in touch with me.

I was sexually frustrated and right handed, two things that sort of cancel out if that's all I wanted out of life. I guess that was the place to start getting in touch with me. Everyone needs a place to start. Scott would rarely initiate sex unless it was poking me with his morning wood. I would have to catch him at the break of day and take advantage of his blood flow otherwise it was too much effort on his part. This only happened quarterly at best.

If it was any other time of day (or year) it was treated like a boring endeavor that started the same way every time, going under the covers and sucking his cock for as long as it took to get him hard, I acquired strong cheek muscles. I would then climb on top and ride him if the opportunity arose. When we would have sex, it would lasting five to eight minutes; he would time it.

I would be flabbergasted when he would be fast asleep right after he came. How was he so exhausted? He would just lay there while I rode him, barely participating. I would lay awake afterward unsatisfied, listening to him snore. I had stuffed away my sexual cravings since I was a teenager and knew there had to be more to sex than what was happening in my marital bed.

As a pubescent teenager with torpedo nips and undeveloped tits, I would hear buzzing in the middle of the night coming from upstairs. I was curious what my mom was doing up there, so I investigated. I found her off white, battery-operated, eight-inch, twist bottom self-stimulator along with a bookshelf full of erotic literature while she was at work. She liked the books that were filled with short porn stories like penthouse forum.

I read some stories and figured out what to do with the vibrator to my enlightenment. I didn't really want to have sex, I just wanted the feeling of release. I found the detachable showerhead handy and in looking back this was my first experience with pain and pleasure. To speed up the body's responses for climax, I would turn up the temperature of the water as hot as I could stand. The pulsing of the massage setting was muffled between my legs, so all you heard was the water running off my body and down the drain.

I soon explored my body more creatively with vegetables from the refrigerator drawer that would later that day be used for salads at dinner. I found that I liked anal stimulation; carrots had some give were a great training tool even though I didn't know I was in anal training. I was never afraid of a carrot breaking off in my ass, a cucumber maybe, and it never stopped me. I always washed the vegetables after I used them and put them back; I knew enough to do that. I had no idea how gross that was then. I didn't even really think about it, I was satisfied and that made me content and satiated in my immature self-centered teenage mind.

I didn't even know what was happening to me when I came or how that intensity could ever happen with a partner. I didn't know it was called something. The stories in the books talked about waves crashing over and over. I love that visual.

I had only experienced my first real orgasm, where I was able to identify what it was and why I liked it was through masturbation as an adult at the ripe old age of thirty-five. I would watch movies or read erotic books and get really turned on. I started to finally get some relief of tension, frustration, and hurt through fast paced, purpose driven orgasms. I would slide out of the bed in the middle of the night and pretend to go to the bathroom. I would throw a towel on the floor and rub myself off in less than three minutes, I'd time it, under the intense fear of getting caught and then flush the toilet and return to bed.

He never touched his dick unless it was to pee or adjust it in his pants so mutual masturbation was not on the table. Toward the end of our marriage I needed an orgasm to fall asleep or I had to take meds to help me. He never knew about my affair with the bathroom in the middle of the night. I was a sexual creature that needed to be fed and stimulated.

After the split there were responsibilities to deal with. I had the three kids and a grandchild living at home and owned my business. I was left with an incredible amount of debt that had been accrued over the years we lived in Minnesota.

He walked away with all the liquid assets and stripped the house of anything and everything that had value. I retained the home and business both in need of some real repair that happens over time. It sounds lop sided, but I was totally cash poor supported solely by our Mom and Pop business. He walked away from the children without any rights, not even a fight about it.

He didn't want them, the cost, or the responsibility. So, I wasn't free really, but the weight lifted by my divorce was enormous. I had removed the thorn in my side, the constant festering irritating pain, the septic infection was deep rooted and needed aggressive treatment. The stress was a great help in losing the last fifteen pounds that were between me and my goal weight after my bariatric surgery. I lost the weight of him too, that was 285 pounds. There's always an upside!

Moving from urban NJ to small town America had been a great change in most areas. Going through a divorce in a town where everyone knows everyone or is married into a big family name, or where church is where people pray for you in gossip circles was difficult. Our personal life may as well have been front page headlines in the five-page local newspaper. It didn't help that my soon to be ex would cry the blues to every customer he would bump into at the grocery store, gas station, and gym. I was amazed at how social he could be when he wanted to be.

I wanted to celebrate my new independence. I was going out with my older girls occasionally, but they were only keeping tabs on me and reporting all my actions to their father. I realized they weren't my friends and their alliances were clear, which killed me.

They were twenty-one and twenty-two now and since they were teenagers they would outright ask me "Why don't you get a divorce, you'd both be happier?". I thought they'd be relieved or at least have expected it. They instead acted shocked and bewildered.

I thought going out with them would be safe and fun, we would bond over shenanigans, stories and shots. I was wrong, we weren't there, my mistake thinking they could handle all this. I told the girls from the time they were young, “I wasn’t put in their lives to be their friend.” I tried it out; now I believed it even more.

I needed someone I could talk to and trust. I had lots of questions and curiosities. I had topics to talk through that weren’t for just any ears. I was at a loss, not my older girls, not people in town, not my mom. I talked to my sister, but she was in Florida and I had my friend back in NJ to talk to, I felt like an island.

I was single and empowered by my freedom. The only thing I knew about myself was that I needed to explore my sexuality before entering any other form of committed relationship. This was a big step toward acknowledging who I really was and what I would expect from others and myself. I had always been a people pleaser, now I declared my pleasure as number one.

This is where my sexual revolution began. This is where the story takes a naughty turn into all things that intrigued me, stretched my beliefs and boundaries, and helped me get in touch with my true Goddess.

I started filling out profiles on match sites looking for conversation. I wanted to figure out what made men tick. I was aware that I would run into a lot of scumbags and losers. I knew there would be a lot of married and separated men to sift through. I also knew that a lot of these sites were hook up sites.

I wasn’t really wanting to get involved with anyone emotionally, but I wasn’t a slut either. I dabbled in flirting and messaging guys all over the world. It was fun to flirt and tease, it was my entertainment. Firefighters, IT workers and Financial Advisors seemed to be the most prominent players. Soldiers deployed overseas were the winners when it came to cheating on their wives. Most felt justified because there was no physical exchange. I felt like I was providing a service to our servicemen by helping them release and stay focused on their assignments.

I had an electronic rolodex of twenty guys or so on a text messaging app that would ebb and flow with chat throughout a day. Some would start casually, most were very forward sending dick pics right away. I would talk through text only. I like to write so being a character and playing a role was fun. I like to talk to people and I was isolated; this was my outlet. There was no emotion involved at all.

I was disillusioned on marriage so my filter on their marital status while sexting was wide open. It was safe for me, and I didn't really care about them. Who was I to judge? I wasn't married anymore. I didn't care about the person on the other end of a satellite signal. If they were sexting while in a relationship there were already issues, I wasn't the problem. I made lots of men cum hard by my voice, words, and occasionally a sexy picture if I really liked the guy. It was nice to feel desired and sexy, and able to scratch an itch for a stranger without touching them.

An old High School boyfriend, my second boyfriend ever and last before marrying Scott, contacted me when I changed my Facebook profile to divorced and we started talking. My therapist said that this was typical, to try to go back to "the good old days" while processing feelings. I knew it wouldn't work because he was the same as he was in school, he hadn't changed a lick. I had changed, and I was going to prove to him what he missed out on after taking my virginity in 1988.

He was an over the road trucker claiming to have been with hundreds of women but never settled down with one. Ron made me feel tiny compared to him in stature. Standing at 6'4", with a stomach that looked like he was 6 months into a pregnancy, he still had that smile that melted me and eyes that spelled mischief. He was my bad boy complex I guess.

I entertained meeting up with him at some point and seeing what happened and we all know what that means. I dated him, while still entertaining my stable of perverts. With him I experienced my first orgasm through penetration that took my breath away and made my face and ears numb. Shit yeah! There was more to sex than what I had been putting up with. The release was therapeutic and riveting in my core. I liked sex and it made me feel alive, attractive, vibrant and buzzing. Releasing all those endorphins into my system made everything seem okay.

In the meantime, an interesting new fellow liked my profile on the match site. His name was Joseph, but I could call him Sir. Interest piqued. He was a professional and well-dressed according to his profile pictures. He had a charismatic smile and his lips turned up on the ends in a way that spoke to my inner naughty girl. I replied, and we exchanged niceties, but he was very stern and direct in his communications. I got the impression that this guy gets what he wants. He wanted me.

I was struggling at the time balancing all the daily tasks that needed to happen around the house. My Ex, had been more domestic, cooking often because he liked to and cleaning when he felt like it or yelling until it got done by someone else. When I had the energy to "manage" my home post-divorce, I would delegate to my children, they hated me and would do nothing I asked at this point. I was working the business front end and back, trying to be Mom and Grand Mom, housekeeper, cook, and the ten other hats I wore. I was starting to see the need for assistance in some form or another.

I spoke with Ron about it and he was kind of hands off about everything, no future there, so it was better that way. Then I talked to Sir about my situation. He said, "You need help." I replied, "I know but I can't hire anyone, I don't have the money for that." The next sentence started me down a path that I would call enlightenment.

"You need a House Boy. There are people that do that. They strictly offer servitude and get great enjoyment from it.", "Really???" I said in my most outlandishly surprised tone. "Oh yes. You will find one you like, and he will answer to you for the daily things, but he will answer to me for his rewards or punishments." Sir was so confidently laying out the groundwork.

I was wet, erotically dripping at the thought of Sir providing a solution for me in this New World kind of way. I was giving him my attention, he was giving me direction. I was tired of being the boss all the time and making all the decisions. The power release mentally was an exercise.

I was being challenged mentally and liked it. With all the minor titillating tasks He gave me, I followed direction well. Examples of His orders included things like telling me what color panties to wear, to not touch myself without his permission, and spank myself with a hairbrush on the ass while he listened on the phone. I felt like I was doing something right for a change. He would acknowledge me with a “Good Girl” here and there and it made me want to please Him more. I was an accomplished people pleaser so pleasing Sir felt good, I was a good girl at forty-five.

I started the search for a House Boy, as I was told. I filled out a want ad for a House Boy on a site for kink, as instructed. I got responses for a House Boys and Slaves, as promised. Now, I needed to think. Maybe I should have thought about it first but then I wouldn’t have had the stark awakening that there was a whole lifestyle out there that I was missing.

Who are these people? How do they survive? Isn’t it dangerous for them? For me? I start perusing the site, looking at all the other ads, writings, profiles, groups, events, Kinky and Pervy oh my! There was so much to see. I am now a student again, studying everything I find. I text Sir with questions because at this point only He understands and admires my complex mind. He only answers when it’s convenient for Him. I figure He is married.

I find that I can stay up for endless hours reading and looking at other people’s pictures. I am fascinated by the multiplicity of kink on display. Looking at one picture or profile would lead me down a rabbit hole of exploration. The spectrum being so wide for some and narrow for others was very accepting in a way.

I had been tired of being labeled or judged. This was a place of self-expression and nonconformity, a well spring of openness. I created my profile, very vague at first. I posted a picture of my sternum strategically stopping just before a nipple on either side. I had gotten my most recent tattoo, a full sternum and under breast piece, a few months earlier that had a honey bee in the center with a crown over it surrounded by ornate scrolling around the base and under my boobs. My profile name was QueenBee.

I had always wanted a tattoo since I was about twenty. I am an all or nothing type of girl, so this tattoo was going to be well thought out and placement was of real importance. I had been a manager in the corporate world and tattoos were frowned upon at that time. I wanted my ink to be artistic and very tasteful. I finally decided on some very beautiful diagonal scrolling running from my left hip to just peeking over my right shoulder.

It was done in two sessions and was done in gray scale to keep it classy and refined. After that healed I fell down the slippery slope of body art. I believe this was a way to declare the freedom I so desperately wanted. No one could change or take this from me, no words would make it less valuable, no manipulation would erase it's meaning. I have seven pieces now ranging from very large to rather small but they all have incredible significance but my royal, flying, creative, inexhaustible leader of a bee was my favorite at the time.

I took a few weeks to identify myself through a narrative. It was very open and vulnerable for a profile. I shared a lot of the conflicting emotions I was having trying to as honest as possible letting the readers know that my life was in turmoil. I was looking for answers and direction.

I posted a few more pictures and showed my body the best I could with lighting and angles being my best friends. I was still very self-conscience of my sagging tummy. The four C-sections I had experienced had left me a fanny pack that hung right above my crotch and if it had a zipper I wouldn't have minded carrying a flesh tone purse for the rest of my life. It did not have a zipper and I was not able to swap it out for a more fashionable style. I hated it.

I got a message from Alex, he was in South Africa and an Online Dom. He warned me about putting too much info on the site. He wanted to talk to me on Kik so that our conversation could be more fluid and in the moment. He was very interested in my story and all that I was going through. His words laced with his thick accent were intoxicating.

He addressed me as "Love", little did I know it was commonplace to use it so freely where he was from. Eventually Kik turned to Skype calls. His camera was never on, but he always wanted to see my eyes. He was very private, shy and married. The time difference meant calls were 7 hours different. We spoke mainly in the middle of the night and for long periods of time.

I was identifying myself as a submissive at this point. Between Sir and Alex, I realized that I was really into not being in charge. The power exchange that is talked about so much in D/s literature was what I craved. I wanted someone to care so much about everything I did that I wouldn't even have to think about what color underwear I should wear or how many peas I should eat at supper. I also realized that Dominants were not particularly fond of their subs having more than one Dom.

It's a possessive thing. Sharing isn't very officious. It was kind of hot, being tugged back and forth between their ownership. I was playing submissive because I could hide behind the phone or computer and do or not do whatever I chose. Ultimately, as the submissive, I was very much in charge. The on/off button, closing my laptop, or not answering my phone meant I could be as selective about my role as my vanilla life would allow.

My search for a House Boy was intriguing but difficult for me to process. I couldn't take this willy nilly. I didn't know who I was yet, so how could I handle another human like a slave? I wasn't from the deep south. I would probably get down on the floor next to him with a toothbrush to help him clean the floor. The thought of a female was never mentioned by Sir, but it crossed my mind briefly.

I related to guys better than gals all my life. I didn't want to feel like I was vying for attention, with another hot female when I was trying to establish my worth with Sir. The idea that I was the only female Sir was directing danced through my head naively.

In the meantime, Ron and I plan a trip to Florida. He was very close to a couple classmates from school who married right after graduation. Their daughter was getting married and Ron was like an uncle to her. With the wedding being in Florida I could travel separate and attend the wedding as his date but also visit my Mother and Sister.

Surprise twist, Sir was scheduled to be at a trade show in Orlando while I was there. A whirlwind trip, the superefficient task master I was wanted to make the most of the trek and vowed to do it all. I was growing tired of Ron already, but it was nice to have a physical person to touch, talk to, and fuck my face numb.

Some strange things transpired in the time span of a few weeks. Ron, being the transient, he always was, started talking about moving to Wolf Lake, MN and starting a life with me. Alex had given me the task of having a threesome. My ex was creating ongoing issues with my children and spreading rumors all over this small town of my heinous actions toward him claiming I was forcing him to move out of the state and ripping him away from his children. I would get an escape from all that.

I had started a sexual list, my fuckit list. I started inquiring about sex positive parties and events. I was working the business I owned during the day and ordering adult toys and erotica off Amazon at night.

Sir was calling less often but when He did it was full of promises of the hoops He would have me jump through as His sub. I'd tease Him, playing coy like I didn't understand his language, however I was reading large amounts of information self-teaching. Sir liked that I was a newbie and that I was turned on by all this. He told me that I needed to practice role playing His Trophy Wife.

He gave me a scenario of how He pictured our meeting to go. He planned to send me into a bar wearing a certain color dress and no panties. While working a convention sales floor all day He would have prospective clients that he would arrange to meet later. That man or those men would be told to meet up with me at the bar until He could join up a little later. My job was to flirt with these men and let them know I was there for them to use however they wished as a gift from Joe. The only hook was that He wanted to watch.

He wanted to watch me seal His deals. He was clear that I wouldn't have any ability to say no. He would speak on my behalf. He would tell me when I was finished with them. He would then consume me to His liking giving me more pleasure than I ever imagined, His words of course. It sounded like a naughty night of debauchery.

I told Him I wasn't trained for this, experienced with sex, or even very submissive in person. Talk the talk or walk the walk? I would question myself, is this really what I want? I went through with booking a separate room in Orlando in case I was repulsed by Sir in person or he couldn't hold a conversation face to face but yes, this is what I wanted. I wanted to experience life and sex on a whole different level. What an adventure I was about to embark upon, a year of exploration and ultimately self-acceptance.

I am open. I am kinky. I am sexy. I am smart. I am strong. I am powerful. I am a Goddess. I am Queen Bee. This was who I was and didn't own it yet.

# Chapter 12

I created my profile on FetLife, a site for social exchanges in the fetish world like Facebook for the sexually openminded. There were fields to fill in about yourself. It asked for your location, I lied and put Antarctica. I had learned quickly from the various match sites to protect yourself or you could have a stalker on your hands in no time. There was a reason a lot of these men were single or "polyamorous". I couldn't assume that mental health or lack thereof wasn't a possibility.

I had left a marriage with a man that was abusive and narcissistic, thinking he was God's gift to women, me especially, and that "I'll never find another man like him." He had profiles up and I felt bad for the unaware women that would swipe right, but that wasn't for me to worry about anymore. I was looking for something totally different, or was I?

I had lived through Scott, I so desperately wanted everything opposite of him. I had experienced Ron, a selfish non-committal rogue drifter that was awesome in the sack. I had dreams about Sir, who mysteriously contracted pneumonia when I was on my way to meet him face to face in Orlando. I had escaped into Alex, married and hiding behind darkness while skyping in the middle of the night. I still had all my sexting buddies.

What was I missing? A man, a man with balls, a man that would know what he wanted and do what it took to get it, a man with integrity to be who he said he was day and night without hiding in secrecy. I wanted someone to take the reins, in all things, so I could rest.

All my daily decisions were zapping my will power, I was overwhelmed by all the choices in front of me and all the judgements I would have to make. I was embarking on a journey that was like an adventure book from the 80's where you choose a direction at a crossroad and the entire outcome of the story changes according to what path you take. I did this texting crap for a month or so and wanted to find so much more. These men were all the same. I needed to find what I was looking for somewhere.

I was in Duluth, in early February, and I knew where I was, but I was lost in my head. That's when it caught my eye, a beacon that shone through the fog in my brain. I was sitting in a line of traffic at a stop light when I noticed a neon sign flashing in my right periphery. OPEN, OPEN, OPEN, COME IN NOW, I AM WAITING FOR YOU, ANSWERS HERE it flashed, not literally of course.

I pulled into the weathered driveway of a small store front. Duluth Tarot, card reading, walk-ins welcome the sign in the front window said. So, I walked in. I had been to card readers before at the shore, at a party at a friend's house once, and with "Star" a mystic that had awards for finding missing people and pictures with celebrities hanging all over her walls. I was prepared somewhat for what one expects when someone glares into your soul and reads your innermost thoughts.

The small tingling door chimes alerted a young man to my presence, her son was the receptionist. Two little morkies ran around my feet with similar bells on their necks as chimed at my entrance. First thought was they needed groomed, that is not why you are here I told myself. A petite woman, slender with long tresses and warm brown eyes came out of the reading room.

We exchanged pleasantries and she immediately took my hand and asked me to sit with her. We went into the small windowless room, decorated with saris and candles, there were multiple spirituality beliefs represented and mild incense was burning in the air. She didn't ask me any questions, she didn't try to lead my conversation, she simply held my hands across the table.

Her face had concern furrowed in her brow lines, her eyes still warm looked sad. "I am so glad you stopped Dear. Your aura is all mixed up and the state of confusion you are in is not like you at all. We need to fix this now." There had been no talk of money to this point. "You have three Capricorn men in your life at once, we need to focus your energy. They are no good for you." I did not know at that point but yes, three of the four men in my immediate emotional life were Capricorns. This still gives me the heebie jeebies.

She didn't read my cards that day, she prayed for me. We made a follow up appointment for the next evening. She said that she needed to sit in my energy for a bit to figure out a plan. This was very surreal to go through and as I returned to my car that first night I started letting doubt set in, "How much is all this going to cost me?" I said to myself.

I called the phone number I found online and left a message for her to call me when she could. I realized that in the whirlwind of her diagnosis the evening before

I didn't even get her name. My control freak mind now wanted to know what the hook was. The money conversation had to happen before I would be open to what the universe was trying to tell me.

She called me back a half hour later. I explained that I was already owing her for her insights last night and that I didn't want to take her energy work for granted. I really wanted to know how she was going to fix me, but I that knew it would cost something and I didn't have a lot of money.

She said something incredible had happened and I needed to come in for my appointment and she would share the news. This was an immediate flash back to the Pastor hanging out the window many years earlier. Should I go? I was excited about planning random dates with men that had ropes and cuffs, maybe she would warn me of imminent danger. I went.

Her enthusiasm was exuding from her face, this no named mystic. She once again guided me with her hands to her reading room. She had spent the morning in Minneapolis at a psychic shop to get supplies for me. For me? She claimed that she walked into the shop and spoke with the owner. The owner, whom I have never met, had an envelope set aside for my "treatment," a trigger word with straight jacket emotions wrapped up in it.

Someone had the psychic awareness of my issues and knew that I would need resources and time for prayer. They gave twelve hundred dollars to the woman sitting in front of me specifically notated for "The Queen." Did you just get chills? I did. I still do every time I tell this part of my story.

The no named spiritualist didn't know about my queen bee tattoo or my profile name on FetLife, we hadn't gotten that far into any conversation. I felt like I was floating above all of this in disbelief, waiting to be punked or on a hidden camera expose. She proceeded to tell me that while she prayed about me in the middle of the night it came to her.

I had been a queen in another life and I fell in love with a stable boy, when my affair was found out the boy was beheaded in front of all my subjects. This was what was broken she proclaimed, "You have been looking for that love lifetimes repeatedly, never finding your fated beloved. You are stuck making bad choices in partners and they are affecting your energy, so obviously you can't attract your King. I will be going away for a period, long as it takes, to pray on your behalf at a Meta-retreat center."

She continued with precise instructions. "You need to sit in a bath tub, burn these cones in order as the colors have different jobs to do, and chant so I can tune into your spirit from afar." I was given an amber gemstone necklace "to wear until you feel you don't need to wear it anymore." She had me practice the "Ommm..." resonating sound with her and she cried. It was a very powerful moment of raw emotion and energy, bewilderment and faith. I didn't understand what was happening although I felt like it was imperative, critical, and magical.

That was the last I saw of her, a week later her store front was empty, signage removed and no answer on the phone. She was a gypsy or maybe an angel, either way I had a glimmer of hope. I trusted this odd encounter as a crossroad and submitted to the universe where it was going to take me.

Over the next few weeks I felt energized and I was all about making this work. By this I meant that failure was not in my vocabulary and I'd be damned if Scott was going to destroy me the way he had threatened. Thanks to Sir's initial directives I had several men applying for my live-in slave position.

I had been a manager and hired and fired many people. This was no different I told myself, but it was different. I prided myself on being a kind and caring boss that would come along side and work with someone to make them feel valued. Sir was becoming less and less accessible. This train was already rolling and gaining steam and I was going to step up and be the conductress.

I was still figuring out the nature of submission in general. I was still identifying as a sub but thought the role of a Domme, a female dominant, could be fun. I started researching owning a slave and justify it by thinking it will make me a better submissive. It turns out that many Doms start as subs and learn true service before expecting it from another.

It made sense in a "I wouldn't ask you to do something I wouldn't." kind of way. I still think there is a business model that could be built around the idea of hiring out men, everyone I suggest it to says it sounds like prostitution when I objectify men like that. I'd call it "The Sperm Bank" or "The Cougar Den". They would have profiles and check boxes of what they would be available for, consents and releases and voila! You have a cute (type specific) handy man at your service.

I needed help taking care of manly maintenance things like yard work, carrying heavy things, and fixing stuff. This was my ignorance as a privileged white woman, projecting what having a slave would look like. I was not hung up on appearance, however a nice view wouldn't be bad up north here. I required the applicant to speak fluent English however knowing a second language would be fun to learn for me and the kids.

The right slave would have his own income or the ability to work outside of my required service to provide for himself. His ability to serve me and having a place to live, in my presence, was his reward or payment. Typing that out sounds so arrogant for where I was in my journey but not surprising. I was thinking of the experience and not the practicality, though it did make perfect sense for my current situation. I was so clueless about who I was, who i wanted to be, or what I'd always been. I put a thought to action. Simple, I was just going to do it.

I kept researching and realized that I wasn't really qualified to be a Mistress, I could be an Owner though. It had dawned on me while reading and researching that with some kids still at home, collaring a man and having him wear nothing but a chastity device and a leather harness might not work. As fun as it might have been to watch my slave push mow the grass in chaps and a bow tie or serve me wine on the deck in hot pink women's panties, I still had a business on my property and neighbors.

My vanilla friends might frown on whipping a slave for punishment on the tree in the back yard as my kids played videogames and snapchatted in their rooms. I switched my ad verbiage to pet, much more palatable and comfortable for me. I had lots of furry pets and I was an accredited dog trainer; this role was workable.

I clarified that I needed a man by day and a pet that would sleep on a cushion at the end of my bed by night. This was not a sexual relationship, but a loyalty challenge, I determined. I imagined, adopting a rescue pet and I would get to retrain him for my companionship and fulfillment. A man that desired to be of substance, assistance and a pet that was fun and obedient would be hard to find.

Out of five serious inquires, did I just say that, out of five serious inquiries, I narrowed it down to two. Rav and Eddie, both were of Indian decent interesting to note, and I could not pronounce their full given names, so they got pet names given by me right away. It was a good first step, renaming them.

Rav was an experienced sub with references that was my first pick until he flaked out and ghosted for weeks claiming he had to return to India for an emergency. Eddie, my second choice, was available immediately, worked in IT so he was mobile, and wanted to eat scraps out of a dog dish when he could.

We spoke extensively on the phone and he was very respectful. I found him interesting and intelligent, two things that I required to even tolerate an employee in the past and he loved to cook! I had a discussion with my kids that I was hiring a male live in Nanny/Maid/Chef to help me fill the gaps we were all experiencing. Eddie was offered a trial. I never heard from Sir again.

With Sir gone, I had cleared out all my Capricorn influences and vowed no more. It became a rule, no Capricorns no excuses. I found rules for myself were vital, they gave me structure and boundaries. Alex was an Aries and he was online in South America, he was spared. Alex found me complex and interesting. He would listen endlessly as I fleshed out the dynamics of power exchange. He was very patient and seemed like he really cared.

In his mind, I was his sub and my pet would also be under his control, as he trained me to train Eddie. I used him to figure out how to handle scenarios; ways I could punish and reward my pet, and mostly be safe and in control. A strange man was in his car already driving from Toronto for a two week stay at my home. I never considered that he might hurt me, I never had that vibe about Eddie. He was a submissive and wanted nothing more than to please the Queen.

I really wanted this to work out. With another adult at the house, I was free to study and delve into my curiosities. Rule Two, came into existence before Eddie even arrived. This was pivotal. This rule gave me the out I needed in any situation that came up here forward. One Year, that was the rule. I was not getting into any relationship besides friends with benefits or role play for one year from my divorce. January 21st, 2016 to January 21st of 2017 I was a free agent.

This was my year of exploration and I didn't want false love or guilt to get in the way. I was looking for a connection, feeling, or look, or action that made a person stand out to me. At this point, I wasn't even ruling out a woman, I wanted to feel something from someone that they felt for no one else.

Rule Three, was that I must have a connection with someone to physically fuck them. It is important to note here that fucking was raw and primal sex. Playing with someone meant flirting, teasing, touching, kissing, sucking and these actions were all needed for me to establish confidence as a woman learning about her sex. The line was penetration, not just any dick was getting my pussy.

I never considered myself a slut ever. There were plenty of sluts out there to satisfy all the fuckers. I was much more of an exhibitionist, and tease and wanted to approach everything as a researcher making a sex documentary or wait for it...writing a book. This was the birth of the notion to share my stories and experiences. I had been told for the past twenty years that I needed to start writing shit down. I now had a back story to go with my persona in case I was ever asked.

Queen Bee is a writer, writing a book about her sexual awakening and the many interesting stories and people I meet along the way. My profile status was changed from Submissive to Exploring.

Rule Four, all experiences are for research and should be documented as such. This rule gave me a shield from participation or an all access pass to every single event I went to. I wanted to go to parties and events and I started expressing interest.

The Rabbit Cage no longer was fun after a semi true story of me enjoying my freedom was being passed around Main St. from several zipcodes away. Ok, yes, I was trying to learn Spanish from a Latino man, in his car, while smoking weed and sucking his cock. He said I need to practice rolling my tongue more, so I did.

The rumor was much more colorful and when my girls heard it from friends. My shenanigans were reported immediately to their dad. You can imagine that this caused some issues for me. The divorce was already frontpage news and I would think my behavior would have been expected after all those years repressed. New boundaries had to be put in place for me to be able to continue my exploration.

Rule Five, the final rule, I would not date, see, play with or participate in any vanilla or kink activity within forty miles of my home. There was a huge problem with making this stick, Eddie was already on his way to my house.

Eddie arrived late at night in a badly rusted out little foreign made car. He had driven for days down through Canada, across the border in Detroit, around Lake Michigan, through Wisconsin, and all the way up to Northern Minnesota. He introduced himself and went to his knees to kiss my feet.

My kids came out to meet the stranger that I had hired from a faraway land to live with us. Eddie pretends he dropped something and got up quickly. I had discussed my expectations regarding the children with “the Manny” at great lengths and they were to suspect nothing, period. We all helped Eddie with his belongings to the room where he would be staying.

It was very late before he got situated and used the bathroom to freshen up. The kids had gone to bed. I told him to follow me to my room. This was the best and only place that was suitable for conversation about our arrangement.

I felt very nervous yet very powerful. I ordered him to strip for inspection, I had read that somewhere. He did. Eddie was a tall caramel skinned man, overweight by twenty to thirty pounds and he was hung like a horse. I had never seen anything but his face on his profile and communications.

I walked around him, looking at his body like it was fruit at the market. I ran my hands over him seductively to make a point, with intention, then took them away. I had him bend over and swatted his ass to see what he would do. I left a hand print on his right buttock that was traceable. I came around in front of him and squatted so his cock was at my eye level. "Is this all there is?" I chided. "Lift it up so I can make sure you are clean and didn't bring mange here." He did. "I'm going to have to send you to the groomer to clean you up." Referring to the man scaping needed. "Yes, my Queen, as you wish." He says looking down at his feet. I could get used to this, I thought to myself. "Put your clothes back on. You've been a good boy, you may lay on my bed while we talk about tomorrow."

I heard someone in the kitchen, so I excused myself to see which kid was up and if they realized Eddie wasn't in his room sleeping. When I returned to my room, Eddie was under the blankets sleeping, on my side of the bed, and he looked so peaceful. I was a terrible Owner already, he slept in the bed all night while I slept in a rocking chair. I didn't want to give him the wrong idea of being in bed with him when he woke up, non-sexual relationship, remember? I certainly didn't want him alone in my room without me.

I woke Eddie at 7:00am and started him on the routine. I expected him to get the kids off and on the bus on schooldays. The process of letting the dogs out; filling their food dishes and changing their water, let them back in to eat, make the Queen her morning tea, let the dogs out after eating, bring the Queen her tea and get assignments for the day, let the dogs back in. He seemed to catch on quickly, anticipate my needs, and used his very sad puppy dog eyes to sway me where he could.

He cooked dinner the first night, nothing exotic which was good because we were anything but exotic. The kids enjoyed talking to him and were very accepting, I was proud of them. They excused themselves and went to their perspective rooms.

Eddie had barely eaten and seemed sad. "My Queen?" he asked. "Yes pet." I responded. "May I eat my dinner out of a bowl, my Queen?" as he scrapes the plates and excess gravy into an old cool whip container like he's saving the leftovers. "Is that why you didn't eat much dinner?" I ask pointedly to show that I was paying attention, "I'm sorry, my Queen, I don't deserve to eat at the table with you and the Prince and Princess." He says, and he drops to his knees.

I take the blue and white flimsy bowl to the kitchen. In the junk drawer there is a sharpie marker which I used to write in bold black letters EDDIE. My pet is smiling, and I picture his tail wagging. "Eddie, Come." I command, and he crawls enthusiastically across the floor to his room. I place the bowl on the floor as Eddie looks up at me for approval to eat. "Good Boy Eddie. Time for dinner, Go ahead." On all fours, Eddie puts his face in the bowl and laps up the food. The sounds of a human eating like a dog are gross if you are thinking of a human eating food. Follow my thinking, if you pictured that bowl as your pussy, the slurping sloppy wet noises are erotic as fuck. I was horny.

I started doing the dishes while Eddie ate. This was weirder than I imagined. I was starting to understand what I had read about the difference between living 24/7 lifestyle or role play. I unfortunately dove into things full on so having an on and off switch was going to be difficult for me. It was already a challenge for my pet.

He can't eat like that around my kids, can he only eat when being treated like a dog, was he abused as a boy? My mind tumbles like this constantly asking questions trying to understand. Eddie leaves his room and goes to the bathroom to clean up and get ready to retire for the night. I take my bath, masturbate and go to bed.

I wake to the brightness of the day at 7:30, I've overslept and so have the kids, shit! I get up panicky and head to the top of the stairs where I hear Eddie making conversation with my kids and telling them to put their phones away at school, so they can learn important things.

My shoulders relax, and I breathe a deep relaxing dose of "This is exactly what I needed". I went back to bed and waited. I hear him talking to the dogs. I wonder if he observes dog behavior the way I want to observe other kinksters in action. The back door opens and closes, food hits the dog dishes, door opens and closes, and I hear footsteps approaching just as instructed. He knocks lightly and enters anyway "Your tea, my Queen." I proceed to pat on the end of my bed. We chit chat and I touch his soft human hair until he goes back to let the dogs in. When he returns, he is naked.

"What are you doing?" I asked shocked. "Don't you want to pet me, my Queen?", "The Prince and Princess are off to school, and the dogs have been tended to, I am here to be your pet now." He says sheepishly and cowering like he is waiting to be beat. "Eddie, that wasn't what we talked about on the phone. I need you to do tasks for me and help me with household chores, and the kids." I say, he interrupts "The Prince and Princess are gone." "They have names Eddie. I just went through a divorce and it's all very fresh. I think we need to talk about expectations some more." I hoped he'd get the idea that he was crossing a line. "My Queen, I love you, you are so beautiful. I wanted to please you. I'm sorry Mistress."

I had to empty my bladder, so I go around the corner to use the bathroom and thought that was the end of our conversation. I no sooner finish urinating when Eddie pops his head around the corner looking at me. Just like a fucking dog, I shake my head and must chuckle at the scene that was playing out in front of me, in my house, that I created. "Can I lick your pussy clean for you, my Queen?" He says with droopy eyes like a basset hound but a twinkle of excitement like a child in a candy store. "No Eddie. Go lay down. GO!"

I wipe with toilet paper and flush. After washing my hands and brushing my teeth I decide to get fully dressed in layers. My body was on lock down, no skin exposed except my face and hands. I secretly wished for a bourka, so I knew he'd understand I was off limits.

I come downstairs to a fully dressed and miffed Eddie. If he was a real dog, all the hair on his back would be standing up on end. He was pacing and frustrated. "Let's have a chat." I suggest as I pull out a chair for him. He sits rigidly on the edge of the seat like he was positioning on a starting block to take off. "Why don't you tell me what's bothering you Eddie? I want to be a good Owner and understand what you need."

I start off. "I need you to touch me and want me, I want to lick you and rub against your beautiful body, I want to hump you like a bitch in heat..." "Well, that's a problem." I interrupt. Honestly, I kind of knew that was the issue. "After all we talked about before you came, what made you think I would be intimate with you? That was never part of the plan."

He answered me in a humble pathetic defeated tone, "After I met you in person, I wanted you so badly. Then you had me strip for inspection and touched me and I got all confused. I'm so sorry, my Queen. Perhaps I'd be good enough for the Princess?" He looked at me totally serious, like there was nothing wrong with the suggestion. I instructed him to pack up his stuff and leave. "I have no money, my Queen." What the fuck was happening right now? I gave him some chores to do to earn some money, I certainly wasn't going to just give it to him.

I needed some stuff done immediately anyway. He left before the kids got home from school that day with his tail between his legs. That lasted for two and a half days. He called multiple times begging me for forgiveness and another chance, I knew that I would never trust him around my daughter again. I had to block him from contacting me after two days. Rule five officially started.

# Chapter 13

So, my profile reads something like this is, attempting to be honest and forthright here are the opening paragraphs. I believe there was a lot more to it, I have revised it many times, so the original content is gone which makes me sad.

"I am an intelligent, thoughtful, caring, woman who likes being desired. I am looking at my life through different eyes these days. My thoughts are deep and run amuck often. I need discipline and focus. I am a people pleaser to a fault. I am afraid of hurting people and being hurt. I have curiosity about people, places and things all the time. I am an artistic old soul that loves to find deep meaning in the oddest places. I am using this outlet for solace and peace. I am sassy and bratty at times but loyal and caring to the core. I long for my perfect match heart, soul and sex. I am not interested in random hook ups and do not fuck on sight. There must be substance or a goal to achieve for me to want to engage with you mentally or physically.

Exploration and evolution are my focus. I don't want games. I am a rare find with value. I want to be courted, wanted, needed, adored, pleased, fucked raw and put to bed with a kiss. I like nice things, flowers sent to me, to be taken out in public and shown off. Therefore, married men and those living a lie in fear of exposure need not waste my time. I feel like I am looking for love in all the wrong places however, sex is very important to me in a relationship so having that in common helps save valuable time and can be fun along the way."

I was spending a lot of time looking at pictures on the Kinky and Popular page. You can love the pictures or comment on them just like on Facebook. I visually categorized my kink curiosity by loving pictures and allowing to let others see what turned me on. I rounded profile out by "joining" a couple groups and being "interested" in listed fetishes.

I can see the push and pull of my self-worth playing tug of war in my writing. I was struggling to define my journey. I am this, I need that, I will this and I won't the other. I think I was trying to establish that I wasn't just a nympho slut, I had substance as a filter. I wanted to be wanted but roses too please. I wanted a match, not just a match, a match that was lit and on fire. I wanted passion in and out of the bedroom. I was questioning my year rule already. I'm ancient and imperfect, am I being unrealistic to be so picky? Am I wasting a year of my life not looking for a long-term relationship? Will sex fill the voids enough to forego my dislike for being alone? Can I get this dream of a fulfilling relationship fulfilled or should I have settled for my old life that I just destroyed my family to leave?

I think of all the people I have met and all the different profiles I have read, I am amazed. I am not amazed in an arrogant kind of way that I am so above other people, the experiences and freedoms they have expressed make them all have substance and truths. Some are so brave, some are blunt, most are vague or afraid of exposure or being too vulnerable.

I see vulnerability as one of my most life changing traits after my divorce. Opening all of me to experience and feel everything was cathartic and life changing. I am thankful for my open heart and willingness to make some mistakes along the way.

Loki came to stay with me and help me with my kennel business. I refer to her as my nonbiological older sister, my soul sister, and my best friend. She was struggling with her husband too, separated at the time, we had each other to lean on. I needed her while I sorted through all the fall out of the divorce and Eddie not working out. I was able to find time and space to really think after she arrived.

I knew everything was going to be okay and I had help. She was my rock and my biggest cheerleader. It was a blessing from the universe for her to want to come back to the States at this crazy time in my life to be the steady for a bit, freeing me to explore my New World as me, not who I used to be.

She came back to work here for the third hot season in a row. It made sense, American money went twice as far in Mexico. She had no idea what I was going through until she called. I kept everyone out of it in hopes of managing the rumor mill. Loki was never afraid to speak her mind to me or my kids. She stood up for me about the narratives my kids were getting from their dad.

She is a wonderful balance of love and justice and walks a tightrope in shades of grey never really making decisions, instead just lingers in thoughts to ponder. She is a perfect person to talk to, cry to, brainstorm with, and she loves me and my life with all its messes and wonder, just like I love her.

I would talk to her about the different men I was communicating with extensively. She was always excited, like she was living it through me. She asked questions and made me think of the things I didn't usually want to address. She unknowingly helped me filter and focus.

She is the reason that I embarked on my mission to experience all I could but not to settle ever again. My amazing friend was quick to point out when I was falling into old thinking that had no place in my new identity. She would warn me of patterns and pitfalls that I was not even aware of through gentle guidance and warmth. Loki was ten years older which afforded her wisdom, just enough to make me listen. Her life has not been easy, her travels around the world and in her life made her a better person, balanced.

She encouraged me to go and do anything I wanted. She was on the home front watching things whenever I wasn't. My kids were never left unattended, or without supervision. Loki was my passport to the Lifestyle. I started to schedule visits to "foreign lands".

Before I could participate in an event I had to be vetted. I had a date to be vetted by a couple for a Bukkake party, hadn't even looked up what it entailed but wanted to go. I was making "friends" that I would get to know in person sooner or later. I was making dates to meet men that were contacting me on my profile. From this point on in this book you will go on a fantastic ride through this erotic wonderland.

If you don't think you can handle graphic sexual details, now is the time to put this book down. If you want to know what happens next follow my flirtatious trance and outstretched hand like the gypsy card reader and sit with me. I have many more stories to share. This is your final warning to step away from the book before things get naughty. Seriously, put the book down Mom.

Think About it…

Ok, you are still with me! Good for you. By this time, I was juggling a lot of balls. My online Dom still intrigued me, I had an emotional loyal tie to him that I would have to deal with much later. Even though I had changed my role from Submissive to Exploring, he still considered me his subbie.

He was insistent that I find another woman to be my Sub Sister or a couple, so we could play together for him while he watched via Skype. I would always be his favorite, main girl, in charge, blah blah blah. I was aware that I was only playing the role of submissive for him by now and it helped pass time, taught me dynamics, and made me feel like someone cared about me. Just the fact that he addressed me as Love made me feel loved.

How starved was I for love? I was so starved that a man in South Africa could make me strip down to my panties and have me hold a half dollar to the wall of my bedroom with my nose while I masturbated.

The rest of the game went like this…each time I would lose control of the heavy coin and it hit the floor he would hear it because he was on the phone with me the whole time. When the coin hit the floor, I would spank my ass with the flat side of a paddle hairbrush loud enough for him to hear the smack and start over with the coin. The object was for me to orgasm while performing the task of keeping the coin on the wall with my nose or beg for mercy. I don't remember if I completed the task with him on the phone, thinking back however I did bruise my ass cheek with the brush. I have pictures which he asked for the next morning with my morning panty Kik.

I had shown interest in an upcoming event in the Playhouse group. It was being hosted by an older married couple. This was appealing to my curious mind, "How does that work?" and "What does that look like?" were legitimate questions to ask. I didn't even know what a Bukkake Party was but if an older couple can do it, I can certainly watch.

I contacted Lady K and Jim via private message and we shared emails, then phone numbers. Jim called one evening on speaker phone with Lady K listening in the background. I was so nervous, like on a job interview. I had no experience at all with an event, other men, other women, sex parties, nothing.

I was fresh meat and of course that lead to us having to meet in person since I had no one to vouch for me. This is how things are done. Safety and identity proclivity are paramount. We set a meeting for a few weeks away in late March, Easter weekend, in Duluth.

I figured events would be a great way to meet other sexually open females that might be interested in being my sister sub. I never asked Loki. I also went back to my classified ad idea with the hopes of having a more positive outcome with a female or couple.

I got a response from a man who said he knew a sub that might be interested. I had a lot on my plate at the time so having another person out looking for another sub filled my management skill set. He of course wanted to meet first. I had to get this first meeting out of the way. It was like an incredible roadblock for my assurance that I could follow through with any of this if I didn't pull the trigger sometime.

I agreed to meet him in a McDonald's parking lot. I was meeting him for the first time, so I naturally wouldn't sleep with him, it was my rule. I can see now how he manipulated me by making me meet him for the connection to this other girl. It was part of my abuse revisiting me, in my past everything was conditional, I hadn't learned how destructive that was yet.

Off I went. Dressed in a cute outfit with layered clothing purposely so I would have to think about my rule if I was put in a position to waiver. I did my hair and my make-up like I was going on a date which felt strange because I wasn't. Who was I trying to impress? I had seen some pictures of this man on his profile. He certainly wasn't my type and I was just interested in this mystery sub he was dangling in front of me.

I was concerned that I look enough like my pictures that there wouldn't be any disappointment or let down by the other person meeting me. I had watched many episodes of Catfish and was often mortified by what was behind the curtain of a computer screen.

I would expect the same consideration except I had a moment of realization about the pool of deviants I was diving into and changed my expectations to be more empathetic to a person's emotional state and their story. After all, I'm telling mine and I'm sure I was judged by many who didn't take the time to meet me where I was.

He texted me the make and model of his car. I texted back mine. I suspected this was what it was like cheating on someone the way we were shrouded in secrecy. His handle was RockCandy. I giggled at his self-imposed play on words for his penis. I pictured a stiffy with hard sugar candy all over it and tried to figure out how I would even try to attempt a blow job with that mess. How is that a sexy picture? Syrupy spit and drool everywhere, my hair a tangled mess that a brush would never go through again, the sharp edges of the crystalized sugar slicing up my mouth and lips, let's not forget the dole rod stick that would be shoved down my throat. I'm sure he thought it was creative and all kinds of hot, but not for this literal thinker. I wasn't there for that, thank God.

He was waiting for me, standing outside of his car, a maroon thing that was old and rusty like him. I pulled up slowly like I was doing a drive by. I felt gross checking him out, looking him up and down. "What the hell are you doing?" I asked myself. "Go introduce yourself, and bee nice." I said exaggerating the e in bee. I approached him, and he invited me to sit in his car with the heat on blast while we chatted.

His real name was Rodger, I maintained QueenBee. I was proud of myself for not crossing that threshold. Alex had warned me that in my quest for play partners I needed to put walls around my identity. Identity theft and security in IT was Alex's professional field and he was very successful at it from what I gathered so I listened.

Rodger was in his sixties and had very thin white wispy hair that moved lightly as the fans blew warm air through the car vents. He was so excited that I agreed to see him. I felt like I made his day just by showing up, then he laid it on me. He told me that he had got a hotel room in case our meeting had gone well. "What else were you expecting really QB???" I said to myself. No wonder he was single.

I got flustered and uncomfortable but then I remembered why I came in the first place. I had a hurdle to get over and a mission to accomplish. I needed to be able to navigate these situations or I might as well pack it in and go back to The Rabbit Cage. I pulled myself together drawing from some inner place of determination that I had never known before. I wouldn't call it an out of body experience or fight or flight, it was task management at its finest.

I determined in my head what I have fallen back on in the past was the way to go, thinking about rock candy got my drool going. I was prepared to suck him off, that was it, like the Latino on the day I got divorced. I would satisfy him if necessary and get out, so I didn't have to compromise my rule and I'd get my lead on a sub.

I told him again about my no fuck rule and he understood. He totally disarmed me when he asked me if he could kiss me. He hadn't touched me or tried anything funny. He was just optimistic and prepared for anything like a Boy Scout. I gulped and took a deep breath, I was going to kiss a stranger. Was this to make him feel good or was I in task mode to break through? I don't know still. I said "Yes." cautiously, with trepidation I watched him reach for my hand. He lightly placed his lips on my skin, they were soft and gentle, he turned my hand over and exposed my wrist and kissed there too.

I feel wetness in my underwear. I am being seduced by a man. What an amazing feeling to allow yourself to freely feel physical delight? I had raw passionate fucking with Ron but never this attentive appreciation for touch. My body temperature started rising and I shed my coat. Rodger smiled.

He continued his stroll up my limb with his lips, added tongue action traced my veins and leaving his saliva wet on my skin. I had a puddle in my cotton, granny panties that I wore purposely so I wouldn't expose them, as if they were my last line of defense, strong and durable with old period stains. I should have thrown them away a while ago, today they were my security blanket and I was glad I had them on.

He finally makes his way all the way up my clothed arm and had found my exposed neck. I know what's coming next and I get tense. I really don't find this man attractive at all. Why is my body reacting like this and without alcohol, hello? It happens quickly and in slow motion all at the same time.

His face is in my face, our eyelashes collide as we tilt to the left and right. He is exploring my mouth like an experienced traveler. Running over my teeth and twisting and turning around my own tongue, I enjoy the wrestling, hot and slippery. My eyes were closed, and I enjoyed the dance, he tasted minty, his breath matched mine, nothing else mattered.

Then something odd happened. Not an inappropriate hand, not a hard on, you'd never guess. Rodger, the sweet man that was so sensual with his lips turned into a commercial grade shopvac. He locked his lips on my tongue and sucked it down his throat. I didn't know what the hell was going on until he let go. My tongue felt like I had burned it, my taste buds were all at attention. I could hardly speak, still gasping for air.

I placed my hand on his chest and forced him back into his seat. He looked like he had Jungle Fever, his eyes were dilated and glossy. I was embarrassed and confused. Was I supposed to like that? Is this a thing now? My tongue was throbbing and swelling, so was his cock.

I think he thought I was going to meet him in his hotel room when I said I had to go to my car. I left and went home without the name of the sub in awe of what had just happened. I instantly blocked RockCandy from ever contacting me again. A few minutes later a private message appears in my mailbox, Meekn3ss reaches out to me. She says "Some dude, RockCandy said he's your Dom and he wants us to get to know each other. I thought I'd contact you to tell you he's slimy and you might want to find a new Dom." I immediately respond, "He's not my Dom." and inform her of my search for a third by private message wishing I had gotten her warning before going to meet him. My tongue was black and blue for days. It was good for losing another five pounds.

Meekn3ss, Gwen, and I become fast friends. We talk about relationship dynamics and religion, kids and careers. She was a swinger with her husband for decades, raised children through it, but now just flirts and fantasizes. I am amazed by how she selectively weaves biblical principles and swinging through her marital bed as if it should be common place.

She becomes a sounding board of reason for me. It was interesting to hear her perspective about my online Dom, she was not a fan. We make a lunch date. She is a plus size model for Target and JCPenney, so she travels a lot for fittings and bridal shows, her schedule is tight. We pick a day that is manageable for her ten days later to meet at her full-time job, for a cosmetic surgeon, where she is the office manager.

In between speaking with Lady K and Jim, my encounter with Rodger and talking to Gwen, I am contacted by MrWantsFun. He reached out as a straight male looking for someone to explore and grow with. He was 36, so I was a cougar in this situation, and he liked it. My new profile was clean and polished, not yet tainted. I hadn't acquired many friends yet, he knew I wasn't very active in the scene by my activity on my wall.

His profile was simple and vague, stressing exploration and worship were his focus. He liked a woman in high heels (check), stockings (check), garter belts (sexy, check), spanking (yes please), nipple play (ehhh, not a lot of sensation there but maybe with more attention I'd find a new pleasure, check), also located closer to the cities 80 miles away just off the highway (super check). We chatted on Kik for ease of conversation and decided to meet.

I was very honest and clear in all my communications with this man. I was not looking for a relationship. I had rules. I was broken and toxic. I had an online Dom, still. He still wanted to meet me. I find out that he is currently separated and going through mediation. This was okay by me because I didn't need to have a boyfriend, just a fuck friend. I still wanted to meet him.

Apparently, accents are a fetish or turn on for me and I didn't realize until I heard MrWantsfun's thick English vocalization with hard and soft tones that made my clit tingle. He was a gentleman but just flirty enough to get my attention and he was willing to drive an hour to meet me that day. The urgency to meet was exciting but should have been a red flag. He had been single and separated for several months with little to no prospects, so he was not going to let the opportunity pass for one more day.

His recollection of that first meeting

"He arrives, nervous but excited about the possibilities of this sporadic impromptu coffee date. 2:00, 2:10, 2:15 he hears a rumbling engine of the beast she drives. They get out of their vehicles. Acknowledge each other, embrace. He hugs her real tight, he shadows over her. The hug was reminiscent of one a toddler would have with their favorite stuffed toy. Not wanting to stop, but knowing slight discretion on her part was needed, due to location. They enter the coffee shop/café...they find a spot away from others. They start chatting both in ease, seems like the connection between the two of them was already magnetized. They comfort in sharing each other's turbulent times. As they talk, he holds her hands, rubs then, massaging the fleshy part of the hand. A feeling that she will never forget.

She explains about her past, truly hurt and needing someone to help with the journey, comfort, and care for her. She was the primary caregiver in the marriage. He wanted to pursue this, she seemed as if she wanted to be a part of his journey. They head out of the coffee shop to pay. The cashier is too busy, they leave the payment at the till. He hugs her, kissing her briefly, due to discretion needed. They go outside, head toward their vehicles, holding each other, kissing, hoping for this to be a new beginning, a new friendship.

He drives away slightly aroused, he knew they were looking for companionship. He does the illegal act of texting while driving, something he never did prior to meeting her. There was something quite remarkable about this woman. He gets home, countless messages later, they crave to learn more about each other. He had to go to a mediation appointment, still committed to coming back up north later that day meeting at the same rendezvous point they decide to go to dinner and Walmart for their first date.

Idle chit chat in the car for a twenty-five-minute ride further north, they are holding hands. Applebee's is a safe location to calm both of their nerves. Lots of flirtatious moments, kissing, waiting for the staff to tell them to get a room. They had no care of what other's thought. It's close to midnight now, Walmart is just on the other side of the four-lane highway. She likes to be efficient and claims it will be a short trip. He is thinking he really enjoys her company, but he is getting tired, his pursuit of this gorgeous lady prevails. He finds it amusing that she considers Walmart a date as they push two carts around the store sans grocery list. She is flirtatious and suggestive throughout the store. At that hour is when the freaks come out, he thinks maybe she's one.

They jam everything into the small trunk of her 1988 green mustang with white racing stripes. The back seats are full, foot wells too. They leave tired, but testosterone flowing. This overcame the tiredness. She drove down a frontage road, whips into a parking lot, kissing, then she feels his growing bulge. She fumbles around unzipping, grasping his member stroking. She said "Well, I think it's time to show you how much I appreciate this." She goes down deliberately locking her lips on his cock, slowly teasing. The guy is fully aware of the act being performed in public.

The excitement of the exhibitionism was new for him. She was busy performing fellatio when he sees a pickup truck approach the turn, the cherries go on. His heart races...scrambling to cover evidence, the officer knocks on the foggy window. "Hello Officer, how are you tonight?" he says to the cop. "What are you doing here?" the officer asks. "We were just talking, we are both going through some stuff." she offers. "Let me see your ID's?" the officer commands. They do as they are told breathing heavy and a sigh of relief they get away without any warnings or anything. That was close. They return to his parked car at the coffee shop, laughing and joking about the incident and obviously the sexual tension has risen. This was going to be the beginning of something that was supposed to be fun, platonic, experiences. They continue to chat, flirting, talking daily. The bond is growing, establishing the friendship. The time invested in this is becoming more of a focal point to them both. The attention, teasing texts, the build-up."

My rendition isn't nearly as romantic in the beginning. I was starting to get the picture that men were fuckers. If they are single, there is a reason and that's okay if I can identify it and determine if I am able to deal with it.

MrWantsFun was attentive, touchy which I liked, funny at times, obsessed with the beer and alcohol industry in which he worked at a liquor store. He was oddly friendly with his future ex and very protective of his kids that were still very young but talked about them constantly. He gave up his house and drove a shitty black VW Rabbit that constantly broke down. He was living on his salary which wasn't much. We would always do Dutch when we went anywhere. This was not my future, I needed to make good choices, I didn't want to raise anyone else's children, I was not going to get sucked into this relationship. Fuck, "relationship", there's that damn word that feels so much more than fuck buddy. Scott's words of accusation would haunt me, "you can't be friends with a man, they just want to fuck."

I didn't find out until later that I had broken a rule, MrWantsFun was a fucking Capricorn born on Christmas Day same as Scott. Loki would point out that he was controlling me just like my ex, manipulating under the guise of friendship.

I kept him at arm's length after that. The fact that we fucked meant we needed to negotiate other playmates, dates, events, etc. Negotiating our arrangement, a word that has found a deep resonance with me, was new and difficult for me. In my marriage, communication often lead to arguments and sacrifices. I learned not to speak my wants, needs, or expectations because the outcome was hurtful and disappointing. I had lost faith in the idea of compromise.

I was free from that now, like a bird set free from the cage. I'll just call him Mr., insisted on full discloser and I rebelled flapping my wings and squawking. I was safe it shouldn't matter what or who I was doing. I wasn't out to screw everyone I met; I wanted experiences, and to fly. My thinking was, if I have a fuck buddy I wouldn't be inclined to screw just anyone because I knew I had a clean, safe, friend to visit. We weren't a couple. This was an ongoing mantra that I would have to say over and over and over to myself and my friend with benefits.

Mr. was also very sexually confused which was a turn off for me. He claimed he was a more dominant personality and in truth I walked all over him. He liked the idea of being in charge and being the boss, but he had no clue how to make this Jersey girl, newly bratty, do anything he wanted.

He struggled with my relationship with Alex which had morphed into just a friendship by now. It was a competition and I found it ridiculous. I prompted Mr.

that I needed more leading from him, and I made a contract like I had read online, in books, and of course from 50 Shades. It was quite comical, looking back at it now. I wrote it with sarcasm and loop holes for whatever I desired to be attainable, he signed it.

This is when I realized this man was not a challenge for me at all. I was not psychologically stimulated by our conversation after the newness wore off shortly after we met. This is the connection piece I think I need, to mentally respect someone, it becomes more important over time.

We had nicknames for each other to try to establish a barrier. The thinking was, by staying superficial, we couldn't go too deep on a personal level. I was Jersey or Madame Secretary because of my accent and because I strongly resemble Tea Leoni, and he was Ramsey like the chef because he cooked a mean risotto. My diet consisted of shredded wheat, bananas and gummy bears so any food was amazing.

I didn't like him cooking for me though because my ex had spent so much time in the kitchen looking for approval. For me, it was a throwback to a grown man, hiding like a child in the kitchen, being moody, arrogant and pouting because help was futile to his agenda. And to leave a mess for everyone else to clean up! My ex's one man show in the kitchen was a metaphor for our dead marriage, you can only do so much to macaroni and cheese, but of course it was the kids favorite.

I was deep into the Game of Thrones while spending time with him, so I would fantasize about that sadistic Ramsey on the show taking me in his twisted ways while I stroked my fuck buddy's ego about his performance. Truth is, Ramsey, had a long thin cock that reached spots inside me that I didn't know I liked. He could stay hard for long periods of time and I would keep pace, never quitting. My stamina and desire for sexual arousal, attention and satisfaction was remarkable. It is with Ramsey that I discovered that I am multi-orgasmic.

We had a lot of fun together mostly sexual in nature. His long pencil like penis curved perfectly to rub the front of my vagina stimulating my g-spot. He could stay erect for a long fucking time, literally. He was not nearly as adventurous as I. I would use his long body to satisfy myself while he laid there with a look of amazement at my raw primal desire.

I was a willing participant in all my own scenes, like a sponge soaking it all in and then exploding repeatedly and he was along for a ride. I learned that I was too much for Ramsey sexually about a month into this charade. I also found out that when he listed nipple play in his profile he wasn't talking about playing with *my* nipples.

He needed so much hard nipple stimulation to cum that my hands would get tired from pinching and twisting that I started using my mouth. I would suck his nipples like a breast-feeding baby, nibbling every once and a while to let him know I was in control. I was very turned on by kissing and moving on to his pale English skin, leaving bite marks and hickies was fun. I got a real sense of artistic license and power, all the time knowing his future ex and kids couldn't know my art existed, was a secret that turned him on.

I suppose with no preconceived ideas of what sex was supposed to look like, or feel like, or manifest itself as, I was open to my body and mind's releasing of energy. A cleansing of my frustrations, sadness, anxiety, all through the amazing act of being in the moment sexually. This was what I craved, to be fucked and used for pleasure, like I was designed and created to do.

I had procreated so my uterus was content. My vagina longed to have purpose too and use its magic feminine potion to lure cock into it like a hummingbird going deep for nectar. Being wanted by men gave me a self-confidence that was linked to my sensuality. I know this appears weak to many people that are reading this. I wanted to be wanted, it was a fantasy to be used, I needed to manifest my inner slut without being one. I had skipped my rowdy twenties to be a mom, I was taking care of business and I was good at it.

I was posting sexually provocative pictures on my profile and driving men and women crazy all over the world. "Friend Requests" poured in and I collected them. I was enjoying being ogled by voyeurs near and far. The attention I was getting was not equally enjoyed by Ramsey, he had deemed me under his protection and was communicating passive aggressive messages to my friends letting them know I was taken, even though I was not.

These pushes of controlling me only made me want to stretch my rubber band more and snap it on his ball sack. I was comfortable in his presence and he gave me enough attention that I could think with my head instead of my pussy, that's why I kept going back. He was pathetic as a fuck buddy as time went on. He would fall asleep while I was riding him often because I just wanted to ride for hours. I cared about him as a person. Caring… I didn't know how to care for someone without having feelings. I was so absorbed in my exploration that casualties were inevitable.

# Chapter 14

As I learned more and more about BDSM, I concluded that I needed to change my thinking. The idea of what I wouldn't do x y or z morphed into I might not go that far, but what would I do? My hard limits were no scat (feces), no children (must be 18 or older with ID), and no hanging from the ceiling from hooks or blood play, I would joke. I really started stretching and growing regarding my personal fears and judgements.

My kinks and fantasies and fetishes were all on a spectrum that was shared by millions of people. I had no place to say that what I liked and what gave me pleasure was any better or worse than someone else. This was my journey, my childhood and experiences in life had created neuropathways that were unique to me. My curiosity got my pussy purring and I understood more and more that intelligence and respect were expectations in a partner, play or otherwise.

I made an appointment. I was nervous. I chose a person I didn't have any affiliation with to do the job. Ramsey came with me even though he knew I'd be off limits for a while. I wore a skirt and no panties. It was late, her last appointment of the day. She had me sign paperwork and pay the fee. He couldn't be in the room with me.

I felt like I was going for an illegal abortion as I climbed into the medical chair covered with sterile sheets and stretched out my legs as she instructed. She donned gloves and inspected my genitalia. She wasn't very talkative, making me wonder if she was disgusted by my procedure. She prepared the medical tray with various items and tools. Changing gloves again, the snap of the latex makes me wet, and I am embarrassed that I am turned on right now. She uses a tool that reminds me of a cross-stitching loom in the form of a medical instrument, stretching the tissue and restricting blood flow while it pinched from both sides.

She prepares the area for what is about to happen. I get lightheaded as she reaches for what looks like an upholstery needle, thick and curved. I can feel the resistance of the tissue against the needle and then I feel the burn. I got my clit hood pierced. A part of my whole being was being acknowledged and was burning literally and figuratively. I wouldn't hang from the ceiling on hooks, however I would experience piercing a body part to celebrate opening my mind.

I got home and said goodbye to Ramsey. His complaining about the ride home was annoying and I still sent him on his way without a blowjob. I needed to rest with an ice pack on my crotch. I call Gwen and tell her about my night and I get directions to her office for our lunch. I feel like I have a special connection with her like we have been friends for years. Her profile was slim, no pictures so when I meet her I will see her for the first time.

My experiences where feeding my brain, expanding my universe, helping me realize my desires, needs and wants. We all have one life. It is divided up into roles where we label ourselves and set expectations according to those roles. Most of these expectations are put on us by our upbringing, our view of religion, our responsibilities, our careers, our children, our addiction to social media and propaganda and sensationalism.

How did I let myself be drawn so far away from my core being? Passion is what fuels us to live, like fire to a flame, adding intensity. I lied to myself all those years, pleasing others, appeasing others, and tolerating the intolerable in the name of my vows to God, being a Mom, being a VP in the Chamber of Commerce, owning a business, sister, friend, daughter. I told myself that being a good person was enough, living a status quo day to day existence was the best it was going to get and that nothing would ever change.

I wasn't depressed, I was being real with myself. I finally got it. Nothing was going to change unless I changed it, expected it, refused it, or acknowledged it. Ramsey was in my life because I still needed to learn. It's true, those lessons just keep coming around until we get them right.

By reducing my divisor (things dividing my attention) I could focus more on me, I figure my experiences individual and shared are the dividends that just accumulate and ruminate, ultimately increasing my sexuality quotient, desired outcome, and fulfillment. This is foundational to tap into the power of an Inner Goddess.

It was necessary to tear off the layers and labels and get real down and dirty with myself. Touch myself in erotic ways, know my body's scent, hear my heart and soul talking to me and use my mind to follow through. It was real progress to see the little things that brought me glimmers of happiness and joy and embracing them. I am a thinker. I think too much as you may see in my writing. I know that I can't possibly be the only one thinking and feeling this way, am I?

My meeting with Gwen was down in St. Anthony at her office. I texted from the parking lot like I was instructed. She gave me instructions to her office deep inside the building. A maze of hallways and two elevator trips later I find the door plaque and slowly enter.

I hear her voice coming from behind the tall counter to the left. There is a waiting room with three chairs and a table. In the corner, a lovely bouquet of fresh lilies and other assorted flowers create an odd aroma of floral flavored coffee you could almost taste. It felt like a Dr. office, neat and tidy, minimalistic in décor. Her eyes lifted, and she sees me.

She already knows who I am because of all my pictures on my profile. I am taking her in as she speaks to the client on the phone very professionally. She is my age and married with older kids, this I knew from our phone conversations. She was a woman with curves, long blonde hair, and a killer smile. She had told me about being a model and I was surprised that she looked so normal.

"What exactly are the requirements for that and why didn't I get that job posting?" I'd thought. She had explained that her body type was used for the patterns of women's plus size clothing. She'd try things on and tell the designer's what she did and didn't like about them.

The part I thought was the coolest was runway bridal shows. She would play the part of the guest, bride's maid, Mother of the Bride and the Bride herself. I never had the opportunity to try on wedding gowns, I put it on my list of things to do someday fiancé or not.

She hung up the phone after politely saying she would ask the Doctor the question and get back to them. She came from behind the desk and gave me a big hug. "Finally, in person!" Gwen exclaims as if we had been pen-pals for years. She must have felt kindred like I did. There was an odd familiarity between us that I wouldn't pin point until later, it was comforting. She hurries and grabs her purse and heads for the door and almost runs into a man standing in the office doorway.

She invites him in and quickly closes the Main Office door from the hallway. She introduces him, he says he was just passing through and wanted to say hello. Idle chit chat and out of nowhere "Oh My Gosh, I have to see your clit piercing. Don't you want to see it? I've always been so curious about them. I've never known anyone personally who has done it. How bad did it hurt?" Gwen rambles without breathing. Grabbing my hand and guiding me back to the medical rooms she leads me to an exam table.

Jack is in tow and very amused by Gwen's antics. He is an older athletic man to us young things by maybe ten years or so. He is a medical supply delivery driver. He is smirking and going along with Gwen's itinerary oblivious to his delivery schedule at this point.

I hopped up on the table covered with the white tissue paper. I was wearing a skirt and no panties. Going without panties is like the most fun sensual thing I have found I enjoy. It's my little secret and makes me feel incredibly sexy, like I'm ready to be taken at any opportunity that might arise. It is a flirty surprise if I was to be kissing some random handsome man and he was running his hands down my body, over my hip and not feel a panty line he might just explode in his pants, the ultimate tease.

I slide my skirt up and Gwen is right there, all up in it wanting to get a good look. Jack is now lingering in the exam room doorway as if he needs permission. Please note that pictures of my pussy, clit, breasts, lips up and downstairs are all over my profile for anyone to see. I trust Jack because, he is what? He is nothing to me, I don't care if he looks. If he doesn't look now, he will when he goes home to his computer and looks up my profile. I'd prefer he make eye contact with me and enjoy my pussy than perv after meeting me.

Jack slowly meanders alongside Gwen, peering inquisitively. He gets closer as he inquires about why I am not wearing panties. "Is it sore? That is some serious hardware." His hand is on my knee as my pussy is exposed and we talk about my sexual exploration. His hand creeps up my inner thigh.

"Excuse me for a minute, can I touch it?" he says like a little boy anxious for permission. I let him. Gwen steps back, but watches. I pretend that it's Alex's hand. My pale skin gets flushed with red, my mouth gapes, breathing intensifies, and I cum quickly. Jack turns to leave, letting us know he won't wash his hand until he masturbates later so he can smell me all day. No penetration just highly sensitive tissue friction, and an experience with a woman present, not a threesome.

"Ugh. I wish I could be that spontaneous. It's been really difficult to say no since I broke Dan's dick." I try to not fall off the table as I am adjusting myself and getting down. "Did you just say broke? His dick? Dan's? WHAT!?! You didn't tell me that." "Well, I don't bring it up with just anyone, I feel like we could be sisters. Not sub sisters, either" she clarifies frankly. "I really love sex and I get really into it. One day, Dan and I are going and going, I decide I'm heading for the finish line and I was on top. I'm riding him hard, came down wrong, and bent his cock. It's been busted ever since, about two years now." I am amazed.

I must have looked flabbergasted. I didn't know that was even a real thing, even with nursing school experience. "So, is that why you swing?" I ask ignorantly. "No, we have been swinging for decades. You want to know why we swing you should ask my husband. Do you have plans for Easter?" She knows things are bad with my kids. "You should come for Easter dinner and meet my family."

I'm still holding out hope that the Easter Bunny will visit me and make my house full of smiles, egg hunts and the smell of Ham. "When do I need to let you know? I'm not sure." I respond. "I'll give you my address, dinner is at noon, after church. Just come. When the kids leave you can ask Dan about the lifestyle." "I'll try." was my people pleaser response, wait..., after church? Oh, yes. I was having Easter Dinner with Gwen, I needed to see this in action.

I had drove two hours to meet her for thirty minutes that turned into an hour. It was a day without clients in the office because the doctors were away at a conference. She would return phone calls after I left. I didn't plan that very well, not very efficiently, I'd get much better at that as time went on. I drove two hours home. I needed to get home spend time with my kids. My vetting for the upcoming party was tomorrow night up north. Saturday was open but now I had plans for Easter. My social life was shaping up. I was keeping busy, not a pathetic lonely single woman at home in mourning. I was making shit happen because it was better than being alone.

# Chapter 15

Holy Saturday 2016, My children are all in camp with their father. They are older kids and the grandson is too young to know about the Easter Bunny yet. I have chosen not to try and compete with Scott but let them go and enjoy the holiday since I have plans to be busy anyway.

The kink community never sleeps, it does have patterns and unpredictable outcomes at times, but you can bank on it that someone, somewhere is getting their freak on even during Holy Week. I was meeting Lady K and Jim tonight at the Sports Bar of the Holiday Inn in Duluth. They travel up north from the cities every Easter and I got to save time and money by meeting them still 40 miles from home.

Loki and I chose a black dress with a pleather jacket for me to wear with my black standard five-inch heels. I wore a black push up bra to create the illusion that my breasts had cleavage. I choose a black lace thong and garter with Cuban Heeled stockings to help me feel sexy for my vetting. It was still very chilly out and the hotel was just off Lake Superior, I needed to appear normal and sexy and not catch pneumonia.

In Duluth, the standard attire for anyone is plaid flannels and starched jeans for the guys or bedazzled and bejeweled ass pocket jeans for the girls, hats, scarves, mittens, boots. I was already going to be standing out, this was business and I already established that I was getting down to it. I decided to park in the garage of the hotel, reducing how far I would have to walk in my stocking covered legs with the seam up the back.

I had researched vetting and it is most commonly used to give someone the onceover before selecting like in the case of an elected official, or a charity chairman, or a trustee of a large estate. I felt like this was a lot of pomp and circumstance for allowing me to participate in an event. It made sense to protect the identities of the hosts and the participants. Just like in any group dynamic, there needs to be a commonality, an agreement of individuals of what will transpire for unity and gratification.

There are rules and suggestions laid out on the event page for all to read. I appreciated all the effort that went into this. It was obvious they had done these many times before. My mind was swirling with questions, not only about the event but about my being there and meeting them.

Was I ready in their opinion? Was it inappropriate or disrespectful if I got there and decided to just watch? Was I what they were looking for? I digressed into a childlike place of wanting acceptance and belonging. In school, I was always the last person picked for teams. This felt similar, would they like me? Would I make the cut? What if someone prettier comes along?

I walk through the bar to the back, left corner where I am drawn by two others, incredibly out of place. I first make eye contact with Jim, he sees me and smiles like he is pleased, and I immediately breathe normal again. My mind settles, this will be ok.

Jim stands to greet me. His hair is long, white and wavy almost to his waist. It accentuates his blue soft eyes framed with wrinkles too many to count. His smile makes his eyes twinkle like a mischievous child. His blazer is tan with plaid patches on the elbows and he wore a casual haughtiness. I notice his dirty white converse sneakers.

He pushes back his hair from his chest like Fabio, exposing his collar, and puts his arms out for an embrace as his metal chain clinks on the table. I see the beautiful long black hair of his wife, Lady K sitting with her back to me, her right hand holding the leash handle as she sips her cocktail. I say, "Jim and Lady K?", she corrects me "Lady K and Jim." And she turns to see my face.

She is smiling, a crooked smile and her face expresses pleasure like Jim's did. I wondered if her lag was purposeful in greeting me, possibly they had sign language or blinked in code to each other for a thumbs up or thumbs down as I was approaching. She appeared to be about ten years younger than him, at a guess she was sixty. Her features and skin tone made her look Hawaiian, or Native American, the lovely brown tones of her pigment were noticeable in this crowd of Norwegians and Scandinavians. Her eyes were dark and small, squinty with crow's feet.

She stands up, petite build, thin and strong. Her power isn't noticeable by her visible muscles, it's the way in which she holds the leash that is telling. She nods her head to Jim and he completes his intention to encircle my body with his arms. I accept the hug, then turn to Lady K to share the love. There, we have all touched each other and shared space. Going to a sex party can't be much different than that, right? I felt accomplished already and there was so much yet to happen.

We had met at nine at night, the bars in Duluth in March are still on Winter's Hours so they were closing at ten. An hour, how do you share your story in an hour? I cannot, that is why I wrote a book. I was reserved but ready for whatever vetting questions were coming my way. I had practiced in the car.

The first question after pleasantries was,

"What is your purpose for wanting to attend our event?" asked by Jim. Purpose, for attending, hmmm, hadn't really thought about that.

"Exposure." I blurt out, "not exposing myself, I mean getting exposed to new things. I am really new to all of this." I elaborate and share some of my history with my ex, my kink and vegetables as a teen, and about my Dom.

Probably much more than was necessary for them to get that I wasn't a rapist or serial killer or stalker, and they seemed very intrigued. I find out that Jim is a Professor of Human Sexuality and has been studying and teaching for over thirty years. His story was fascinating because he evolved his mental sexual state and allowed it to morph his physical needs and desires.

He challenged me about labeling myself, instead to just be. Lady K was a relatively new bride of seven years to Jim. They had met online, met in a park, fucked in the same park on that very day, and decided they were meant to live the rest of their lives together. They married and blended families and throw kink parties in their down time. They prefer to just add a third here and there, heavy hinting via eye contact as they share.

The bar is closing, surprise, the reason they chose this bar was because they had a room in the hotel and apparently Jim makes a mean Green Apple Martini.

"What do you say we move this conversation up to our room?" Lady K suggests.

Jim and I share a love of photography and he wants to show me some of his work. I am aware of what is happening but feel like I am unable to chart the course home. I start to perspire and get fidgety, accepting the invitation with,

"Ok, but I can't stay too long." He is going to be making martinis and I am driving an hour home, what the fuck are you thinking? I ask myself.

My friend with benefits is aware of this meeting, he also knows it is primarily to satisfy Alex, he has insecurities and anxiety about the whole idea. I tried to ease his mind through hours of conversation earlier in the day.

He would toss all different questions at me which I had no answer for because I had never done anything like this before. My adventurous side scared the crap out of him. He had his own issues to focus on and I kept redirecting him off what I was doing to throw him off my scent. Instead, he needed to be searching for the Easter Bunny for his kids.

Ramsey's visitation order allowed him to have his children Friday into Saturday, his wife would have them on Easter. I have mentioned that he was on a small budget and his car was a piece of shit. Well, his car broke down Holy Thursday and he just decided the kids weren't going to have Easter with him at all. He couldn't afford it and the kids would be stuck to him from Friday night until they went home, they were especially clingy with the uncertainty of the roles they played in the divorce.

"My oldest doesn't believe, but Ollie still does. This will probably be the year that they both find out the hard knocks." said in his thick English accent.

I tell you this information because this, is why I couldn't stay late or overnight if it was offered at the hotel over green drinks. I decided to be the Easter Bunny and keep the kid's mystical childhood lies alive earlier that evening to encourage my fuck friend.

I told him to take his kids to breakfast in the morning on Saturday and I would text him when the coast was clear for him to return. I hadn't really thought this through with drive time and stuffing eggs and how much it was going to cost me all by the end of breakfast and likely with a hangover at this point. I like to fix things; my kids didn't want anything to do with me. This was something I was going to fix so maybe someone else's kids would appreciate it someday.

Back to the hotel, I grabbed my coat and followed them, the black- and white-haired couple, through the bar to the hotel lobby and into the elevators. Third floor button is pushed, and some soaking wet kids get in the elevator with us coming from the pool. They are dripping wet, so am I, not sweat. I am excited by the unknown and proud of myself for doing what I was doing.

I wasn't doing anything great, but it was a real stretch for this catholic raised, former born-again Christian to follow a sex positive couple up to their hotel room for drinks. That was a lot. I find myself walking seductively, leg over leg, the hips were swaying like they belonged to someone sexy. Was it the stockings making me feel so sultry or the pheromones being released between my legs?

My feet walked lazily toward the door as Jim slid the key card through the opening, getting a green light to enter. That sounds so sexual, funny. She removes his collar as we enter the room and I immediately scope the lay out. I see the bed, laid open and ready for anything.

Sitting area by the door, bathroom in the middle and bedroom in the rear, no windows. Decorated in seventies avocado green and grey but with a modern twist in the art on the walls. Jim retrieves the ingredients for the cocktails and proceeds to mixing and shaking. They seem oddly prepared for anything from my point of view then I remember who they are and what we are doing.

Lady K and I graciously take the first two pretty, green drinks, in the appropriate martini glasses, might I add. We wait for Jim to make a third and continue with small talk like we never changed locations. Clinking our glasses, Lady K proposes a toast,

"To whatever happens next…", we tap each other glass making eye contact, no more talk, and the drinks slid down so smooth they were gone quickly.

That was all it took. I felt the warmth cascade down my throat into my stomach. Lady K felt the warmth too, she took off her shoes, pants and socks, in that order as if her very life depended on it. Her flowing top hung like a dress now.

Jim got out his camera and started taking pictures of his wife, documenting the energy in the room. I took my heels off and released my stockings from their holders. I removed my garter and panties and stuffed them in my purse while I was in the bathroom. I hadn't practiced casually undressing in front of strangers. I left the stockings on, they were giving me super human courage. "You can do this." I persuaded myself not knowing yet what I was about to do.

I emerged from the bathroom to Jim in his boxers and Lady K in nothing but her panties. She was so uninhibited, so aware of herself and yet comfortable that I was seeing her. She sprawled out on the bed, her hair like ribbons, looking at Jim with lust and he was clicking the shutter repeatedly.

It was like a porn shoot between lovers and instead of being a fly on the wall I could participate. He called her his beautiful slut and his whore, words that were once derogatory to me sounded like a love song or a poem. He would talk to her and point out all her features and what he found so incredibly sexy about them. His appreciation for her body gave me deeper understanding of their love. This love and connection and freedom to be was exactly what I needed to see.

I eventually offered to take some pictures of them together. Jim was almost always behind the lens, he appreciated the offer and proceeded to lose his plaid boxers to the floor and lay with her. They make eyes at each other and the camera. The flash of the camera highlighted the waves and single strands of grey on both of their heads. As I adjusted the lighting to make it more artistic Lady K starts rubbing my inner thigh and I don't stop her. She slides her hand between my legs further looking for a green light for entry just like the door to the room. I hand the camera back to Jim and ask him to help me with the zipper on my dress.

The alcohol had warmed me sufficiently that the dress coming off was now a necessity for my comfort. I was intoxicated enough to not care about my body image, this was happening, no going back now. Jim lifted the dress over my head and left me with just my tattoos and stockings on. Lady K is grinning, Jim is in full photographer mode.

"Let's get some shots of you two beauties together." Jim chides.

I scooch onto the bed like a virgin on her wedding night, knowing what's supposed to happen and hoping it's more than anything I could imagine. This is the first time I ever touched another woman intentionally. My body spooned against hers, our hair tangled together, inhaling each other.

We flirted with each other for the camera. This, I knew how to do. I had been the subject of other shoots, I mastered selfies. This was great subject matter for Jim, he knew what he wanted to capture, and the nervous energy was palpable, making for authentic images. We kissed.

I closed my eyes to pretend she was a man, then I opened my mind and allowed myself to feel her soft sensual lips as a woman. I wasn't lost in the moment or whisked away, I didn't turn into a lesbian in room 305, I just went with it. I had never been with a woman and Lady K knew it. She used her body to pulse against me which helped me settle down my anxiety. It is very hard to be anxious when you are being so suggestively stimulated. She wanted to use my body for her pleasure.

She climbed her naked smooth body on me and a little to the left for better pictures, always considering her husband's view. We kept kissing as I felt her pubic mound brush against my thigh. Jim put his warm hand in the crook of my knee, bent and placed my leg a little lower. I thought he was arranging a shot.

Sometimes photographers make things very unromantic as they intrude to set a stage. Lady K spreads her legs over my knee and starts to slide her pussy up and down my leg, leaving a snail trail of moist sticky wetness. She would hesitate on the upswing and grind hard over my knee cap, that part that slides with pressure, and I could feel the pearl of her clit throbbing. Her husband knew the song, I was the violin and her body, the bow. Jim enjoyed the notes being moaned. They were tuning my pegbox and teasing my bridge. It was rhythmic and sensual.

She gracefully dismounted and settled her knees between mine on the mussed hotel bed. I knew what was coming next, I swallowed hard from nerves. Her hands went to my non-existent breasts and taunted my nipples, pulling on them. She folded in half and all I see is her long black hair in between my legs. I am focusing on Jim and the potential shots he could be taking to distract my mind from a woman's mouth probing my sex.

I think randomly of Medusa with her wild snake hair. My mind was trying to analyze or compensate, anything except acknowledge. What would it look and feel like if Medusa went down on a man or woman, phallic and sensational, I suppose. I become present and pay attention to my body, closing my eyes to quiet my mind. It doesn't work.

The control freak Virgo rears her head, I calculate that there will be expectations for reciprocation. My performance anxiety kicks in already and I tolerate her attempts to bring me to climax while my brain is coming up with a plan. I kick into task mode.

Using my shoulders and torso, I lead my body to roll over gently, breaking her rhythm. She is aware of the flip and lies on her back in wait. Jim is still clicking away, hundreds of pictures taken at this point. He is one of those photographers that just takes and takes and takes pictures and hopes for a bravura shot.

K is relaxed, not nervous or preoccupied, she is enjoying this. I kiss her, with my eyes closed, still pretending she's a man. I taste my nectar on her mouth, sweet and light scented. It brought back the vision of her between my thighs, she is all woman.

"No fooling you!", my id and Super Ego start going at it in my head. Meanwhile, I was surprised because man cum tastes so odd and the consistency is thick, and the pussy juice was thin and slippery like dog drool. My observations regarding my own essence gave me the courage to go to The Lady K Juice Bar and sample hers.

Oh, how my mind starts to wander as I drag my lips seductively down her body. As I kiss her neck, I smell her perfume. As I kiss her breast and stomach, I taste salt. As I approach her mound, I smell her.

"If it smells like fish, it's a dish. If it smells like cologne, leave it alone." runs through my brain, "What will you do if you get a pubic hair stuck in your throat, you know that gag reflex of yours isn't pretty?" another thought. "I should have paid more attention in Anatomy and Physiology or watched some girl on girl porn before this." yet another contemplation.

I determined right there and then, this was not something I was necessarily into and Alex was going to be disappointed when I wasn't as enthusiastic about sister subs.

I buried my face in her folds and start to lick and flick with my tongue. Lady K gives me direction,

"Think back to what I was doing to you. What did you like? Do that or what you imagine that was, to me." I accept the advice and orchestrate my own moves. She had been soft and tickly adding a humming like a vibrator. I found it distracting and fake feeling like porn. Are noises expected when giving too? I inquire of myself. This is something I never considered, I'm learning new things and my tongue is in a woman's vagina!!!! YEAH EXPLORATION! I exuberantly acknowledge my ego.

The mini celebration of progress gives me the will to press on and finish this task well. As I would approach anything else in my life, I dig in to do my best. My ass is in the air, stockings still in place, lost the shoes a while ago. My upper body is intensely engaged with K's lower limbs for leverage. I find a rhythm and start to lick from bottom to top like an ice cream cone alternating to the left and right of her large lippy hood.

I am thinking of a hot day licking a cone and trying to embrace the mystery flavor. I feel Jim touching me all over, running his hands along my spine, pushing back my hair from my face. I notice not as many pictures being taken. He rests his hand on my left butt cheek and is sneaking toward my anus with his thumb. He takes his hand away for a second and I hear a pop as he sucks his thumb and slaps my ass.

His thumb hovers still, the camera flashes. I am very aroused and want him to play with me, I push my ass further up in the air like an animal in heat, flashing my pussy, wafting my scent. He puts his camera down and returns.

He is encouraging his wife to cum as her moans get higher in pitch as he services my snatch with some vigorous finger fucking. As he pushes into me, my nose and chin press into her, I add my fingers inside her slit and rub the ribbed lining of her walls. My orgasm stops my activity as I quiver, Lady K signals her husband to her, with a look that is primal.

Jim stands at K's head and she extends her arm to grab his cock. She moves and hangs her head over the edge of bed and leads Jim's willing cock to her mouth. He is partially erect and there is moisture leaking from the tip in a droplet form.

I roll along side of her for warmth and a good view. She licks the underside of his cock and then looks at me, it's my turn. I know what I'm doing now, no insecurity in this moment, I run my tongue around the rim for a few laps and pass him back. Like sharing a joint we take a hit and pass him back and forth until he can't handle it any longer and takes matters into his own hands. He strokes and moans while we kiss each other sloppily and he exclaims he's ready to cum.

Lady K takes her husband into her mouth and he exploded. She gets up on her knees, cum dripping from her mouth, and kisses him deeply sharing his load with him. Intensely intimate and accepted graciously, I sense this is a thing between them. I slowly slip away to the bathroom to get dressed and leave them alone in the romantic afterglow for a few minutes.

I was a third, technically I had accomplished a threesome without being entered. Was that legit, could I mark it off my list? I didn't expect anything that had happened. I was reeling through all my thoughts and senses, my clit was throbbing, still slightly intoxicated but feeling very proud of myself.

I enjoyed myself in a learning kind of way, would I ever be able to just let loose and be sexual? Had my years of repression and bitterness ruined spontaneity and reckless abandon? Was two company and three a crowd? Did I like being a part of another couple's arousal and satisfaction? Was I open to doing that again? Did I get an invite to their party? I'd have to wait to find out.

# Chapter 16

I start to drive home and check my phone. Ramsey had left numerous texts and voicemails wondering where I was. What was supposed to be just a get to know you and put a face to a name, became a very different kind of getting to know you type of encounter. It had never occurred to me that I needed to check in with Ramsey. He knew I was meeting them, I gave no parameters for concern. I felt violated by the notion that he felt he needed to keep tabs on me. This was ex-husband behavior to a tee and I didn't respond to him until morning when I was on my way down to North Branch.

His kids didn't do anything to me, on the other hand, I didn't owe him or his kids anything either. This was purely about me giving back or a psychological side step based on the grief I was experiencing about my own family demise. I felt very compelled to do something special. It was a coping mechanism.

He kept asking me questions about the vetting and I kept telling him we would have to talk about it later. I stopped at Walmart on the way down and bought the kids a basketball hoop because they had no toys at their dads. Basketballs, one for each and three hundred eggs all that got stuffed in the parking lot of a grocery store where I cleaned out their candy isle of half priced Easter candy. I went to his split-level rental and coated the yard with a rainbow, any kids dream for an egg hunt.

I thought about parking and watching the surprise unfold. No, that wasn't what this was. This was me doing something selfless; it fed my sense of worth as a person. Am I capable of being selfless? In all the acts of kindness, generosity, charity, heroism there is a fulfillment after or a drive that was instilled long before, that brings a sense of goodness to our spirit. Was this about them or me? I get caught in this humility vs. pride battle often.

I felt good about what I had done in the moment however I didn't see the interpretation coming. I was starting to live, in the moment, I didn't have to carefully analyze the ripple effects of my actions. Perhaps I should have. Ramsey saw my appearance as an act of love. He was falling in love with the Easter Bunny only I didn't have a fluffy tail, yet. I knew where to buy one though.

My kids are with their dad. Loki is with her family for a big Easter gathering. I'm already in North Branch, half way to the cities, headed to Gwen's house. The mighty green mustang with the racing stripes grumbles down the road, roaring louder than the music.

I follow my GPS to a beautiful neighborhood with big houses and well-manicured lawns, reminding me that lawn mowing season is coming. There are early spring flowers blooming amidst the small residual snow patches in the shaded areas. The houses are all unique in design.

Gwen's house is a Tudor, to their left is a Colonial, and to the right a Cape Cod. The area smells of affluence, even the trash containers all match and look clean enough to eat off. Keeping up with Jones, who swing with the Smith's and the Kitchello's around the corner.

Who the heck knows what sexual activities go on it a neighborhood like this? How many of these houses have a play room with plastic sheets and toys neatly displayed on a wall? Who might have a cage in their living room for a slave? Who might be living a life of sadistic indifference, not even knowing about the kink spectrum? My mind is expanding with possibilities and fantasy.

In her front yard, chained to a huge oak, is Bunker, their dog. Bunker stands out because he is a St. Bernard and his whitish tan, red and brown coloration is bright against the brown house and the green grass. He has been digging a hole to lay in the size of a small crater. The small dark ring of dirt around his pink nose gives him away as a recent culprit.

He barks repetitively in a consistent tone of an alert. I approach him slowly and cautiously, avoiding eye contact and extending an arm for sniffs, as expected his nose goes for my crotch. He is very excited, and his big back end is swaying like a pendulum independent of his front half that is bouncing and pawing.

Gwen comes to the door and yells at Bunker to settle down, "It's your friend. Don't you remember her from the dog park?". "What dog park?" I ask. "Oh, that's my cover story about how I met you. If anyone asks, we met at the Dog Park. I'll tell Dan about Fet sometime, I needed a reason for why this stranger, you, would be coming to Dinner." she says as she gives me a hug. "Oh, okay? I'm not going to get you in any trouble, am I? What do they know about me?" I become panicked in an under the microscope kind of way. I don't want to say something wrong and wreck this beautiful, strong, honest, family in Christ. My brain is having a field day with all this.

I feel like I am living a soap opera or having an ornate dream. The cast of characters sort of resemble those of my family. She has three children, well maybe four. Clara Jean is her best friend, who is also very dependent. She lives in their basement from time to time, participating in Holiday meals and activities but not church.

She has been an active swinger with Gwen and Dan at parties they have attended, but mostly she is an attention whore. She is the least stable of all of Gwen's "kids" and needs her ego stroked with reassurance that she will find the man of her dreams someday. She arrives very late and it appears her only reason for coming at all was to size me up, her competition.

It was a very normal family holiday feast. Her children were all grown, or in college and out of the house, while school was in. The kid's rooms where all still decorated with trophies and posters, whimsical colors and matching comforters, waiting for them if they wanted to come back. Her kids picked at each other with comments like daggers meant to provoke, they were all very good sports and would answer sneeringly with quick wit.

Dan was very busy in the kitchen. He is an industrial chef and kitchen manager in the city. This was a small meal in comparison to the portions he usually makes for thousands.

He was shorter than I imagined, “Why?” the inner mind conversation begins. “I don’t know. I just thought to swing you would have to look the part. Like a porn star, tall, long cock for viewing pleasure, and somewhat attractive, cheesy conversationalist.” My self-thought would reply.

I jumped into full on task mode and sidled up to Dan to see if I could help. It is a natural way to break the ice, jumping in to work alongside someone. This man was an enigma to me. Scott had been so controlling, jealous, and insecure that Dan fascinated me.

He is very comfortable in the kitchen and directing me in how to help, he manages a kitchen and a holiday meal this isn’t metaphysics. We chit chat about how good things look and what the secret ingredient may be, and my future trip to South Africa in September for my birthday. He is evaluating me, I am confident in my persona, even if Gwen has made it a lie.

Clara regularly draws the attention back to her and what she’s doing or wants out of life. She let’s me know multiple times in conversation that she is part of the family and the basement of their house is her crash pad. She has no filter and makes Gwen blush; her children aren’t phased and find it entertaining and it seems normal. She is searching for purpose and meaning in life, it’s palpable. Her excuses and expectations of others creates a thorny hedge around her that would be difficult for anyone to get through.

It is curious that Gwen and Dan’s house is riddled with religious figures, crosses, and wall decals sporting bible verses with references. Or is it? I start thinking about Song of Solomon in the Bible and “The Marital

Bed". Am I in the Bermuda Triangle or on Fantasy Island? "Maybe, they are unequally yoked, 2 Corinthians 6:14" I mention to myself, explaining the duality of their life through a looking glass. I am can't wait for the kids to leave so I can ask questions and have my braingasm.

We all play UNO for a while, except Clara who hates that game. The adults and those children of age with a designated driver are imbibing on various wine varieties. The bottles pulled out of a cabinet were dusty but were perfect for such an occasion. When else do you break out all those miscellaneous gift bottles?

It was like a wine tasting drinking game but with UNO rules. Skip, Drink 2, Wild (Card holder picks who drinks), Drink 4 (Pick three others to drink with you), and Reverse were the cards that we all mischievously played. This is when Clara realized I'd be spending the night in her room. She left in a full pout about having to work in the morning, instructing me to take care of her cat, Tuxedo, then hugging all the kids and telling them how much she loved them.

Clara's leaving started the momentum for a mass exit of the rest of the guests. I had packed a small suitcase and retrieved it from the green beast while leftovers were divided and put in toss away containers, one of the best inventions ever by the way. Goodbye's weren't hard here because they all lived close. It was more like a calendar revision of when each one would be coming to do their laundry. They each make special requests for a meal when they return.

Gwen and Dan where great parents. I was hesitant to give them the Parents of the Year Award until I got deeper in, penetration of the façade was my goal. Did there have to be a dark side? No. I wasn't there to judge just learn and challenge my thinking and knowledge. All distractions are gone.

The dog has been put out. We all have a light buzz from the wine. There are dishes from the day to wash, that's where I start. I wash and set pots, pans, dishes, glasses, aside and Dan dries them and puts them away. Gwen is tidying up the house and starts the conversation.

"I told Dan about you being curious about "The Lifestyle"." she offers. It suddenly hits me that maybe they think I am there to play with them, oh shit.

"What do you want to know?" Dan replies.

"Well, how did you get into it? Did you meet that way? If not, how did it come up? What was your worst experience? Are they long term partners or just playdates? What exactly is "Swinging"? You know, those kinds of questions, and probably a billion more."

"You are thinking too hard already." He answers. "We didn't set out to be any kind of way. We attended church services at a non-denominational fellowship. We made a lot of close friends. It was some of those friends that introduced us into swinging much the way we were given the gospel. Word of mouth, come and just watch, if you don't like it you can leave, we are just everyday people loving every part of each other." He candidly shared.

"Gwen and I saw their relationships as solid and happy and functional. Nobody was sneaking around, cheating on each other." Dan was reaching up above the refrigerator to put away those dishes you only use for special times.

Gwen starts talking about the first event they went to and how it was considered biblical because the husband is over the wife and if nothing is hidden then in the eyes of God the act of sexual satisfaction was being fulfilled uniquely by the husband. Twisted I thought.

I tried not to be judgmental and it was a tug of war. "What a stretch?" my mind would say, "Why do you care?" my kinder me would answer. Back and forth like an auto-correct setting in my brain. First, I'd see it or think it, maybe even say it, then my empathy and desire for an open-mind would change what I saw completely to make it acceptable. This is their story, let them write a book about how it all works together for good (Rom 8:28). See, I can do it too.

I was mostly interested in what was the situation post cock injury. He is still identifying as a Swinger, yet the he has taken a hard right, at about 130 degrees. He encourages Gwen to find a man she is interested in, that man then needs to meet him for an interview, then if he passes, he gets a shot on goal. They explain, if the third is a good fit he is expected to be around the house a lot, hold a conversation with Dan, man to man, and love dogs. Between Dan's physical issue and his work load, he admits he doesn't have much left to give Gwen. This is his way of maintaining a happy, healthy, satisfying marriage.

It is obvious that they love each other in that husband and wife of 30 years kind of way. With this detour around norms and expectations, I see a very creative and devoted husband. I feel like he would have liked it to be different but when you are given lemons make Soy Lemon Flank Steak with Arugula, a specialty in their house.

"Aren't you afraid of falling in love with someone that you are so intimate with regularly?", I say with concern. Then it happens, the rest of the story. I remember Paul Harvey's radio snippets and chuckle. Dan shares, and I knew there was more to it. Gwen used to play with a third with permission from Dan until they caught feelings for each other and it turned into a romantic pull, jeopardizing the marriage. Dan put an end to it. That was the deal, the agreement. Gwen's struggle was real, not play, taboo. She liked connection too.

As Dan explained a situation gone bad, I knew who he was talking about from talking to Gwen. Dan referred to him as a friend, no name. He was very matter of fact about it and kind of proud of himself that he identified a pitfall and averted the destruction of their marriage.

What an amazing triumph as a couple? Working through an issue instead of throwing the marriage away, old school. It was inspiring that two-willing people, that love each other, could put the needs of each other before themselves and cross the river of complexities. Fascinating concept that I would apply in my future search for a partner. I want that kind of love.

We chatted over emptied, colorful glass vessels with artsy whimsical labels until very late. I was glad that I had taken Gwen up on her offer of Clara's Liar. I snuggled into bed and Tuxedo joined me kneading his feet and purring. I touched base with Alex and

Ramsey, saying goodnight with a video of me massaging my clit and then cutting to the cat, "Do you like my pussy?" I teased. Neither answered, I passed out.

I woke up the next morning with 10,000 grapes screaming in my head. Mixing all the wine varieties didn't sit well. The happy couple were already at work and they encouraged me to take my time leaving. I showered and spent some time with Bunker. I took him out to pee and was on my way home. I spent a lot of time on my ride home thinking about what I had learned the night before.

Learning to discern between a relationship and play is not easy. It's easier for men than women, my humble opinion and not saying all men or all women fall into that. I do also think we are becoming so calloused fighting for equality, as women in all things, that being a player is just as fitting for women as men these days. Does that make us more evolved really, better somehow? Why does that make us equal?

The acts of intimacy and the level of closeness involved in sexual act needs clear communication between partners and boundaries defined and understood by both parties to reach bliss. Is it more a level of consciousness than closeness? Are sexually open people further along the path of enlightenment than someone like me? Even perverts, really? Emotional attributes generally caused me to be jerked back to reality and live in the real world, addressing my insecurities and desires with erratic outcomes fueled by other people and their fucked-up lives, addictions or falsehood.

This is one of the very deep waves of doubt that I had planted in my mind by this time. Was what I wanted even possible? This open sharing about sex, with and without feelings? Do you have to live an open lifestyle to do this? If lust and love can comingle freely with or without a partner or fuck buddy or husband/wife, why do I need a connection?

"Relax, you're thinking too much again. Your orgasms will show you the way." my pussy reassured me in a Yoda way. I was approaching North Branch and my little head took over driving. I didn't bring myself to completion with Tuxedo watching me, in Clara's bed. I needed to cum badly. I start recognizing tension in my body for what it was. My desire for information and experiences would often leave me pent up. I called it. This. is. Horny! Ha.

Look at me identifying my feelings. I can't get over how such a small thing, knowing what I feel, is taken for granted by many. Two steps forward, one step back, I go to Ramsey. I got a fuck and a thank you, in that order. It was a great Easter.

# Chapter 17

The month between the vetting and my first event felt like an eternity. I was still fielding messages from match.com, kik, and FetLife. My profile was still very open and telling of my newbie status. A lot of men and a few women sent me messages asking open ended questions about how I came to be kinky.

My story wasn't that unique, 50 Shades of Gray had unleashed the wild in many mid-forties women all looking for their own Mr. Gray. I still hadn't found mine. I knew he didn't exist. I knew I was looking for something different.

I expressed interest in choking in a couple groups I joined, and Alex instructed me to get a belt and keep it by my bedside. It made me wet wondering why. Telling a Dom that you want to experience something is giving them the power to tease you with it. The mental pregnant pause between suggestion and anticipation is an intelligent subs undoing.

Time went by, he knew I was waiting. One day, out of nowhere, he texted me to have it around my neck when I Skyped him next. I put on a pretty lacey black bra and panty set and I draped the 2" wide black belt around my neck with the buckle dangling over my collarbone.

"Good girl." He says before even saying hello. I am immediately dripping wetness through my undergarment. "Loop it through the buckle but don't fasten it. Hold the loose end tightly in your left hand. Now."

"Yes, Sir." I quickly do as I am told. He is watching me from the shadows of his screen, like The Banker on Deal or No Deal.

"Get on your bed on all fours." I start to move and let go of the strap. "Did I say to let go of the strap?" he asks sternly.

"No Sir." I adjust my position with the leather in my left hand facing the screen of my laptop. "Does this please you Sir?" I am on edge, the edge of a fantasy and ecstasy. I am visualizing the belt around my neck as a collar and the long lead as the leash and he is holding it ready to lead me to Orgasmville. He has different plans.

"So, you like being choked?" "You like the idea of someone having that much control over you that they hold your very breath in their grasp?" He sounds annoyed.

"I'm interested in what that would be like. I have read that it intensifies orgasms. I want a relationship where I can trust someone to know me so well that this could happen. You know that I am exploring my interests." I justify.

"Rub your clit with your right hand. While you are joining all these groups, it makes me realize that there are many things I want to do to you that I can't. That does not please me." He says. "If you had a sister sub I could do more things by using her to be my hands."

"It hasn't been as easy as you made it sound, Sir. I am trying to please you." I am not really sorry. I don't want to share Him.

"Sit up on your knees. Rub that clit harder. Faster, now finger fuck your pussy with your other hand. I want to see your face as you apply pressure to your own neck while satisfying Me." He knew exactly what he was doing.

I looked down at my left hand and it moved toward my mound all on its own. In slow motion, like time was standing still, I feel the belt tighten and pinch my soft skin. I feel the metal buckle cold and uncomfortable applying pressure directly under my chin. There is still a gap there, I feel safe. Of course, you are safe idiot, you are holding the damn belt. I didn't let on to Alex that I was in my head, that wouldn't be very polite after He went to all this trouble to satisfy me.

I was instructed to remove my bra and slide my panties over, so he could see everything. I was getting close to orgasm when I hear the front door and a bunch of commotion in the kitchen. Before I could cum, before I could black out, Before I could have died unintentionally, I hear my son start up the steps. I quickly close my laptop and grab my thick Turkish cotton bathrobe with my initial embroidered on it and cover myself up, bounding to the door. Did I lock it? He will think it's weird that I locked my door. I fumble with the door knob and open the door.

"What's up Honey?" I ask nonchalantly.

He looks at me quizzically "You ok?" he asks.

"I'm fine, what do you need?" I offer trying to act normal.

“We are going to ride the four wheelers around the property, ok?” He is trying to communicate, which I acknowledge with favor.

“Sure. Be safe and wear helmets. Don’t do anything stupid.” Said in my best Mom voice.

“What’s with the belt?” he asks

“I was trying it on with an outfit.” I lied.

I picture my mom in a similar conversation with me, and I try to keep a straight face.

“I want to try affixation with a man on another continent, ok Mom?” I would inform her.

“Oh, that sounds fun dear. Be polite, say your please and thank you. Wear clean underwear in case you pee yourself or need to go to the hospital. What’s your safe words? Is he a nice guy?”

I decided from that day on that if I was curious about stuff I needed to take on learning it on my own until I had a real Dom, live and in person. How was Alex ever going to bind me or do beautiful rope ties on me from South Africa? How was Ramsey ever going to take me to subspace when he was not dominant from the get go? How was I going to manage being a single kinky Mom and having a Dom that wasn’t invested in my life? The search goes on.

Alex understood the abrupt cut off, he’s married and ghosts on me for days at a time. Life happens. Meanwhile, I am ordering toys and implements from various places, eBay and Amazon as well as the Fetish Factory and good old Adam and Eve. I wanted to be ready for "The One" with an arsenal of tools at His disposal. If I found someone I trusted to experiment with I wanted to be able to act in the moment and not have to put it off any longer. I had waited long enough. I only had nine more months to figure this shit out.

The postman, UPS driver and FedEx delivery drivers could probably write very interesting books based on the houses they visit, seasons of spending, guessing what is in that brown paper wrapped box? They are probably more informed than local grocery store clerks or the local PTA. I fantasized about answering the door naked or propositioning one of them to come in for a glass of iced tea and then seduce them. I never did.

Rope bondage was beautiful to me in an artistic way. The intricacies of how to weave and knot were an art form. The rigger, person tying up another, needed to have subjects that could withstand long periods of discomfort, pain, meditation, cold, heat, exposure, and with the bladder like the humps of a camel that could hold it for hours if needed.

I went to Home Depot and went to the rope aisle. It dawned on me that I had many choices and I wasn't really prepared for shopping. I had worn a sexy outfit. I dressed up every time I went out, you never know when you'll bump into the man of your dreams, your next husband, or someone that is willing to tie you up to the rafters of his garage. I found a worker, typical mid to late 50's guy with the orange apron and started asking some questions.

I'm guessing that Steve, the employee, had a good idea why I was asking so many questions. How do you clean it? I touch every rope on a spool, I am very tactile. The question that I am sure gave me away was where are the safety scissors? I was blushing when I asked.

I pondered how great it must be to be the Rope Expert at Home Depot. Was this guy a rigger? Did he know any others? Do they sit around the break table and tell stories about the best questions they got that day? Do they fantasize about what people are really doing with the products they purchase? Do it yourself had a whole new meaning to me and I have never looked at a hardware store the same since.

I bought thirty-foot pieces in the prettiest colors available in a big box store. I ordered more online. I wanted to have enough rope around to be tied to the bed spread eagle and helpless. I also wanted to be dressed in rope accentuating my body in some places and using rope as a curtain to mask other spots. My true Dom would have rope skills.

It was like finding a needle in a haystack. Finding a Dom, I could trust and that wasn't just wanting to fuck 24/7, was hard. Rope skills fall on a more introverted Dom personality, I found. The rope is their pleasure, the time, the finished product, the photo. I guess I had romanticized it thinking that I would be like a fly caught in the spider's web and we would comingle there for hours and bond before he devoured me sexually. I needed a more rounded individual, riggers were out.

I found a site on the internet on how to do self-ties. I decided if I wanted to be in a rope dress I could do it myself. I didn't need a relationship with a man to creatively wrap me in mauve nylon. Step by step, the paragraphs and illustrations gave me the way to assemble this interesting macramé on my body. It took me a long time to get it just right for taking pictures. I tied it tight and kept it on while I was home in my room.

I get a phone call from a close friend bringing me back to reality. Her mother was dying of Stage 4 Breast Cancer. Joi has reached out and let me know that this call was about a hospitalization. She isn't doing well and has been talking about me. I feel like I should visit because her days are numbered. I put loose clothes on over my binding rope dress.

The excess rope is hidden easily in my sweatshirt and sweatpants. No bra because my tits are supported by the upper rope and the rope with well-placed knots create a thong. The rope dress is a lattice work that supports itself and doesn't move. I have a secret, no one knows what I am doing, like not wearing underwear, my exhibition side smiles. I wonder if I am a bad person for enjoying my kink while visiting my dying friend. I decide not to let that voice have any power.

I get to the hospital and I am surprised to stumble into a room full of people. Like I said, her days were numbered, no one knows when the last breath will be drawn. As I enter the threshold of her room, her husband and daughter stand and approach me for consoling hugs. I have an "Oh shit!" moment as Hal hugs me. He is a good hugger, firm and holds it so you know he means it, this time there was an inquisitive back rub incorporated. I am a hugger too and it would have been weird for me not to engage. I have no clue what he felt or thought. It has never come up. His daughter hugs me lightly, whew.

I sit as another friend of theirs is leaving and offers up a chair. I descend quickly, comfortably used to my nylon netting, the knots have moved ever so slightly rubbing against my clit briskly and causing me a jolt like a sat on a child toy accidently.

I settle in with a little wiggle and the knot flips over my button each time I change position. It is so habitual for me to constantly cross my legs from one side to the other that I almost orgasmed in the hospital. The room was warm so being flushed and swallowing hard were acceptable and appropriate actions you might see from a visitor.

Ruth was only awake for about five minutes of my visit. She was in the pain management phase that left her high a lot. She was a recovering alcoholic and had done terrible damage to her relationship with her daughter because of it. She considered me a daughter and at her funeral I met many others that she mothered and nurtured. When I left the hospital that day, there would only be one more time that I would see her.

Her biological daughter and I found that we really enjoyed each other's company. While her mother was a raging alcoholic, Joi was looking for connection in biker gangs, Sons of Anarchy type stuff. She had a daughter out of wedlock and had lived a very hard life. She settled into truck driving as a career surrounding herself with men always looking for self-worth in a gang mentality.

She knew Scott and was unsure why I stayed. She hadn't reached out to me before the divorce because she didn't like him, no one did. We shared stories and struggles later, after that day at the hospital. She could sense my confusion and her intuition was spot on. She was real enough that I could be honest with her, she was guarded enough that I could trust her.

Had her father felt my ropes? Did that make me just kinky enough to hear the biker life she came from? She wanted a friend, a connection. We became like real sisters. She would listen when sadness and pity were entering my scene and she would kick me in the ass and let me know pain was ok but to get over it. I would assure her that she was right where she needed to be, with her estranged mom.

I drove home from the hospital thinking about death and life. The big picture, where am I in all of it? I zone out to some music as I am hurling toward home. I will be passing Cloquet which reminds me I need some things at Walmart. My brain is still feeling sort of spacey in deep thought.

I refer to my list in my phone but can't concentrate. I end up walking the aisles up and down, in no hurry to go home alone with my thoughts. About a half hour into my shopping I feel something weighty in my gait. I turn around quickly as if to catch someone watching me and I see two long pink ropes dragging behind me.

In my haze and somewhere between the car and the shopping aisles my excess rope had slithered out of my baggy clothing wanting to be seen. I was panicked at first. I gathered up the two ten-foot or more pieces still attached to my body and quickly wrapped them around my waist several times and tucked them in.

I looked around for people that were watching or cameras, of course there were cameras. Was I going to be on "The People of Walmart" clips that were popping up like crazy? When I started breathing normally again I owned what had happened and laughed. After I slowly and sensually removed the rope from my body, I wrote about my adventure on my profile and chalked it up to another experience.

I got curious about other things that I could do for myself. I was always yearning for someone more experienced to be guiding me like a Shaman. I could lead a conversation in a direction with some of these online guys and have an audience which I enjoyed.

I did anal training all by myself, graduating to a "Big Girl Plug" named Bertha. I would wear her for hours and she would vibrate in my ass every time I went over a bump. I tried self-fisting because I saw videos that intrigued me. I was assured by many men that it was possible with a lot of lube and patience. I realized quite quickly that either my hands were too big, or my pelvis was too small which is probably why I had four C-Sections.

Since I was become less dependent on Alex and Ramsey I figured I needed to meet more kinksters in person. I started attending munches. These are gatherings of likeminded people from groups advertised through FetLife and group posts. There was one group called The AlphaDen. I surmise that perhaps I would find an Alpha personality in The Alpha Den, how smart right? Could it be that simple?

The group met at a bar in Superior, WI. It was known as a gay club and it was very popular before the internet because that was how you met partners. I attended alone without knowing anyone. My brain indexed the group members that I had looked at and said they were coming. They seemed harmless enough, a lot of couples or people in dynamic relationships.

I was a single, a milficorn, middle-aged hot Mom with a libido on fire who knew who she was and were she had been, and what was on her fuckit list. Unicorns were single, cute twenty somethings that were useable and expendable like ass wipes or tissues. Singles were a threat, period.

I would be objectified and judged. I didn't care. I had survived the waves so far and was ready to cause a tidal wave and take down anything in my path. I wasn't designing to be destructive, more like unstoppable.

I parked around back and came in the off-street entrance. The smell of urine hit me hard, like a wall as I walked through a narrow hallway with red worn carpet into the recessed seating area at the foot of the stage. Beyond that were tables and tall barstools and a coat check area. This is where The Alpha's Den was having their munch. On the counter where someone would accept coats was a spread of hot dishes, crockpots and bars. Arranging the food was the organizer, Jewel.

Jewel was wearing a belly dancer outfit and bangles on her arms, jingling with every movement. She directed me to the area of reserved tables and told me to help myself to food.

“We will begin when Master gets here.” She said like he was my Master too.

“Who is that?” I asked

“He is the owner of the group, The Wolf” I felt like I should have known that by her tone. “You'll know him when he arrives.”

And I did. Treasure, a sixty-year old hippie type sub, giggled, jingling like Santa's sleigh, ran toward the front of the establishment past the bar and around the pool table to get to Master. If I didn't get it was him by her enthusiasm perhaps her screeching “M-a-a-s-s-t-t-t-e-e-e-r-r-r!!!!” throughout the place over her jingling would have given it up. I couldn't make out his features because of the time of day, everything was shadowed. How appropriate, coincidence, who knows? The Wolf walks into the light.

I am underwhelmed. I think back and shake my head, what was I expecting? Here this thin, elderly, worn down looking man in his sixties. He comes in looking like he just came from working under an engine all day covered in grease. He goes to his spot, all set up by Treasure, and sits. Other people have funneled in through the front and the back and there is a group of about twenty-five people including me, the odd one, the milficorn.

No one reaches out to me, so I start playing pool, alone. Two crossdressers at the bar come over and start talking to me about my hair, they are not part of the group however. I have had a couple glasses of wine by now and start to wonder why I came. In my moments of vulnerability, I text Ramsey and he encourages me to leave and that he will attend the next one with me.

I am too drunk to drive so I get my things and go across the street. On to another LGBTQ bar with two locations, one in Superior and the other in Duluth. I am too drunk to drive so what do I do when I go to a new establishment? Have another glass of wine, of course.

It was a Tuesday night, it was very slow, but the music was good, there was dancing. I could burn off the alcohol if I stopped drinking it. I decide to put a call out to my kik friends to see if anyone wants to join me and then take me home. They could take me home to their place and fuck me. A one-night stand, open invite for sex, and none of the boys I was talking to could host. This would become my biggest pet peeve.

I danced and chatted with some strangers until I felt like I had sobered up enough and I proceeded home. I felt like the night was a waste of my time and didn't see anything coming of that in the future. The Alpha's Den was a closed group with established relationships. However, I did see a flyer for another newbie gathering the next week in Duluth. Ramsey was on the hook and I was going give munches one more try. Maybe it was just the people in Superior that I didn't culturally jive with. It was worth another shot.

# Chapter 18

The time between these two munches is very important because I conversed with two of the most interesting characters I have ever shared time with, Fuzzy Sweater Guy and ArchAngel. I received messages from both men and quickly started traveling down the rabbit holes of their kink journeys which I told them I would share.

Fuzzy Sweater Guy

I get a message, out of the blue, inviting me to an upcoming event. The theme of the party is fuzzy sweaters. Okay, I think to myself, there's something for everyone. The guy that is hosting the event is very engaged and sends messages asking to see the sweater I am planning to wear. I inform him that I don't own a fuzzy sweater and that I will have to buy one. He directs me to thrift shops or Good Will and I tell him I will go the next day. That next evening, like clockwork, I receive another message inquiring about my sweater purchase. I am curious about his persistence and ask him to move to kik for a more fluid conversation. He agrees and away we go.

I ask him "What's the deal with the fuzzy sweaters? Will everyone be wearing them?"

"Do you really want to know?" he asks.

"YES, please." I say.

"Will you still come to my party if I tell you?"

“Sure.” I am now hesitant to commit but want to know.

He proceeds to tell me an amazing and disturbing tale. He was attracted to his teachers in school when they wore pencil skirts and heels. I am thinking, oh yeah there ya go, that makes total sense but there is more. After high school he worked as a front desk clerk at a motel.

He worked the shifts no one else wanted and had lots of prostitutes as friends hanging at his place of employment. Over time, he really liked this one Latino working girl with big boobs and killer lips. He would upgrade her room for her to show her he paid attention to her. One day she started a conversation with him and asked him what he liked, what he thought was sexy. The next day, she shows up with a john in a pencil skirt and fuzzy sweater and heels which blew his mind.

He upgrades her room per usual and waits. After about a half hour Fuzzy Sweater Guy gets a call to the front desk from a room next store to the one he gave his heauxfriend. “It sounds like someone is being killed in there, call the police!” Fuzzy Sweater Guy assures the customer that he will tell them to quiet down and as he hangs up he thinks to himself they must be having a real good time.

He calls the room, no answer. He goes to call the room again and he looks at the camera and he sees his heauxfriend stumbling in the corridor with both of her hands over her mouth. He can tell something is wrong, he calls the police and then heads to the room. The beautiful girl is slumped over in the motel hallway, blood running down her arms and all over her fuzzy sweater.

Fuzzy Sweater Guy looks around for the john in the room; he grabs a blanket from the bed as he follows the blood trail back out to the hallway where she sits gurgling. Fuzzy Sweater Guy slowly pulls one of her hands from her face and is in shock himself. The police arrive, she can't talk and now he is covered in blood too. He comped the room, he went in and walked through the blood getting the blanket, he is questioned.

The girl with the beautiful lips had her bottom jaw ripped off, torn in the corners of her mouth and dislocated at the joint. Fuzzy Sweater Guy was able to show the video of the john entering the room and leaving only a minute before she had stumbled out into the hall. He lost his job, he lost his heauxfriend, and never got closure that she was okay.

To this day he can only ejaculate on women wearing fuzzy sweaters. I told him he needs professional help, like seriously. The next day the party was gone from the calendar and I never spoke with him again. I still have my fuzzy sweater that I found at the Good Will the day of our conversation about all this. I can't seem to throw it away; this story haunts me.

ArchAngel

"Are you into Watersports?" he asks vaguely.

"I'm from the Jersey Shore. What kind of water sports? I haven't lived there for a while, so my interests may have changed a little." I playfully respond.

"You are aware of what I am asking, aren't you?" he snarks.

"Umm, skiing, surfing, parasailing, boating…" I reply. I then bring up my page for definitions of all things kink and look it up.

"Have you ever been marked by a man's scent?" he is still being coy

"No. I don't get this even a little." I get a weird acid taste in my mouth and a disgusted expression on my face like I was smelling poo.

I had determined that my hard limit was poop, I never listed pee I suppose he isn't out of line to ask. My rational explorer reemerges and provokes a query on the topic.

"Where did this kink start for you? If you don't mind me asking." Again, we move to more fluid conversation this time by email.

ArchAngel as a handle now makes much more sense. I think of this dude every time I pass a McDonald's. I find out that this man, in his early thirties, was raised in a Baptist church as a Preacher's kid. He sends me a long email with long paragraphs and references from the Bible and other books.

He has done his homework. He informs me that this is not a homosexual thing, so he must get that a lot, his tone feels defensive. It could be degrading or humiliating in a D/s relationship but that's not what he is about and that's good because those things are hard limits for me. I don't know why I keep reading, but I do.

He informs me through his research paper. Some people are exhibitionists that like to pee in public in front of others, even if it is just one other person. The act of peeing on someone can be a unique bond between two people, a special experience that's secret like a pinky promise. Some people believe that allowing yourself to be peed on is bringing down all your barriers, exposing yourself like a puppy that exposes its belly or pees everywhere when excited.

Some people associate golden showers with an event or activity in their life that involved urination, so it's a positive association with something else. Some find the warmth of pee flowing down their body warm and erotic. Some like the fear and exhilaration of not being able to make it to the bathroom in time only to release in an inappropriate place. In Archangel's case he liked to mark women with his scent like a dog.

The smell of urine, strong urine, can stay with a person for a week or more depending on how well they wash and what kind of soap they use. He was very into the idea of a woman submitting to him and being protected by him and he felt his scent would keep other men away. I was educated. I had no idea this was such an in-depth study. I declined his offer but didn't move it to my hard limit list. Done in the right way, with the right person there could be an interesting theme for a night of play.

I told Alex about these two guys and he told me to stop talking to strangers. Later, Alex gave me a writing task. Here it is - If we were to do something like that what would it look like? He told me to set up the scene being that I had learned so much, considering my own thoughts and fantasies. He wanted me to use my imagination because the mind is the most sexual organ we have, spoken like a true online Dom.

So here it is - Hypothetically, we would have to be at a hotel, somewhere that I never planned to be at ever again. I would steal an extra set of bedding sheets and comforter off the housekeeping cart. I would bring a shower curtain liner and drape the bed with it and then lay my contraband set overtop so I would be comfortable. I would lie in the middle of the king-sized bed and have rolled towels placed around me where pee may pool up.

I would wear my hair pulled back tightly in a low bun and my head and face would be covered in a black latex hood with only a straw for breathing. I wouldn't want to see or feel anything on my face, in my eyes, running down my scalp or in my ears. He would apply cuffs to my wrists and ankles and I'd feel him secure me to the bed with rope.

He would seduce my body with his hands first lightly running them up and down my limbs, grabbing my breasts and squeezing them confidently in his whole hand. One hand would linger around my neck and collarbone while the other headed South of the Border and would clutch my pubic mound like a bowling ball, lifting my hips with his thumb on top and third and fourth fingers inside.

This scene would be for His pleasure, so I would expect a crop or flogger drug across my skin and some well-placed licks from the leather. I didn't know his impact style because we had never been in person to play. Would he be a sensual Dom or a Sadist? Would he get enjoyment out of me writhing in orgasm or writhing in pain? Did he want to leave marks or pee on open wounds?

I think about going to the beach on the Jersey Shore and knowing that if I got stung by a Jellyfish I may have to ask a random stranger, "I just got stung by a jellyfish. Would you pee on me?", which I never had to do by the way. Here I am fantasizing about being stung by a man with a whip or a cane and getting peed on by him afterward, funny how my mind correlates these things.

Not having ever seen him play makes the idea thrilling and unpredictable especially if I would be wearing a hood. I'd never wore one before. The idea of sensory deprivation and helplessness are ways for me to let go and not allow myself even the thought of being in control. That is what I would get out of wearing an oversized balloon on my head, in case you were curious.

I imagine the constriction and tightness, the heat and then add the random things being done to my body at my Dom's will. I'd give ultimate surrender and use of my body and when he was finished playing with me, he would climb up on the bed and stand over me. I'd feel his weight indenting the well-used mattress.

My initial realization and shock of what is about to really happen would give way to the sensation of warm fluid running over my body. He'd get down and let me sit in it for a few minutes. The fan in the room would be blowing soft currents of warm air over the wetness ultimately making me cold, goosebumps appear like a wave and my nipples are hardened.

My control freak mind wants to clean up right away afterward, is it over? I anxiously await a cue but instead I feel him remove the excess towels and he starts to wipe me with several warm washcloths where I had felt his crop, I wince, my skin is raw and sensitive. It stings where his uric river flowed, yet I wait, not moving.

He unties me from the bed and removes the cuffs, leaving the hood in place he directs me to sit up and come to the edge of the bed. He is close to me and I feel his erect penis poke into me as we move. He leads me to the steamy bathroom blind.

He taps each leg as I am to step into the warm cascading H2O. He lathers me up and I let my hands roam feeling very slippery and sensual. My hand dips into the folds of my labia and the wetness there feels distinctly different. He encourages the attention to the front of my body while he turns his attention to the back.

I feel him standing behind me, in the small shower my sense of touch is heightened greatly without sight, smell, or taste. His right shoulder dips as he reaches his wet, slippery hand down the crack of my ass and lingers there. He circles my crinkled star with his middle finger and slips the tip in, tugging a little like he's hooked a fish. Using the same fingers that had grabbed my pussy earlier he rhythmically strokes my rectum.

My noises are muffled because of the hood and I am breathing heavily ready to cum and he unzips the hood with his free hand and peels it off my head. The cool air, the free oxygen, the water on my face, I'm ready to explode. He forbids my orgasm.

"Don't you cum yet, you aren't done cleaning up this mess. Get on your knees and wash my cock with your mouth." I obliged obediently licking, stroking and sucking. The trick to giving a blow job in the shower is to not break suction and breath through your nose or you'll take on water. I am in a state of hyper sensitivity and sucking his cock with my eyes closed, I see white where I usually see nothingness. He tells me to cum, and I do just as he delivers his second load of bodily fluids during our session.

"Good girl." I hear him say as he lends me his hand to help me off my knees.

I grab the last remaining towels available in our room and as if watching someone else doing it, I dry Him. As I dry myself off between quivers he has grabbed the corner of the shower curtain liner and slid everything on top of it off the bed into a heap by the window. He pulls back the clean bedding and we crawl into bed together still slightly wet but wrapped in sheets and blankets and arms and legs. We don't talk, I feel my orgasm diminish and just slip into sleep. When I wake, he isn't there because none of this happened. It never will.

Alex asks me if I would let him pee on me? I said no. I would have.

It seemed like an awful amount work when I look at it. I guess ejaculation takes less time than peeing in most cases. It's the build-up, the anticipation, thinking about the details for days that make a scene so much more than sex. Having a partner that is as into it as you are, is cosmic.

The fact that he is pondering what could be if he was closer, lets me know that my power was growing, he was losing the ability to contain me as his sub. He knows I'm strong and my future doesn't have him in it for long.

The second munch happens with Ramsey in tow. I am affected by his insecure energy and it makes me on edge, less outgoing. I don't like being hindered and he is being clingy. I walk away from him often to allow space and invitation for interaction. The leader of the group is very organized and has handouts. She likes to be informative, I find out that she is a sex educator in her full-time real life, way cool. I like the professionalism and the crowd that shows up is returning her effort. This is more my style.

The door opens, and someone keeps it open long enough for the cool night air to creep across my ankles. First, I see the wheels, then hands pushing them, then I see HillsideDmnt. Jonas is his name. Hillside because he lives on a hill in Duluth, Dmnt because he is a Dom. I am intrigued to the point of fascination.

Jonas is a handsome, young redhead who loves trees. He loves trees so much that he climbed a tree in the middle of a forest to get a clipping. The clipping was going to be used for genetic splicing of two variations of evergreens to create a new breed of trees. He is a professor at a local college and has a fully funded lab and assistants and students but can't walk. He fell thirty feet attaining the perfect specimen and was instantly paralyzed.

The old question "If a tree falls in the forest does it make a sound?" Well, Jonas fell and used his phone to call 911 but because GPS hadn't been incorporated into the Emergency Call System yet, the operator was limited to taking crossroad info. Jonas had his exact coordinates, but they couldn't find him for hours. For this reason, he sued the city and won, but did he really? He was dominant before and he is still dominant now, his subs are generally brats and ironically walk all over him. He can still eat pussy and loves it. Ramsey is jealous that I was befriending the man in the wheelchair. What an asshole?

September was still six months away. My ticket to Cape Town had been bought and I was going to photograph Table Mountain. I would hopefully catch a seasonal cloud effect and a spanking if I played my cards right.

The clouds and the mist rests just over the mountain and falling over the sides like a tablecloth. I picture Godzilla coming out of the Cape and having his morning coffee. I am a registered numbered member of The Cloud Appreciation Society, such a geek. Anyway, I feel like if it's meant to be we will meet, me and the Tepui Mountain. Alex and Godzilla were secondary, that's what I tell myself.

# Chapter 19

I am certainly not monogamous with Alex mentally or physically which I think attracted me to him even more. How could he conceivably be jealous with a wife at home to cuddle with every night? I found four additional Doms that were weaving in and out of my existence keeping me entertained and learning. All were very different, another on line Dom from France, a Dom that was very mysterious and was on the phone only, and two that I met in person. I was test driving, don't judge.

Guy from France was a Professor, another very intelligent man, he was well spoken and direct. He was a verbal Dom, using his words to coerce my limits. He called me slut and whore a lot, I let him. With him, I did candle play, I envisioned his sexy thick French accent as the wax dripping all over me. He had me hold the lit candle in my mouth and calculate how to get the drops of heat to his desired points of interest which made it a challenge for me.

I was nervous about catching my hair on fire and I was very concerned about the mess wax would be to clean up. I used candles especially made for play. It was more of a turn on for him than me. I gave myself a pat on the back, I tried it. Candle wax was checked off my list with a note that it would be more fun with someone else delivering the sensation.

De Fleur, as I would later call him, also had a shoe fetish. It was not uncommon for him to have me dress up before a video chat, which I loved to do, just to slowly strip off my clothes and when I got to my black patent leather stripper heels he would have me suck the heel off like it was his cock. Again, not really my thing, but it made me feel powerful to get other guys off in such interesting ways. He was short lived. I think I only liked his accent, Ramsey had an accent, so did Alex, the real fetish.

The Caller Dom was interesting. He was very nice to talk to at first, we chatted a couple of times about sexual and non-sexual things. I thought he was a person that had some substance, maybe a friend if nothing else, until things got weird.

This guy is probably out there somewhere with a girl locked in a soundproof room shackled to a wall. He had an aural fixation and would ask uncomfortable questions and prod for an answer to get a response. I think it got him off to catch me off guard or hearing my breath change because I was uncomfortable. There was a lot of awkward silence where I was sure he was whacking off. I don't even remember his name.

One call was very disturbing and as much as I would try to change the topic or deny him satisfaction he kept pushing in the name of understanding myself. He insisted that I look at my secret perversions to understand myself better. Mainly, he wanted to know what drove me to masturbate. The things that triggered that primal need response that is what gets the better of sexual deviants and predators.

I would identify triggers for me as the buzzing of my mother's vibrator when I was a teen, seeing animals strut in heat and then get taken with no regard by a male, the visual insertion of anything into an ass, and a damsel in distress or a female hostage situation. The calls would be quite graphic and detailed. I would be panting and needing my own vibrator until the call ended and I think that was what turned him on.

After those three distinct phone calls he started asking about my kids. He knew I had four, he knew how old they were, he knew two of the four were sexually active, and that they had been while living in my house. This is where I drew the line.

OutdoorsMan meant business. He was a salesman for a large outdoors superstore that I had never heard of. He lived in Wisconsin about 6 hours away and was married but traveled a lot for work. He traversed the I-35 corridor a couple times a year for big meetings in Duluth but was often as far north as North Branch. Ding Ding Ding!

I arranged a meeting at Perkins and was given specific instructions to wear a blue G-string. If the meeting was going well and I felt like we were a good match I was to remove my panties and put them on the table. He had intense ice blue eyes that were in black and white on his profile. I got the feeling that this man was more of a real Dominant than anyone I had met so far. Game on, panties off!

He got my cue and paid the bill. We walked out to his big truck with huge wheels and big black bars all over the front to reduce deer damage to his vehicle. I wasn't expecting things to happen right then. I gave the green light and that's all he needed, he starts driving. He is making lefts and rights all over the place, I lose my sense of direction after a bit. I small amount of panic starts in my throat, I am gulping hard thinking what did I just do.

"Why couldn't you leave your fucking underwear on?" says the logical part of my brain to my left anterior cingulate cortex which was making my clit swell and prepare for sex. He pulls over the truck and loosens his belt, button and fly.

"You've been teasing me with that mouth since we said hello. It's time for you to do what that mouth was made for." He states in a calm matter of fact voice. It resonates with me how even toned a lot of these men's voices are. Like singing bowls in meditation, vibrating through a woman's body leading her as if in a trance. I twist my body for my approach and wrap my lips around the head of his erect cock.

Surprisingly, he starts driving again. He left hand is on the wheel, his right is on the back of my neck forcibly controlling how deep his muscle goes down my throat. I open for him and the special spit is extra slick and copious. The truck is on gravel now, I can hear the pebbles tinging against the wheel well which I happen to be close to. He is getting close, I feel him tensing as he steps on the gas and then the break. The roomy cabin has stopped moving, everything is quiet except my sloppy blowjob.

He pulls my head up and off his member by my hair. I like this. He tells me to get out. What? Is he going to leave me here? He is coming around the front of the truck and I meet him there. He grabs my hair again without a word. I flash back to animals, I had strutted like I was in heat and he is taking me.

He forces me down on my knees and face fucks me. It is pitch black, except for blinding headlights and I feel rocks digging into my knees. Tears run down my face, not from pain but pleasure. There is something with your tear ducts that are stimulated when you gag. He cums hard, shooting his load down my throat, holding his pulsing cock in my airway extra-long.

He is grunting and exercising demons through his release, it is all muffled to me as I struggle to stay conscious. He pulls out and gasp for air. He puts himself together and helps me up. Giving me a big hug and rubbing my back. He kneeled and brushed off my knees, they were bloody. He offered a napkin from his console that he dampened from the water bottle I noticed in his door when I got in the truck.

There wasn't much conversation as we found our way back to the Perkin's parking lot and my car. I was exhausted, my mouth was well used my pussy was not. I am already texting Ramsey for a place to sleep for the night, but I am not wanting to tell him about my evening. I start withholding information from him.

IluvGreece was an executive in the financial investment world. He was global, doing business with big companies that looked at other countries economy as precursors for making moves. He told me once that when Greece stops picking up the garbage the stock market is going to drop. Is this true? I didn't really care but it sounded intriguing. Honestly, who watches the trashcans of Greece? This guy. He was married and in a sexless marriage…blah blah blah. He had a son with a severe disability that would have him living at home all his life and a self-proclaimed sex addict.

We met on a whim at a Leather and Latte, a coffee shop in Minneapolis. We got our drinks and secluded ourselves in the basement lounge area. I liked being alone, that way I could be frank and open and not have to worry about other ears and he didn't have to worry about being seen. I was getting tired of this other woman routine. In the quest of exploration, this was not a relationship, I was able to deal with it. He asked if he could hold my hand while we talked. I agreed, and he didn't let go for almost two hours while we sat and talked.

He was slightly older than me and towered over me in height. Dressed in expensive business attire, shown by the details, he was put together on the outside. He spoke well, had a soft side with his son's condition. This one was well rounded and more accessible than OutdoorsMan.

IluvGreece liked the release that sex gave him, it helped him cope with the other much more stressful aspects of his life. I wanted to be used so I could forget about the pain in my life. This could work, I thought. He left that afternoon with nothing more than the smell of my perfume on his wrist. He called me later that night and we are unsure when we will meet but our coffee date assured it would happen.

A weird series of cancellations, opportunity and desire happen that make an encounter plausible. Apparently, I am a preferred member of the Grand Casino, which I have been to three times in my life. The status gets me a special deal on a midweek room. Not the nicest place, not my usual style. I am tired however of having to pay for rooms to have a sessions or meeting in a car so, the motel it is.

I enter the space, assess and start to undress. I dressed like a business woman trying to appeal to my counter-parts professional side. I wanted him to know I respected him and his position of power in the office and here, in room 111. I remove my flowery sheer blouse and drape it over the lampshade to warm the atmosphere energy. I wore my black beaded corset underneath for him. Black was his favorite color. My thigh high Cuban heeled stockings make an encore appearance and I adjust the seams in the long mirror making sure they were straight up the backs of my calves and thighs.

He texts me to lay out all my toys and to be on the bed waiting. Just a by the way note, this is a difficult task to complete correctly because of answering the door. I flip the security brace in between the door and the metal frame and the door clanks as it closes against it. I will forever be curious what is going on in a room with the door propped open like that from now on.

I am vulnerable, open, ready for whatever comes through that door. I did not know what to expect. Had I asked the right questions? Did I tell him too much about all my disappointing Dom experiences? Would he have something to prove? What if all the others were posers and they took it easy on me? Is this what I really want? No, this isn't about want anymore. This was a need.

A slight knock and he enters. Tall and commanding, handsome, distinguished, powerful in mind and body. He has skeletons in his closet like I do allowing complete trust in a very convoluted way. We share a welcoming kiss; the energy is palpable. He tells me I am beautiful, I don't believe him.

He inspects my toys. I had dumped them out on the bed in a heap. Rope, clamps, anal plugs, crop, flogger all tangled together like my pent-up emotions and thoughts ready to be counted and organized. He slowly separates them and puts them neatly in a row at the end of the bed, His Command Post.

He looks at them, now laid out neatly, and straightens a couple just so, meticulously planning the tools needed. I purposely left the paddle at home. I was afraid to have it used on me by someone I knew so little about. I am such a control freak.

His first instruction for me is to get on the bed on all fours. This is an uncomfortable position for me always because of my body image. My tiny breasts dangle like upside-down choir bells of the smaller variety. My nipples point down and hang like pendulums. Out of my comfort zone, I am already submissive and knowing this is not about me but Him.

"What are you wanting today, pleasure or pain?" he whispers in my ear. I am quiet for a minute while I think this through. I am lucky I didn't get a swat for hesitating. I respond pleasure, apparently my logical rational brain is on duty today. I don't know what pain would be to Him, therefore what it would look like to me. I am such a control freak again.

I immediately wish that I hadn't been the one to choose, my mind wanders, I wonder what the other option would have brought. No longer in the moment, that quickly my brain travels to options and scenarios that might have been. He senses my preoccupation and gives me another task.

He tells me not to move while he gets ready. I hear him undressing. I look away because I was told not to move but I want to watch so bad. I get a special moment while I am staring at the ivory wall. The light glowing from the bathroom and the blouse covered sconce project his silhouette on the wall as he removes his belt holding the two ends together in one hand and the open loop laying freely in an egg shape is ready to snap. I am instantly wet but that isn't for today. I chose pleasure.

After he is undressed, I suck his large cock. I hope I am a pleasure to him with my small mouth, taking great care to wrap my lips over my teeth. Pleasure for Him too. He redresses me with a blindfold and a ball gag. He touches me all over with his big strong hands. He likes touching me, my skin is hyper aware and tingling with sensations. I flash back to him massaging my hands and wrists while we talked as strangers and how intimate it felt in the basement of a coffee house.

My thoughts have been wrangled back to the present through pleasure. Interesting, I have been relying on pain to keep my attention. His touch is genuine, not an act, not just play, pleasure pure and simple. He adds the cloverleaf silver nipple clamps from my collection to my already pert pencil eraser like nipples from behind as I lean against his strong chest. They grab like an animal trap that has engaged. He tugs on the chains that are attached and I wince. I wear them like a beautiful accessory to my naked body. He folds me back into doggie style and the weight of the clamps make my nipples throb.

The fucking of my pussy and my ass is a pounding that we both wanted from the time we touched. It was hard and fast, then slow and sensual. I felt some thrusts that had intent, provoked by my “HARDER” cry with the ping pong ball in my mouth. I moan and squeak with every deep drill. I can feel him inside me to my belly button and my back aches from the actions in my core.

We change positions and I ride his cock on top and he drives deeper still. Does my vagina have an end? This internal ache is from him ramming my cervix. There is talk of an A-Spot located on the anterior side of your most inner wall. It drives my orgasms deeper and deeper stimulating every part of my female anatomy from my brain to my toes. He holds the chains of my nipple clamps again holding them like reins on a horse steering my every move. The pain is pleasure too.

After the intensity of our play session the aftercare was more intimate than the play. I was raw, nerves exposed, pleasure was achieved and appreciated. He starts talking me down from my experience in the most haunting way. I felt like I was outside myself still quivering and shaking. His hands again running all over my body, it was pleasure. I enjoyed it immensely. I wanted that, but in a partner, for the rest of my life, not just when the stars aligned for a play date.

# Chapter 20

It was during all these various episodes and the anticipation for Lady K's Bukkake Party that I decided to host a party of my own. My younger two children that lived at home had their plane tickets to visit their dad in Delaware for the entire month of July.

I talked to the Playhouse Coordinator about how something like this is done. We looked at the calendar and picked dates that wouldn't clash with any other events in the group to maximize attendance. July 17-19th it was planned.

I called it QueenBee's Beehive Party. I chose a full weekend to allow people to come and go around their other commitments or family. I knew I was far from the heart of kink, living up north. I knew people would have to plan and wouldn't just drop by. I had to make an event page and hope for the best. Yep, I was inviting the kink community to Wolf Lake for the weekend. I was really shaking things up now.

One of my older girls was still living at my house on and off when it was convenient for her. I informed her that I was having a party, gave her the dates and told her she would need to make other arrangements to not be crashing at the house anytime that weekend.

Apparently, this piqued her curiosity. It bothered her that I wouldn't tell her who was coming. She knew I had become a hermit as far as the people from town were concerned. She knew I was off "making new friends". She was also a spy and informant for her father who was trying to provoke me wherever he could by text, Facebook, and our kids.

I had a large cabinet in my room. Not the pressboard kind, Ethan Allen solid walnut, large, meant to be used as a desk with big doors so you could hide away your unsightly mess. My real closet was small and couldn't hold my regular seasonal clothes, never mind all my new outfits, corsets, catsuits, and toys. I removed some shelves and added a few hooks to the back wall of the mammoth piece of furniture and installed a clothes bar.

On the back wall of it I hung my crop and floggers. On the slide-out keyboard shelf was my array of dildos and vibrators. In one drawer were my books, and in the other my lubes, lotions, candle wax, etc. I had jewelry organizers for my nipple clamps, chokers, collars, and anything else small that might get misplaced. I used zip lock bags to hold and organized my bra and panty sets that I invested in for play and pictures that laid neatly on the main desk top area.

Everything else was hung from a hanger or draped over one. I installed a security hasp lock, two pieces that overlap and then you put a padlock through it. I thought I was being very careful and protective with kids in the house.

The lock, what was supposed to be my security, became an unequivocally goading draw.

I didn't even realize it was so noticeable, the stainless-steel hook and clasp against the dark walnut finish. I guess I could have painted it to camouflage it. I didn't see a need, it was just in my room. I was foolish to think my kids were only in my room when they were talking to me. I remember now, being a kid and going through my Mom's clothes and jewelry and books. I remember finding hundreds of dollars stuffed in a book from her Sugar Daddy, "George Winston", who I now know is a pianist my mother loved at the time. I didn't have anything like that in my space.

One day Daughter No. 2 decides she must know what I have in the cabinet. I still don't know if her father played a part in the debacle. She goes to the extreme of dismantling the doors to get around the lock, taking them off at the hinges. She's a smart one, I give her credit.

Imagine the children in the book The Lion, The Witch, and The Wardrobe. Lucy was so drawn into what she found inside the wardrobe that after returning to the real world, she got her three siblings drawn into another world. My Daughter No. 2 went and got Daughters No. 1 and 3, as well as my son, and showed them the contents of my private collection.

The horror doesn't stop there, oh I wish I could have stopped the bleeding there. All my son's teenage friends were paraded through my room for the show as well. I wasn't the Queen of Narnia, I was Queen Bee and it was decreed far and wide through all the lands, and bars, and campfires of the Northland.

I didn't find out what they had done until three days later. Daughter No. 2 lets it out, she can't keep it buttoned up. She was dating a guy that kind of liked the idea of a Dominatrix and wanted her to fill a fantasy. She started asking me random questions and telling me about her sex life. I thought it was odd.

Why isn't she talking to her sister about this? Are we cool? Have I passed a test and now I'm in friend zone? My heart wanted to believe that she was growing up and maturing, my gut told me something wasn't right. She makes references to the piece of furniture that had held my passions and exposed my kinks that had been raped by her. She was proud of herself.

She proceeds to tell me that she knows what's in there as nonchalantly as possible, like it was no big deal and she had a right to know what her mother was up to. I was in shock and awe at the invasion of my privacy, and the exposure to her siblings. I answered her questions about being a Dom verses filling a fantasy because at this point to save face at least I needed to act like I knew what the fuck I was into.

Later that day, I sat at the table with the three children living in my house and Loki and had a sex conversation like I was coming out of the closet owning my sexuality. It was more like me wanting to crawl into the closet and never come out again unless I needed more batteries for my vibrator. I felt like a selfish, stupid, bad mom. I had been made to feel that way since I long before the divorce.

The next day Loki and I have a long discussion about what happened, how it was handled and what's next. She again is my biggest supporter and tells me to shake it off. Lady K's event is coming, and Loki won't let me miss a beat. She wants to know what I am going to wear if I get invited and keeps bolstering me telling me how brave I am. I told her to come with, she refuses stating she'd be too nervous, and it would make me inhibited to have her there. It is true.

I check my inbox and there is my invitation. I was picked to attend, I kind of thought I would be since my vetting process was so stimulating. I was given the intimate details of the event. When, where, who could come, what to wear, bring and do. It was all very Eyes Wide Shut like. They invited me to stay the night if I wanted to and to be a cohost. There it was, engagement, I was now not attending but part of this living, breathing, fucking event. I couldn't chicken out now, people were counting on me.

After speaking further with my new friends throwing the party, I decided I was indeed still too shy to be fucked by random men that I didn't know. The Universe helped me out with my monthly flow starting the day before. We certainly weren't looking for a Carrie scene with blood everywhere. I wouldn't fuck, but I would most definitely suck.

This is when I was given the role of Fluffer. A job, something to concentrate on and manage so my anxiety didn't get the best of me. In porn movies, there are girls off set sucking and fondling the male stars to help get them hard and keep them hard for their big shot. That was my next big gig. This was a role I was designed to play.

I kiddingly search jobs for fluffers on the internet and find that in the right market a fluffer makes 42-45K a year, which is more than a social worker, plumber, or kindergarten teacher with a lot less work. Just imagine how toned your face would be from working out all the muscles daily. No turkey neck here!

I would be dressed seductively and be the best tease I could imagine. I would manage the boys and weed out the early exploders. I would be fair about time, not play favorites and be an equal opportunity Fluffer. I would take time to examine the different nuisances of each man in front of me, I wanted them to feel special, good customer service. These were my standards, my mission. They would start with me and finish on Lady K, the ultimate tag team of catch and release.

The day finally arrived. For my comfort, I decided to book a hotel room for an escape if needed. I did my routine of bathing and shaving and packing. I was nervous for a split second and then I remembered I had a job to do. If I didn't feel comfortable I could leave, no one was going to make me do anything I didn't want to. In the days leading up to the event a fellow reached out to me and asked me if he could be my Daddy for the night, no sex, he just wanted to take care of me. Harmless enough, I hadn't experienced a Daddy yet, I said yes.

When I finally checked in at the hotel and then got myself together to get to the secret address, it was another hotel. If I had known I would have booked there so I could walk back to my room, hindsight. The event started at 8:00 pm, I arrived at 7:00 since I was a cohost. I helped them carry totes up to the condo hotel rental. They brought lots of stuff, it felt like I was a groupie setting up for a band.

They were professional sex party people. This was their thing. They had luggage like you would expect but they also had a blender for drinks, a light machine to set the mood, and lots of other accoutrements that I never would have thought of. I made mental notes. Of course, they were traveling from their home to a rental, so it really was like a traveling show. An old beat up and rusted van carried their haul, Jim's long white wavy hair supports the disheveled look.

The condo rental, furthermore referred to as Suite 69, was a beautiful set up. You walked into a sitting room with a full kitchen to the right, a large double queen bedroom and bathroom through pocket French doors to the back, and a set of stairs that led to the off-limits area. Upstairs is where Lady K and Jim were a normal married couple with things that were strictly in their space, like purses and wallets, toothbrushes and a stash of special tequila, Cabo Wabo, for her.

She doesn't need it she assures me, "but it eases the process and warms me up from the inside out." she says.

"This really doesn't bother you? Preparing your wife to be fucked by other men, doesn't it sound different to you?" I ask. "You must have people that try to get in your marriage and fall in love with her, don't you?" The idea of people just fucking to fuck was still a very odd thought process for me. "Do you have Rules of Assurance? How do you know she won't fall in love with someone else?"

"This is not Love, my sweet QueenBee, this is letting go. A beautiful, confident, release of her sexual energy, being shared in the way we were designed. We choose to be together inclusive of these activities. We have grown above sexual repression alone and as a couple. I get to share my whore wife with other men. Do you have any idea how powerful that makes me feel?"

I feel as though he is poignantly stating his point for an award acceptance speech. I had thought about the power dynamic in Dom/sub relationships but was struggling with the Swinging/Gangbang aspect. Jim enlightened me. It was one of many moments that strongly impacted me during my journey.

The stage was set. The bar was in full swing as Jim, fully clothed, started making his famous Apple Martinis. Guests started to arrive, I scurried to the bathroom to change into my first outfit of the night. I could pull off lots of lingerie that covered the stomach or had padded bras to give the girls a lift. I especially liked corsets. I was very thin, having dropped another ten pounds from stress and just plain not eating. I hoped the guys found me attractive.

Getting into a good quality corset is no joke. You see the pictures and movies where it takes another person to cinch it tight. I didn't have another person. This really annoyed me because how are you supposed to surprise your man with a corset when it takes extra help to get the damn thing on right?

I loosen the strings as far as they can go without unlacing it, that's a whole other bitch session. I wrap the whale boned red silk half shelf corset around me like I am giving myself a hug. Part of wearing the corset was to hide my c-section pouch so it needed to be tight and just in the right place to conceal my insecurity. The metal clasps were rigid and unalterable.

The front of the corset had little handles on the front to the left and right to allow you to see what you were doing yet still pulling the front together. It was the first time putting on a corset under pressure and it proved very difficult. As people were showing up, they wanted to use the bathroom after driving.

"One more minute! I'll hurry." I'd say as I was breaking out in a panic and sweating, thus making it more difficult to fasten the contraption. I accidentally catch the middle hook and eye and was subsequently able to latch the top two and then the bottom two easily. I should have watched a YouTube video.

I pulled the strings tight and tied them behind my back, securing them so it wasn't a repeat of Walmart. I put on my stockings and heels and freshen my makeup. By this point, I know Lady K and Jim have started letting people use their upstairs off-limits bathroom by the foot traffic going up the stairs over my head. I make my exit, or entrance depending on which side of the door you were on.

There are, a dozen or more men in the sitting room, naked with just their socks on. Weird, weird, weird. Really just like that, this happens? How long was I in there? It is 8:20, not that long. I come around the doorway to the main area and Jim announces me to all present like I am a celebrity. I visualize Jim naked with nothing more than a red and black vest, coattails and a top hat, maybe a phallus shaped baton. "Ladies and Gentlemen, I present to you a specimen recently discovered in the Arctic Tundra. She is a wild beast of unfathomable passion and inner beauty. Locked away for a quarter of a century in the harshest of conditions, QueenBee70 has a need to suck cocks for her survival. She is a seductress and supremely intuitive therefore only choosing to mate with one partner at a time. Enjoy her succulent, wet, oral, primitive, tongue dances while she displays her natural slut state."

He didn't say it like that though, more like "Meet our new friend QueenBee." Men of all ages, shapes and sizes are groping and wanking their cocks while they nod at and fuck me with their eyes.

More people arrive, and the drinks are flowing. I do an inventory of the space. Twenty to twenty-five men and six females were present. Funny that I joked earlier, but I felt like I was at the circus. The men were the clowns, all shapes and sizes, walking around with their penis' in various degrees of arousal. They walk around with ease and pride, giving off an illusion of confidence and simplicity. They had no substance in this realm, I see red noses on all of them. Jim starts taking pictures.

Lady K and I were in the center ring, we got the bedroom, as co-hosts we got good billing. On the floor in the front room were two young women. The Ethical Slut and DaniSweetheart, in their late twenties, both were thickly built and curvaceous with beautiful milky pale skin and exuberant smiles. They sit like sphinx on their knees, back to back, on a shower curtain liner covering the floor. They have their hair pulled back in ponytails and they have on no make-up.

Jim uses a marker and writes on one "Cum Dumpster" and on the other "Cum Slut". They held each other's hands behind them like they were making a pact and opened their mouths with their tongues sticking out and eyes closed. It was a beautiful picture. Jim's camera clicks ferociously.

He documents them clean, untouched, not yet vandalized with random semen. These girls were to help with guys that had multiple loads in them. Lady K would get her share and then some. It was good hosting to keep all entertained.

Nasty Nancy was the token girl for the party. An event all her own, a man that had surgery and became a woman. On her profile she listed her age as sixty, when alone with her she confided that she was really seventy-two.

She was very comfortable in her female body. Her D cup breasts were drooping from gravity taking affect decades after her plastic surgery. Her entire trunk was covered in tattoos, every inch from her shoulders down to just about mid-thigh where shorts would end. A flowing, V-neck neckline drapes her collarbones drawing attention away from her Adam's Apple.

She refers to her tight little girl pussy, which is also covered in tats, often on her profile and is very selective about the size of a male that enters her. Man-made vaginas have some limitations and challenges. I had no idea, why would I? I was taking in all the information like a sponge, and not the contraceptive kind.

I was really all about transformations and change and Nancy was fascinating to me. I could have left with her and gone to dinner, picked her brain for hours and not even blinked an eye about missing a party. Not Nancy though, she was a self-proclaimed evolving slut. Nancy was bi-sexual and preferred playing with women, so she was very flirtatious with all of us sister snails.

So that makes five girls. Let's introduce Madam Mysterious sitting on the steps observing everyone, speaking to no one, wearing a mask. She is approached by several men one at a time and she makes direct eye contact and moves away. She toys with them. She is in charge, no randomness happening with this one.

She was dressed in a teddy and garter set, also heavily tattooed, and half her head was shaved with graffiti art etched in like the boys back in Philly. She carried a flogger, a thuddy one. It added to her power play. Some guys stayed clear away from her, afraid of her gaze even, revealing their submissive nature and feeding her, like red meat to a lioness. She was the Lion Tamer.

As I am observing the dynamics of this organized fuck show, Lady K has sprawled out on the bed to left. Her jet-black hair is flowing off the side like a waterfall. She is playing with herself and the men are circling like birds of prey. I see some fellows sitting on the bed to the right, watching.

I assume my position on my knees and put myself in front of the one closest to Lady K. I look in the man's eyes and ask him if he wants a little help to get ready for that, nodding my head in her direction. He doesn't need to reply, his cock is engorged and jumping at my touch. I lick my lips and lower my head into his lap. He relaxes and leans back on the bed to get a better view of my mouth on his member.

I usually close my eyes when I give a blow job, but I didn't want to miss a thing. Eyes wide open. I look to my right and there are men lined up hip to hip down and around the corner of my workspace. They want my mouth on their cocks. They find me attractive enough to get enjoyment from. My Inner Child feels accepted and wanted and is erotic dancing as my mouth finds a rhythm on each erect pole. They know I am laser beam focused on getting them ready to explode.

It was a Flufferganza! The guy that was my Daddy for the night, Brad, would watch me with each receiver and made sure they didn't touch me. If I chose to Deep Throat someone it was because I knew I could handle it not because some ass was pushing my head down forcing me.

Brad was very attentive. I would spend three to five minutes with each guy before I would come up for air and tap them to move on. Brad would step in if a guy was being greedy and not taking my hints, very protective and I didn't even know him. He would put breaks in the line, so I could get a drink, brush my teeth, or gargle with some mouthwash.

I took advantage of a break to stretch. Getting up without looking old was a real concern, however I didn't let it stop me. Brad came in and helped me up like a true gentleman. Who was this guy and what did he want from me? I was getting that weird stalker/rapey feeling.

The night was about half over and the need for fluffing had declined. I am waiting to use the bathroom and observe the event space differently now. The visual stimulation and pheromones released enthusiastically by the piles of bodies, the Cum Twins covered in gizz, and Nasty Nancy was being fingered in an arm chair were effective enough to keep the long-distance fuckers going.

The bathroom door opens and it's the girl with no name. She asked me if I could get her a bottle of water and I did. She opens the door enough as to invite me into her world. She has removed her mask and is fixing her make-up. We exchange names for the first time. She knows who I am, she introduces herself as Voxie. I am carrying my backpack that she takes it off my shoulder and sets it down on the floor as if to say, “Stay a while.” I pee in front of her and start to undress.

She asks if I want some help getting out of my corset. I had tied the bow into a knot, so her help was greatly appreciated. This was the second time I was completely naked in front of a woman. She had changed outfits as well, and we were both wearing nearly nothing when we exited the bathroom.

Voxie was desiring to use her flogger and I told her I was a sub but had an Online Dom. She was not impressed with that idea at all. I offered to get a scene going. The guys face’s about hit the floor when the two of us re-emerged and I assumed the position against the wall for a flogging, the post intermission act in the Fucker’s and Flogger’s Circus.

Most of the guys were just there to fuck or blow a load. The girls were really into it and soon the four of us that weren’t either fucking or flogging were lined up on all fours wanting for a spanking. It was a unique bonding experience, making small talk with Nasty Nancy while getting our asses turned red. I didn’t move a hair and Voxie was impressed. The other girls bowed out, one at a time, as the heat of the red skin being licked by leather over and over got to be too much. I won, by pride and by hide.

Several people had left after the BDSM stuff, which made me curious about the mix of energy in an event. I am feeling no pain, very tipsy on

Green Apple Martinis. Jim proved to be the ultimate multitasker as his wife was getting showered with load upon load of baby batter.

Don't these guys know about sperm banks? They could be loaded, pardon the pun. Jim asks me to come with him, and I follow him to his wife's side. She is being eaten out by a man while her husband strokes her face lovingly.

"May I have permission to be serviced by the Queen?" Jim asks humbly.

"Only if she will swallow your load." Lady K responds.

"Would you be so kind? I don't usually get to cum for anyone but her. My cum is very valuable to her like an essence, she says. The fact that she wants you to have it is special." He is giddy.

"I would love to show my appreciation and gratitude." In my head I thought it was the greatest tandem pick-up lines ever.

He hadn't participated with his cock before. He had just directed and used his camera and hands. I had been so wrapped up in my first girl on girl experience that I didn't give him a thought. It wasn't until he was laying between both of us that it was discussed. His fetish pleasure was voyeurism, and we gave him a show never to be forgotten. He probably played that over and over in his head, looked at the pictures frame by frame up to the event. I was learning that tease and denial were very powerful tools to keep in my toolbox. He erupted quickly, and I swallowed every drop of elixir.

When I lifted my head, there were several people standing around us, but they were all looking at the other bed. I turned around and there was Voxie on her back being fucked by Mousterbater. He had won the prize of her affections and her hole. He was a twenty-something lumbersexual that was tall, hanging off the end of the bed tall.

I was slightly irritated that she couldn't wait until I was done. It bothered me to be bothered by her. Brad, aka "Daddy" offered to take me back to my hotel since I was in no shape to drive and it was on his way home. I no longer felt weird about him, the alcohol made me less concerned. I rationalized, worst case scenario, I get drunk fucked. I was horny after all that sucking and blowing.

We got to the hotel and Brad walked me to my room. Got me undressed, aha I thought, he's just another fucker, but no. He got me into bed and then put some Tylenol on the nightstand, charged my phone, gave me a bottle of water, and left. In the morning, there was a note in the bathroom.

"I really enjoyed taking care of you last night. You are beautiful and amazing to watch in action. Call me when you get up, so I know you are okay. – Brad"

I text Loki, all is fine at home. I text Brad, all is fine with me. I text Lady K and Jim and arrange to go help clean-up before heading home. I check Facebook, out of habit. I check FetLife and I have fifteen friend requests and several messages which I suspect are from the party wanting an opportunity to fuck. Out of all the messages the only profile picture I can identify with certainty is thecurvedcock, because it is a pic of his dick which significantly curved to the right. I'll read them later.

I compose a message to Voxie through her Fet profile. Thanking her for the help with the corset. We had talked about our mutual love for photography, so I suggested we might get together and shoot sometime. I was drawn to her, like a moth to a flame. Our paths were meant to cross at that party. I wanted to learn about her and from her. I was opening myself up to her world, letting the universe direct my path even then.

I didn't know that it had been her first event as well. She had asked if she could just come watch and bring some toys. While we cleaned up Lady K and Jim shared, that is a very common request that usually ends with the person participating once they see there is no threat.

They were thrilled at the outcome of the party and Lady K's skin was glowing from her facials. They mention that there was a music festival going on somewhere and invite me to go with. I decline, knowing I needed to decompress and report to Alex and Ramsey about my adventures.

On my way home, I contemplated what had just transpired. It wasn't so bad. The people were accepting and there for sex, not relationships. How would you even be serious about dating someone you literally met at a sex party? I guess, if sex is important to you both, and jealousy and competition aren't a driver, it could work.

I was wowed at how outwardly comfortable with their bodies everyone was. I suppose when sexual release is the goal and there are no strings attached this is the perfect place to be confident with your body. Every dick needs a hole, every hole needs to be filled. This makes the sensation of a real women, verses a lunchmeat hand job, more desirable than the appearance of the woman.

I could look at every profile on any event page that said they were "going" to said event and many of them wouldn't have even been invited. Instead by clicking going they merely had shown interest for the hosts to weed through. And on top of that, most profiles are dick pics or memes, so you don't know the appearance of attendees anyway. It means that unless you are hosting and making the list, attendees fucking get what shows up, literally.

Sometimes the more desperate someone is the more sexually admissible they are too. If you haven't had sex in months and you go out to a bar, you might get someone's number. If you haven't had sex in months and you go to a sex party, you will get action if you want it, and you might get a drink. I have found that there is someone for anyone sexually. There are groups and events for people with breast cancer or other cancer survivors, a huge crowd that's into amputees, age gaps, vampires, big guys that dress up like little girls, tits, ass, curves, flat chested, etc.

The vanilla world was much more judgmental and difficult to weed through. If a person could be open about their sexuality, I believe it is a good window into their view on other things. A good rule of thumb in any party situation, sex parties included, don't bring up religion or politics and you'll have a blast.

Alex is interested in my take on the party and asks me repeatedly if I have found a third. Voxie piques his interest and so does DaniSweetheart. He encourages me to reach out to them and I do, but only to Dani. Alex wasn't in the bathroom with me to see the look of distain on Voxie's face when I mentioned an online Dominant. She clearly wasn't going to do anything to please Him.

Dani was another story. A single mother of one amazing little girl that was eight. Dani lived with her Mother and Grandmother, so dating was next to impossible. She would go to events for a release and to meet other people than family.

Her job was very demanding and stressful. We had exchanged phone numbers through private messages after the party.

Dani was into sex, she wasn't very sure of the D/s power exchange. She was bisexual, and we had enjoyed each other's company at the party. She knew I was a safe bet and she talked to me like I was her big sister. I talked her into putting on a show for Alex. I was feeling very pressured to deliver this one task that was like my white whale.

We planned out matching outfits, and even a routine sort of. Picture a tag team wrestling match. Me, being the manager and control freak that I am, wanted to be sure she knew I was in charge. I wanted to give Alex the stuff I knew he liked and mix it up some with props and toys, so we didn't have to be girl on girl the whole time.

I felt very insecure when I found out that Alex was contacting Dani directly and I knew he was doing his thing behind the screen with his sexy accent. I booked a hotel near her to make sure she could follow through. No excuses, I want to get this over with. She agreed to the date, even if it was just for a small window of time, she assured me we would make it work.

I had let Brad in on what we were up to. He of course wanted to watch. I checked with Dani and she didn't care. He was to sit off camera and not say a word. Alex did not know that I had leveled the playing field to two on two. It was kind of thrilling to me to have this little scenario going on. I had kind of hoped Brad and Dani would hit it off, getting me off the hook all the way around.

We spent fifteen or twenty minutes performing for Alex before he had to go. It was perfect. There was teasing, and nipple play to start, rubbing and stroking of each other, then I spanked her ass and left a perfect hand print on her pale skin as a souvenir.

The big finale was a sixty-nine with me on the bottom, my choice. I knew after this that I was for sure not a lesbian and not even bi. Doing this again would be strictly for a partner's enjoyment or total surrender to an orgy type environment of hedonism.

Alex was pleased. DaniSweetheart ghosted shortly after the tryst, claiming that her life was too busy for a sub sister. I was totally relieved, and I told him that was done. I had delivered. I wasn't going on the hunt again. I think we knew at this point that I was not very submissive and too bratty, or maybe even a switch.

A switch is someone who can play both parts, top or bottom, give or receive. I was also losing respect for him and it came out with me trying to take control of our situation, being bossy, or just plain saying no. I didn't hide things from him, I just told him less. So, it surprised me when he asked if I could make a trip to London and Ireland work and meet him in person.

# Chapter 21

I was torn. He was married, fact no future here. This meant no Tabletop Mountain trip, I couldn't afford both. The South Africa trip was booked for my birthday in September, I didn't really see our relationship going on that long at this point.

I did want to see his face, let him touch me and explore our chemistry, have conversation about everyday things back and forth in the same time zone. I called the airline and for another three hundred dollars on a credit card was able to book tickets and match his itinerary within twelve hours of coming and going.

I was excited and scared, but I was doing international travel all by myself, well, kind of by myself. Alex would be working long hours and have meetings. I would be alone a lot. I always liked the idea of traveling alone. No one else to consider, no time pushes aside from what you alone want to do. See a show, don't see a show, who cares.

A co-pilot would inevitably want to do touristy things, fuck that. I was going on an adventure to places that were never even on my radar to visit ever. The story was that I had a friend who offered me a free place to stay if I could get there. It was true. Alex's company would pay for all the accommodations and food.

My youngest daughter was livid that I would travel anywhere alone when she would be happy to come with. Loki thought it was fantastic. My mom thought I was nuts but was sure to remind me to carry my passport with me everywhere and to break up my money. My sister was cautiously concerned but went with it. Gwen and Voxie were not happy with my decision at all. Of course, they knew a lot more details than most listed above and that freaked them out a bit.

Ramsey was questioning everything all the time. He was trying to have a pissing contest with Alex, and he was losing. We weren't getting together as often but he called me a lot. The conversations were like comfort food for me, emotional crutches, he wanted me to know he cared.

Familiar tone, I knew what to expect, his insecurity was blaring. I kept reassuring him that I was still exploring and doing what I set out to do, which scared him even more. I told him we should take a total break until I get back.

Brad asked me to be his plus one at another event. It was a great distraction to kill time until the trip. We attended together as a couple, without any couple expectations. It was a hotel suite take over. People that were invited were encouraged to meet in the bar of the hotel ahead of time. I found that odd, how would we know if someone else was there for the party? Oh, you could tell. There is something about women who are preparing for an evening of fucking that just makes them glow.

People in the bar that were just there for a beer were dressed in jeans and flannels. Not us sex party people, dresses, suites, fancy shoes, make-up and hair done we stood out like sore thumbs. But where would those thumbs be later? In someone's pussy or ass or mouth is the answer. This party was a Swinger's Party.

After mingling at the bar for a little, we get the okay by text to start making our way upstairs. Like a choreographed dance, couples' pair off and exit stage right. I was getting nervous and had to have the talk with myself again. This is what you are here for, to find out what you like and don't like. Suck it up Sunshine, no hiding behind fluffing this time.

Brad places his hand on the small of my back and gently nudges me in the directions to go. This is Brad's niche, he has a buddy that throws these party's all the time. As I hear this I connect why he is so good at being attentive. He has attended close to a hundred hotel take-over parties and seen some wild stuff.

His family owns and operates restaurants which he helps with, so the hours make it hard to have a committed relationship and go to all the parties he wants. His mom has called four times in the two hours before the party. Trying not to listen, I red flag some serious Mommy issues between the way he ineffectively communicated with her and his attraction to MILFs. He will never pass the friend zone.

We enter the suite. Our donation of twenty dollars a person or thirty-five for a couple is expected upon arrival. Brad pays. There is a small snack table to the right with cheese, crackers and pepperoni and punch. My brain wrestles with the thought that pepperoni isn't a very orally pleasing taste for kissing and often produces gas, but that wouldn't be for a couple hours. Now I'm hungry for pepperoni, damn it.

I have a flash back to my first real French kiss, not the practice kisses with my cousin under the steps at my grandmother's house, my first boyfriend kiss. Peter was his name and he ate a mounding plate of taco slash nacho and liquid cheese at Great Adventure before planting a kiss on me, pressing in hard with his braces on my lips. Not the best in my life, but he gets points for making the move.

There were men and women milling around talking all over. Brad introduces me to the host, who looks hungry as hell and like I had dinner written on my forehead. A late fifties short guy, balding and boisterous. He jumps on the bed a few times, showing everyone, he can, or that he is just that free-spirited, or childlike, or energetic or high. Pick one, or two, or three and make your own conclusion. I conclude to stay away from him.

I decide to check out the terrace. A gorgeous wrap around patio type space where there are more new and interesting fuckers to meet. This was very different than the last party, people are peeling layers off slowly as not to jump in too fast or be the first whore out of the gate. I sense judgement. Men are ogling the females coming through the place. The wives are glaring at the same females knowing that piece of ass is what my husband really wants tonight, maybe more than once.

These people have no idea about the Fetish world, they just know about the Alternative Lifestyle. I introduce myself by my name and that I am a writer. I am a writer. By this time, I have started compiling many thoughts and details for my book and written several shorts about experiences. That was all these people needed to know about me.

I am looking out over the balcony and a very tall Chinese man, odd to point out more but unusual to see. He sidles up to me and says he overheard that I am a writer. He is a professional published author of several books and is probing me on my subject matter, and I didn't even care to remember his name.

I share briefly, and he is intrigued to think that ironically, he may be in a book talking about his books and the fact that I am writing a book. He is obviously a deep thinker; his wife has found him with me by now and introduces herself.

Augusta, is a busty blonde in her mid-fifties, dressed in a bright red satin nightgown slip thing. She has beautiful brown eyes that smile when she does. She offered that she is a Neurologist. I was taken back, but why? Brain doctors need releases too. Female brain doctors are entitled to pleasure, and good for them as a couple getting their needs met. I was ashamed at my critical thinking. Just because they aren't into BDSM doesn't make their kink, sex, any less authentic or beautiful.

She suggested that perhaps I play with her husband later, not even concerned about herself which prompts me to look for Brad like a security guard. Inside, I find him sitting in a corner of the room with his cock out just stroking away. He gives me a devilish grin and a wink. I know he is fine, and I am free to do my thing. What is my thing? I walk back out on the balcony and go to the far end alone. I park myself in a comfortable industrial made patio chair that is oversized and stiff.

"Why are you over here all alone?" I hear over my left shoulder.

"Oh, I am just enjoying the view and the sunset? What a great place for a party?" I reply

And as I turn my head to acknowledge the man's voice he is standing right behind me with his hand in his jogging pants. His dick is getting hard, as I look beyond him and there is no one outside anymore. This man was ready to party, and I was there to participate. The way the next half hour went down was like an out of body experience.

My subconscious mind must have played a part because I have no recollection of making choices. I hadn't been drinking much, I had to be sober, I was the designated driver tonight. I was supposed to stay in contact with Voxie and possibly stay at her place to save some money.

The man was an African American in his late twenties. I saw my first big black cock that night. It was big, more a light brown with pink low lights, and it did holler cock-a -doodle doo by the time I was done with it. That was only part of what was going on though.

Brad had migrated out and stood tall and wide to block the view of other hotel guests, so the party wasn't busted, watching of course. Another fellow came and placed my not busy hand on his cock for a rub. My mouth was full of BBC so that saying no wasn't an option. The tall China guy had appeared ninja like with his head between my legs and up my dress.

He was burying his head into my pubic mound and rubbing his chin and nose all around. Eventually exposing my clit and started sucking it. At the appropriate time he introduced his fingers in my pussy and my ass. I had to adjust a few times while multitasking to allow proper efficiency and aerodynamics.

I start being distracted by a whimpering noise. Like a fussing child, crying, not a temper tantrum, more like weeping. A high pitch, weeping, sad and sorrowful sound. I know that Brad is here, and he is looking out for me, so I don't stop. I am totally focused on what I am doing and the glowing bright white light that had taken over my thought space slowly fades bringing me back to reality.

Brad breaks things up and says we need to go inside. Too many people were moving in and bringing attention to our little oasis on the balcony. I am pulling myself together, wiping the drool off my face, and the guys all disappeared that fast. It was a crazy drop.

I hadn't finished my release, it was hovering right on the edge, that damn crying was overriding my pleasure center. I walk into the hotel room with that "oh yeah, I was being molested by many men" look. I get the evil eye from the heavy wives holding up the wall by the chips.

The tall Asian was sitting on the couch next to his wife while a young woman sucked his cock. He had a micro penis, I caught a glimpse while walking past. I noted it for my book, I had never seen one before. Now, when I say micro penis I am talking that it almost looked like a clit. It was about an inch tall and as thick as my pinkie finger.

When I got home and researched it I was shocked at the percentages of men with micro cocks. In my limited, but various cock sucking escapades, this was the very first. Amazing irony that I would see my first big black cock, and I would be talking about the Asian's micro penis sighting in the same night and being a part of my book, right!?! I can be a deep thinker too. He started to whimper with excitement. It was him!!!

Tall Asian Writer Dude was crying into his wife's bosom. Augusta was stroking his head like he was her child, consoling him and encouraging him to cum. What the hell vortex did I fall into here? This beautiful girl on the floor was happy to suck him off and was upset that she had done something wrong. Augusta directs her to keep going. Almost in a tantric rocking motion, Augusta and her husband explode together, erupting in moans of pleasure and release. Holy fuck, intense.

That night culminated in a full out orgy style pile of fucking and sucking on the king size hotel bed. Every inch of surface space was being used and I somehow was on the bottom of the pile. Moaning, groaning, writhing, throbbing, shaking, quivering, gushing, licking, probing, and so many more things were happening all at once.

It was uncomfortable being at the base of the pile because I got a little cluster phobic and wanted out quickly, but I had to surrender my panic because there was no organization to deconstruct the mass of limbs above me. I laid there, sober, watching. I look to my right and the host of the party offers his cock to put in my mouth. That was the first time I declined giving a blow job, another first. I look to my left and there's Brad, watching. I feel friction on my pussy and I let myself go, I deserved that orgasm.

# Chapter 22

The next day, Loki asked me, "When you go to these parties or orgies, breakdown the attendees? Like what are your first impressions of people?"

The question took me a moment to answer. I struggled with myself and being honest. With my measly two parties, I didn't want to come off judgmental or snobbish. Throughout a night, I am open to meeting and talking with everyone.

I learn so much more about people that my first impressions no longer mean shit while their face is between my legs or I am sucking on their glorious cock. She asked for my first impressions or thoughts, so in my humble opinion I attempted to break it down. I am sharing in hopes of encouraging someone to go to a sex party without the anxiety of the unknown.

10% pervs…

10% 20-45-year-old men who will fuck anything

30% 46-60-year-old men who will really fuck anything

10% 20-29-year-old females that are self-proclaimed sluts and will fuck anything.

30% 30-60-year-old women that will be fucked if they want to hook up with one of the men above.

5% voyeurs standing over in a corner or around the bed just taking it all in.

5% people that I would fuck including men and women

Loki says, "Where are all the young beautiful people? Are you just not getting invited to those parties?"

Where are all the hot bodies. Young perky titties and hung like bull cocks with great hair and teeth? Where are these people sauntering across the room naked and confident of their beauty, fit and strong?

Masks add intrigue. Discipline and control are romantic ideas and not seen often. It is obvious that the extra effort for the purpose, of looking and feeling sexy, has left the market long ago. Again, romance isn't the objective here at all if we put it back into the frame of reference. It's a sex party. It's easy. They show up and pay twenty bucks toward a room and it is expected that some form of sex will happen for their enjoyment in one way or another.

Most of the people attending, appear old or tired. They are going through the motions to have an active sex life. Let's face it, if you go to a party and get fucked by five partners in one night and that happens once a month, you are already getting sex 100% more than most married vanilla couples between the ages of 38-60. Way to go! This is living life to the fullest for some, living a life of passion for some, and others it beats being lonely and drying up crusty.

There are endorphins released during sex that help with depression, circulation and healing illness. There are endorphins released during sex that help with your psyche as well. An individual's confidence, release of anxiety, anger, and tension, self-worth, sense of belonging, sexual fulfillment and sensuality are just a few. I wonder how different the world would be if we could all just fuck a lot more. I was already a lot more relaxed and satisfied.

The real question is, why do I go to these parties? I go to experience the dynamics, meet new people and hear their stories. I get energy from the collective sexual tension. I feel good about myself when I am chosen to be someone's partner in a weird, sort of hunk of meat kind of way. I also get a sense of belonging, a social leveling I guess, that this is who I identify with at this stage of my life.

I will deal with my disappointment, pain or hurt outside of the events. I am learning that these group events are soft for me. I'm not sure how many more I will attend because I like a connection with who I'm fucking, swinging seems random and cold. I'm sure if you got into a circle of swingers that you could find more regular outlets however then you teeter on the edge of relationships and affairs which I don't want to be a part of.

I think to myself, the young people are just out fucking. They don't need a label to go to a bar and go home with a stranger every night, it's the norm. It's more about us older folks trying to hold on to our youth through crazy parties that are reminiscent of the 70's and 80's. Let's call a spade a spade. They are what they are, an orgy. Being an anonymous participant is very freeing. Stripping down to nakedness in the presence of strangers is difficult but once you can come to terms with your own body and needs you evolve to a new level of power.

This is where the Inner Goddess begins to find her strength, and where men cannot deny that they are fuckers. Women find acceptance in tribes and cohorts, our counterparts are about finding their Eros energy like a man, alone in the wilderness.

I mean that with respect, and without it. We all strive to be what we were told we should be. We are all shaped by norms and negativities of society and religion. We all want to be wanted and accepted. Most of us came into the world through a woman's womb, were identified as boy or girl, then our health and appearance would be assessed.

We were born with only two fears. One, a fear of falling which is remedied by holding the baby close and swaddling them in a blue and white blanket with a pink pinstripe here in the United States. The other is loud noises. A loud noise innately means danger and spurs a fight or flight response. All other fears are learned through our lives by exposure, example, irrational responses, shock value, and the idea of good vs evil.

When I was a child, sex wasn't talked about, it was inappropriate to touch yourself, boys were bad and only wanted one thing. Worse, I didn't know what that thing was, so it made boys even more scary. I always was to respect my elders, even if they were grown men touching me in questionable ways. I was fat shamed. I was taught through looks and tones of voice that my feelings weren't important.

I learned that my parents preferred me to be seen, not heard. I was taught that I earned male affection, my father's particularly, by doing tasks that a boy would do, or following orders. I learned to bend over the bed and get spanked willingly with the belt, it would be way worse fighting it. I learned that I had to work to be loved. These lessons were all received before I was a teenager.

My parents did what they knew, the best they could, at the time. They taught me the things I would need to know to succeed according to how they were raised. You see, it isn't until time passes, and I reflect as a parent that I see the patterns and repetitions, the nuances that would imprint and affect my choice of ever being present at a sex party.

It made me second guess my body image and shy away from exposing my flesh to one man, none the less ten or more. Coming to terms with your fears doesn't really get easier the more you do it. My fears are still always there, in my mind, rolling around like a rock in a tumbler. It will take hours and hours and days upon days, with just the right abrasives and agitation, orgasms and stimulations, principles and wisdom to come out all polished and shiny, but still there.

In this period of my life, I was choosing to put my fears on a shelf. Like a beautiful polished stone or crystal, I would appreciate that it came from somewhere and was part of the old me. I guess, my transformation into QueenBee let me get fierce on my shit. Not being afraid was what I was holding onto for dear life; I was afraid of failure. Yep. That's how it works.

I have worked through life graduating through levels of acceptance of fears. I have "Fear Buckets". I have four bright orange, five-gallon buckets, and they hold me back when they get too heavy. They are labeled on the bucket's loss, failure, rejection, and the unknown. Every single fear I have falls into one of these buckets. When the bucket gets too heavy to carry I have to deal with what's inside.

I had to deal with fears before a sex party or be willing to shed them like my clothing. Each piece coming off, making me lighter and lighter. A sex party is no place to have a meltdown. It is very charged by the energy brought to the place. Erotic energy is very powerful and positive, intimate in a mutually appreciated space. My tip: Know your sex party, leave your judgment at home, and leave your fear in a heap on the floor with your clothes. I had to do some research before the Bukkake Party because I didn't know what the word meant. I needed to know my own understanding of swinging by asking questions of Gwen, Brad and Google, of course. It helped to have an example, she enters dramatically, Voxie.

Voxie and I became fast associates. We were together a lot. Through texting and phone calls we would arrange plans that spanned Thursday night through Monday before the school bus came so I could sneak in like I'd been home all night. I was still feeling shamed at home so it's no wonder I wanted to leave.

She is a Metropolitan girl, she knew all the cool places to go, what was hip and happening, she had connections all over. She was my in. I was intoxicated with her nonchalant approach to all things sexual.

With retrospect as my filter, I saw her as a sex dripping hero, however she was being entertained by my presence too. So, Who's Muse, is the question? I did not know from the beginning that she was bi-sexual. That alone may have intimidated me when I was having sleepovers in her bed, with her and I both naked (that's how I sleep). I was thrilled to not have to pay for a hotel, and she was fun, we were great company for each other and I didn't even consider that she might be anything more than a friend.

I was never allowed to have fun girlfriends in my past, so, I just pictured this as normal stuff I missed out on. She was so confident that it rubbed off on me and made me more confident.

She had “boys” bringing her flowers and chocolates, taking us out to dinner, and sometimes they would get to sleep between the two of us. It was expected not chased after, not pined for or whined about, expected. She had an uncanny vibe that would entrance people male and female. I fell into it for a summer of sexploit and adventure that changed me from a woman to a Goddess. I am not referring to an inner awakening, this was total transformation.

Voxie turned out to be my rock tumbler. She was very much in control of herself and me whenever we were together. The other stones being tumbled with me, by her, were mostly men traveling in and out of her life. They wouldn’t last long. Her intensity and demands were intense and demanding. Most guys found her intriguing and a challenge. She would fuck with them a bit and then send them on their way with their cock between their legs begging for another chance at her approval.

We both loved photography and would have random photo shoots some with clothes but most without. Embracing the light and angles through the lens and filter of another woman was palatable. She would regularly tell me how pretty I was. I would scoff it off like she was seeing someone else.

What did she see that I didn't? She saw me, the insecure, wounded, adventurous, trusting, authentic me. I wouldn't know that person for a while. I liked who she thought I was. I liked who I was around her.

We were causing quite a stir in the kink lifestyle. She listed herself as protecting me. This confused the fuck out of men, they would deal with her before messing with me. There was a lot of speculation that we were a couple. That became part of my elevator speech when I'd meet someone. You know, a little about yourself to grab their attention and set boundaries out of the gate. Mine went something like this:

"I'm QueenBee70. I'm new to the lifestyle and I am exploring all things sexual. After a bad marriage and worse sex for over a quarter of a century, I decided to put myself out there and see what I can find out about myself. So far, I know that I am straight, I don't do animal play, child play, or hang from the ceiling on hooks and no watersports or poo. Otherwise, I'm ready to try anything with a person I feel connected to. I am all about experiencing everything. I am writing a book about all of it. Oh yeah, and I don't share so if you are into her (referring to Voxie) you don't want me."

I must have used this little intro hundreds of times over the summer. I was proud of myself for having my own standards. Guys were drooling over the idea of threesomes with us. I was not going to compete with my new friend and in my mind that is where it would go. Instead of enjoying an experience my competitive nature would override and I would fall into a negative spiral of self-doubt, self-loathing, comparison and unworthiness. I still hadn't figured out my needs and wants. What I did know was, that I wasn't a Voxie.

Voxie demanded from her submissive and pets that she was always first to fuck in any situation. I wasn't into the idea of being a sloppy second. I broadened the rule to if they ever fucked her, they weren't fucking me. Period. It kept motives pure, just friends. We looked out for each other without jealousy or pride getting in the way. I think she thought the rule was stupid, to me it was sane.

We were constantly on the go or getting ready to be on the go. It was a revolving door of thrills and excitement. We regularly would go dancing or to a drag show in downtown Minneapolis. I loved to dance, like until my hair was saturated with sweat, a glass of wine in my hand always. Voxie has some health issues that keep her sober most of the time, so it was good that she was protecting me. We would go to the alternative clubs and they all had their own thing, but our arrival made nights fabulous.

The Gay 90's had the Drag Queens and the giant penis you could mount and have your picture taken on. They also had cages and stripper poles to play with. I suck at stripper poles, but the cages gave me just enough support to grind all the way down and get back up without help.

There was a room that they would fill to chest height with bubbles on occasion and people would have sex right at the bar hidden by dish soap. The crowd was diverse, and the music was more hip-hop. It was the place to be after midnight.

If it was a Friday night, there was First Avenue home of Prince fame, the place had great energy and multiple floors that came alive with the various kinky theme nights. I remember one specific cold night there. It was Lingerie Night and I had purchased a gorgeous off-white vintage body corset, complete with the bullet boobs and inserts.

I wore my new purchase and stockings and a G-String for clothes and some high gold glitter stripper heels. Voxie borrowed an outfit of mine that barely covered her front and totally exposed her backside through strips of fabric that I adjusted like playing a harp.

It is Minnesota so early summer still had nights in the forties which ironically was the era my girdle was from. I had a coat that was a short trench style and I lost it half way through the night. I hope the slut that took it was warm. The light was purple and there were young men gliding across the floor on roller skates with bright green light sabers. There were women hanging from brilliant red silks anchored to the ceiling. The highlight of this night, over and above my lingerie throw back, was this was the night I danced on a man.

You read that right. His name was Ron and he had no legs. His fetish was to have women walk on him in their heels. “The higher the better” he said from his custom-made box. The box was lined with pillows, a cushion for his spine. There was a frame that held parallel bars to it like you see in a physical therapy room. The bars were steel and sturdy but only for balance.

He insisted I walk on him with my full weight like I was walking on a human carpet. I was instantly self-conscious of my heaviness at the lightest weight I ever was. I was fascinated with this encounter. I strutted over his body as sexy and provocatively as I could muster.

If this was a turn on for him, I didn’t want to disappoint. I dropped it low, my booty that is, at his face with nothing but a ribbon of fabric between my crotch and his chin. The visual was not nearly as exciting for him as all of my weight being shifted to those 6” stripper heels on his chest.

After my turn at erotically dancing on a legless man, I bent down and sat in his lap and chatted with him for a few intimate moments. I gave him a tip, for the pleasure of checking another thing off my list of things I never imagined I would ever do.

Ground Zero was my favorite because they had a Bondage and Domination Show that fascinated me. People would pay a donation to the Mistress and they would be put in a cage where they would wait to be called on the table. The facilitator of the show was one of the many professional Dominatrix that were there to put on a show.

I found this amazing bold and brave, later I recognized that they were entertainers. Up on stage playing the crowd and feeding the energy of the room, I watched the patrons that would pay for a spanking or teasing. A lot of them were the normal everyday folk coming to a wild bar and having a night to remember for a birthday or Bachelorette Party. The true, behind closed doors fetish people, were out on the dance floor or at the bar, meeting people from social media or embracing the idea that the Dom or sub of their dreams was in a corner or nook somewhere in the dark macabre interior.

These locales were always a point of the night but what would happen before and after often made the nights most memorable, mainly after. Voxie always wanted a boy with us. She taught me that they are valuable for watching purses and coats, buying drinks, and making sure we got home. Chivalry was not dead, in most cases the guy was honored to be escorting us around town.

The night that changed boys to fuckers happened after one these fun outings. Voxie knew a guy from the scene and introduced me. He was taller than me with a long black beard and was wearing a kilt the first time I met him. LeFreak was his name, sort of an odd name for this guy that seemed rather put together compared to some other freaks I had met.

He was an artist and loved photography too. We hit it off as a group of three. This night we lost our coat boy and didn't have a set way home. Lyft or Uber was always an option and we would always make the driver blush with our stories or antics. This night was different.

In hindsight, I almost feel set up. Freaky offered to drive us back to Voxie's place. He had been drinking along with the two of us. I was along for the ride and intoxicated per our norm. When we got to the apartment I was asked to sleep on the couch. It wasn't my place to argue. I had nowhere else to go.

I had been drinking. The couch it was. Freaky was in Voxie's room and came out. He wanted to fuck, and I was an easy target. He started rubbing my shoulders, my back and my feet. I told him I knew what he was doing, and he didn't deny it. Soon we were kissing, and I didn't like the beard, so I predictably dropped to my knees and started for his cock.

He was hard and throbbing as I put my lips around his head very gently, teasing. I do remember thinking to myself that this was going to be a problem with Voxie in the morning. Freaky sat down on the couch and I continued to seduce his rod with licking and flicking of my tongue. I hear a female voice, it's Voxie. She is kneeling next to him with a look of pride on her face, saying see what I provided for you.

She whispers in his ear some filthy perverse phrases about him mouth fucking a slut, is he turned on by the sloppy sounds of that bitches cum dumpster, and tonight you will be inside of me. She said these things loud enough for me to hear but like she was a phone sex operator, throaty and hot. Humiliation and Degradation are Hard Limits for me. This was a power play.

She leaves and goes back to her room telling him she will be waiting. He decides he won't wait for her and urges me to get up and bend over. There were condoms all over the coffee table, like all over the place. I was horny as hell and dripping wet, I felt my juice run down my leg. He wants to go bareback, and I say no and to use a condom, and even open it and hand it to him. He takes the rubber from me, stops momentarily and fumbles around, then proceeds to insert himself into my hole from behind.

It was a fast and furious type of fucking. I think he was afraid to get caught by Voxie with his dick in me. He pounds into me with his shaft hard and I was so wet the friction was intense. He isn't making any noise other than our bodies slapping together until he erupts and shoots his gizz all over my back. This is when I put together that he had intentionally violated my consent.

I tried to reason why I would have gotten a load on me if he had put on the condom, trying hard to think the best of this stranger. I asked him if it ripped or fell off as I fingered my pussy for remnants. I look to my left and the condom was sitting on the couch, still rolled up and ready for application. He acts oblivious and goes to the bathroom to clean up before going in to see Voxie.

I start to cry. I certainly wasn't raped but it felt that way. I had been so careful to this point to not play with random people. I thought LeFreak was okay because Voxie and he were friends. Not only that, but I couldn't approach her about it now, it was the middle of the night and he was supposed to fuck her. He disappeared from the bathroom to her bedroom without another word. I showered quickly and as I returned to the couch I pass her room.

I heard her moaning. She was complaining about having already fallen asleep. There was some flirtatious giggling and rustling of the linens. She groaned like a lioness falling into a restful pose of contentment. The growl is unmistakable.

I yearn for a guttural release without having to work through it while sucking someone off. It's not them, it's me. I always feel like I have work to do. I should never be the main course of a man's attention, that was a falseness I needed to overcome.

Voxie expected to be delighted orally, she didn't come from penetration. As I stood outside her door, my heart raced for her sexually, for me mentally, and for what he had done but did he even care with his head in her snatch. Will I have a disease in the morning? Thank God, I'm beyond pregnancy concerns. That would be a real kick in the teeth, a miraculous pregnancy.

I grappled with the violation of my body. As a woman, I felt that everything was my fault. I drank too much. I was in a sex positive culture and the company of sexually assertive men. I wanted to be fucked by him, I had flirted with him all night like he was there purely to entertain me. He desired me, and I liked the attention. He chose me first, I won, validation for my ego.

There was nothing I could do. Who would care? The deed was done, and the consequences of MY actions would follow. I chided myself that the words I had repeated thousands of time to my children were coming back to haunt me.

Truth was this wasn't my fault, yet I was fully taking responsibility. He would be judged someday and get what he deserved. I was not a vengeful person. I was above being a victim any longer. I'll deal with whatever happens with grace. I couldn't dwell here, hanging here would mean regret. I don't do regret anymore.

LeFreak and Voxie fucked for hours. I heard the bed frame banging against the wall as I was trying to sleep on the other side of it. She was loud and wild, uninhibited. I heard her yell out commands and obscenities. He was able to go a long time because he unloaded his first cum on me.

I get aroused as they approach what seems like climax. I went to primal prey fantasies in my mind. She was the sloppy seconds for a change and that made me extremely turned on. I hadn't come during his fuck frenzy, I needed to.

I reached my hand under the blankets, down the center of my breasts, over my belly button, into my wet panties. I slide them down to my ankles and kick them off. The only way I was going to get any sleep is to have a monster orgasm now. I start rubbing my clit in circles. I am still very lubricated, and I don't know if it was from Freaky, or from listening to the rhythmic wall beating like a drum.

The wetness dripped down my crack. I reached around with my other hand and massaged the opening to my ass. I would come harder if my ass was engaged. I wiggle the tip of my finger in the forbidden opening and with intent and I pound my pussy to peak energy build up. Getting off for me was never really a sexy thing, it was more deliberate and necessary than that. I came hard, waves of vibration crashing over my body, no longer tense. A punishment.

That orgasm pushed me over the top to dreamland and I crashed hard. When I woke it was late morning, Freaky was already gone, loser. I gathered my panties and grabbed some clothes from my bag and walked down the block to Cuppa Java for my morning tea infusion. The caffeine would help me function and navigate the conversation I needed to have with Voxie.

It was a beautiful morning and the fresh air felt good, I was still feeling violated but felt helpless. All I could do was fess up to Vox about how things went down and hope she understood. I brought her back her favorite beverage and a piece of cheesecake for us to split. I took my clothes off again and crawled into bed with my well fucked friend.

She opened her eyes sleepily and smiled. Her blue hair was sticking straight up, and the light shown on her beautiful blue green eyes from the window. Her morning breath would have ruined the cheesecake, so she brushed her teeth before I fed her a forkful and then I'd take a taste.

Another forkful with some strawberry drizzle is waiting for her when I tell her how much I heard last night. She laughs boisterously and shrugs it off because that's how she is. I asked her if she heard anything that happened last night. She looked at me puzzled.

I told her how one thing led to another, she had wondered what was taking him so long to come to bed. Another forkful of cheesecake, and then I told her about the condom fake out. Her eyes flashed fire. The cheesecake was set aside.

I was immediately uncomfortable, not for me, for him. This was an apparent hot button for her, not surprising with her domineering tendencies. She felt terrible that she had brought such a "Monster" home and encouraged his interest in me. She felt that she knew how to handle these types of men, I was a novice and wasn't ready. She was right. She said she would handle it and that we needed a distraction. I trusted that it was handled and felt better telling her.

Her friend James had a motorcycle. It was a beautiful day and it was warm. A motorcycle ride sounded great but there was only one bike and one driver. Voxie said she would handle that too. I kind of wonder to myself how this could even start to pan out. Two hours later we are both dressed to kill and ready to ride, in traffic stopping outfits, as if it was a normal occurrence.

I had not packed for a bike ride, I didn't even have a bra. My outfit was a black miniskirt, a plunging white bodysuit that was cut nearly to my belly button, black heels and a faux leather jacket in case I got cold. Fortunately, my tits are small and flat, so they are pressed against my body with the tension from the snap in my crotch. I didn't think we were going to end up riding that afternoon, but I had to be ready for anything as usual. Voxie is answering texts and phone calls and walking out of the room to talk. This doesn't red flag me since she had so many suitors constantly after her attention.

She leads us out of the apartment as she is giving someone turn by turn instructions to her place. James arrives and removes his helmet to expose an early thirties thin man with glasses that couldn't keep eye contact to save his life. He's a submissive of hers. She doesn't really have any connection with him, he is a good fuck toy and he has a motorcycle to entertain her. I say hello to this shy puppet and I hear another loud motorcycle engine in the distance.

A roaring rumble vibrates through my chest as I see Voxie's face light up with a devilish grin. A man with a flat black crotch rocket pulls up revving the motor with a spare helmet attached to the seat behind him. I know without a shadow of a doubt that this is the chosen steed and his black horsepower.

The man embodied the typical bad boy look. Taller than I expected when he dismounted, wearing black riding boots with a thick heel and lots of grommets, skinny jeans that accentuate his tight ass. He chose a white ribbed wife beater undershirt that exposed his mulatto skin and framed his wide muscular shoulders in relation to his very fit waistline. Well, I owe one to Voxie, she did good. This was a distraction from my worries.

He loosens the chin strap with ease, off comes the head armor and I wait for it to speak. Everything was going too smoothly, something had to be amiss. Where in the hell did this gorgeous guy come from? Why wasn't he wrapped up with a lover in sheets pulsing his hips to some smooth jazz? Was this a joke, Voxie is going to ride with him, right!?! He is introduced to me as his riding partner for the day. She laughs, I smile, he winks. Then he introduces himself as Nathan. All I could see were his voluptuous lips and I determined that I would kiss them today. Swoon.

He gets on the Honda CBR something or other and there is a seat that is specifically up a couple inches, this allowed me watch over his shoulder while we rode. I have been a passenger on motorcycles, wheelers, horses, it's all the same. You never lean into the turn, find the center of gravity and enjoy the ride.

Nathan was complimentary of how relaxed I was for riding with a stranger. I held barely, loving the thrill of danger as he went faster and faster down the freeway weaving in and out of vehicles. The drivers had agreed on a destination and independently knew how they wanted to get there. We separated from James and Voxie and took the route through the city, more to see, he informed me.

Oddly, I wasn't scared that I was away from my friend or had no idea where we were or where we were going, it was too late now to revolt or object. I had to go with the flow. I would think about the night prior and how out of control I was yet again, embarrassed. That thought was dismissed quickly as my Inner Goddess would take over and empower me. I was a hot milf, riding on the back of a hot bike, with an incredibly hot man. I was immensely turned on as I lightly played his washboard abs with my right hand.

At stop lights we would make idle chit chat. That had to stop. I didn't want to know about him. I just wanted to enjoy being this close to him and the huge engine vibrator between my legs. I started saying innuendos in his ear that piqued his attention and his eye's smiled through the shield.

I wanted to thank this Adonis for his time and tour guide like skills. I started by catching his eye in the side mirror with a flash of my tit and playing with my nipple. He let me know that he approved with a nod of his head. I continued holding his gaze while I caressed my longer strands of hair near my face and pulled them near my lips drawing attention to my mouth partially open and breathy. He was paying close attention now. I let go of the hair and nibble lightly on my pointer finger sensually feeding my oral fixation. My nails had just been done recently and still tasted of acrylic and soap while I flirtatiously played with my lips and mouth.

I sensed that he might want a taste of me, so I obliged. My hand went from my mouth to his as we jetted down the road. In this moment, I needed to free my orgasm that was rolling up inside of me. The hand on his abs slides down to his crotch and I held his erection while my other hand found the reverberating bodysuit snap that pulled tight against my clit. I slid it to the side. To unsnap it would have reduced my sensation that had me on the edge of climax already. I used my moist fingers from my mouth and his to feel my pulsing mound and lower lips. He couldn't see what I was doing so I shared a taste of my nectar with him and then brought myself into a sexual spasm that peaked as I pressed hard and firm into him and he could feel me quiver.

We met up with Vox and James and took a trip around Lake Minnetonka. I was thankful that I wasn't going to have to be alone with my escort or I would have felt obligated to get him off. I wanted to be selfish, just like Freaky had been. I got dropped off back at Voxie's after stern instructions to follow her home to avoid traffic around a sidewalk festival that blocked the most direct route.

My knight had a date with his daughter and couldn't be late, chivalrous and cute but totally negated any idea of me seeing him again. He was so into his child and I was so selfishly into my exploration it was silly to even humor the notion. I never saw Prince Charming again and will never forget having sex with myself for him on the back of his Honda.

I go back to my house and regroup. Voxie and I plan to attend another event together the following weekend and I have some lose ends to wrap up like the one with Northland's Finest.

This unique fellow contacted me through a message and was very interested in photographing me. This is an easy entry point for most pervs. They get women who are searching for affirmations about their body through art or accolades. Once you get naked then they seduce a woman through teasing or touch until it feels too good to say no.

Northland's Finest was an elderly man and this was his way into a woman's vagina these days. I met him for coffee, because meeting strangers has become a hobby for me at this point. I am so curious about other's stories and pasts that I don't see sexual intent as a deterrent, it's just managed.

A very thin man, in his late seventies, with dark rimmed glasses and a wide brimmed straw hat sits comfortably in the corner by the fireplace, away from others. This must be him, the only single man in the place. I am taken back by his age only because it hadn't been discussed at all, he seemed frail. Now I am feeling sorry for him and proud of him at the same time.

I sit across from him and he asks me to move closer. I slide over a seat, he's harmless. He proceeds to tell me his whole background in environmental sciences and planting trees for the state of Minnesota. He loves to work with his hands, he reaches for my knee.

This man had a spark in his eye when he talked about women that was eerie. His approach was unique in that he charged you for his time. I assume to get buy-in and create legitimacy. He also said that he had a studio full of medical equipment. I probe, pardon the pun.

He starts telling me how his first meeting with any model he does a through physical examination. He claims he needs to know the model's body better than they do. He starts using his hands as he explains nothing is off limits.

He is starting to perspire as he shows me with a napkin the way he splayed the labia to expose the pearl of her essence, a weird cross of Anatomy and Physiology and origami. "This," he says, "is the Beauty Button." I chuckle internally as I remember the wind in my hair a few days earlier while finding my own Beauty Button, and now I am here. I sense the sun going down with the lack of light and start wrapping up this meet and greet.

As we walk outside he lights his corncob pipe that was packed with cherry tobacco. A sweet smell in the air that reminds me of my father. My dad was a brilliant ecosuperhero, this man thought he was too. Odd that I entertained him from the start, maybe he reminded me of my dad. I had nothing better to do that late afternoon. I listened as if he had a chance, said goodbye with a peck on the cheek and went home and blocked him from ever contacting me again.

The next item on my agenda is getting some work done on the house in exchange for a sexual friendship. I had a short in the lighting in my bedroom since 2011. Scott was not interested in the work associated with finding the cause. Maybe with the right motivation this issue would finally be resolved.

Heygetoverhere was the guy I found. He was married, so no relationship wanted, outside my 40-mile bubble yet still willing to come up and check out my mess. He was not an electrician, he was a House Inspector. He assured me that if it was a minor fix he could handle it and he'd bring tools.

There was a lot of sexual inuendo in our conversations. I met him in the parking lot of a grocery store halfway to make sure he was okay. He had a beautiful bouquet of flowers waiting for me in his car. He was super sweet and funny, I brought him home.

Heygetoverhere got right to work and checked every possible thing he could think of without reaching a conclusion on my light problem. I said goodbye with a kiss and sent him on his way. I was learning to get what I wanted out of these encounters of the first kind and that I didn't owe the fellow a damn thing. I'm sure he left with blue balls and that wasn't my problem. I know water and electricity don't mix but I would have been wetter than hell if he had gotten my lights to work.

Voxie informs me she has got me a ticket to the Rubber Ball. A BDSM fashionista's dream come true. Rubber Ball USA is hosted by Bondesque, my favorite upscale kink and fetish shop in Minneapolis. The event is a Latex and Fetish wear Gala, people come from all over the world to get dressed up in Leather, Rubber, Latex, Electrical Tape, and extravagant costumes ranging from goth and vampires to geishas and babies. I pictured it being like a feast for my eyes and brain. What better way to be exposed to various things than participation in an organized colossal apex of power exchange?

I had heard about it on the radio but was starting to watch my money. I had a party to host and it was going to be a classy event. I told her I didn't think I could afford to go. Voxie rarely takes no as an answer, she had one of her suitors buy us the last two Gold Access Passes. I felt like Charlie in Willie Wonka.

Immediately, my brain starts to obsess over what I will wear. There was time to plan but I knew that Voxie would have the final say. We chatted about options in my closet and hers while I FaceTime her from my bubble bath. We talk about the itinerary for the weekend and said goodnight.

I hear my Skype ringing at 2 am. It could only be one person, Alex. He didn't call me often. We had set times for talking so he would be clear from his wife. It startled me out of my sleep and I answered.

"Hey Beautiful. I'm sorry to call you in the middle of the night but I needed to hear your voice." He says.

"I wasn't really sleeping anyway. What's up? I mean, what do you need Sir?" I replied sleepily.

"Good girl. I can't wait to hold you." He says. "Good night Love." And he's gone.

I knew I was going to meet him although I hadn't confirmed the changes with him yet. I wonder what's going on that he felt compelled to call unexpected. I'm sure he is waiting for the confirmation that I am coming. "I can't wait to hold you?" was planting a seed. I realized I had power over him.

I think I wanted to meet him to call his bluff, challenge the fortitude of our dynamic. I had an attachment to this pixelated face on a screen. I guess this is what my ex went through with his bimbo in Iowa when I was pregnant. This is different, I'm not married, and I have no intention of stealing him from his wife. Was I really going to do this? Was it nuts? Yes, and yes.

The next morning, I matter of fact like message to Alex is short and sweet that I made the changes and that I couldn't wait to meet him in person either. We didn't talk much between that day and my departure which had me nervous. I stayed calm and if nothing else I was going on an adventure to places I never would have chosen to go and by myself.

Ramsey was still noise in the background and checked in on me regularly, even after the “break”. He was suspect as to why my trip was happening so fast. I didn’t have the heart to tell him that I was meeting Alex. Instead, I shared that I was getting a Brazilian Massage from BigHands40 on Thursday he flipped a lid. I then had a reason to say I needed to get away from him for a bit and that he’d be blocked until I got back. He didn’t like it.

Thursday night came fast. I drove and drove and drove for what seemed like forever to BigHands40’s apartment. He was a Brazilian bronze color about 5’8 with huge hands. He was very muscular across the shoulders and had no neck. I was surprised by his teenager like smile complete with braces at age 40.

His apartment was small but clean. Upon entering, his massage table was obviously positioned in the middle of the living room with the appropriate linens and support pillows. Everything looked legit, he is a masseuse just like he claimed.

As I turned to put down my coat something catches my eye over my right shoulder. On the wall, arranged neatly, are swords of all shapes and sizes. Also, against the wall, a table is set up with all kinds of toys and impact tools.

I confirm that I wanted a massage and that I wasn’t there to play, he understands. I look for a place to undress and it occurs to me that this man has already seen me naked in my pictures from the profile where we met. No need to hide I mutter to myself. I start undressing and neatly lay my clothing on his couch. He helps me onto the table face down first.

I have had many massages. I would get them mainly because of my back and hip, today was for enjoyment purposes only. Big starts moving his hands through my hair to relax me. He has an accent and a lisp, so conversation is distracting. I opt out by moaning and cooing letting him know I'm into what he is doing.

He responds like a puppy given positive reinforcement and rubs and kneads my shoulders and neck with strong intentional direction. He moves down my spine and fans his fingers around my ribcage and sliding up along my side boob. Down to my outer butt cheeks and down my legs.

I read his profile, from it I understood that he loved the female body, the curves, the soft skin, the small of the back, the dainty feet. When he made his way to my feet I was surprised when he bent my knee to insert my toes in his mouth. I giggled. His hips were level with the table and I could feel his erection as he brushed along my hands loosely hanging off the side. He slurped as he sucked on my long second toe, longer than my big toe by more than a centimeter. He lingered on my feet for a while before his hands started wedging between my upper thighs in rhythmic oiled movement that cleared the way more and more with every stroke.

Here it comes, I thought. Big is a trying to make his move. He did not. Instead he glided his hands all over my thighs and butt even through the crack. He instructed me to roll over and I did. This time he started back at my feet and my feet massaged his package conveniently because of where he was standing. I found this cute. Hands started up the legs one side then the other. We made eye contact and he slipped his hand between my legs and moved it briskly as if massaging my inner thighs inching closer and closer to my clit.

I could have said no, I didn't. After all, I was there for a Brazilian Massage. I didn't Google it to see what it included, I assumed this is what makes it special. Big brings me to several orgasms with just his hands. It was amazing. I was a quivering puddle of oil, pussy juice and sweat. I needed that. I needed a man that could do that for me all the time.

As I say goodbye and thank you, Big accepts a gratuity and a hug. He flounders over himself at the pleasure of serving the Queen. His parting wisdom was offered as a gift to my Royal Highness.

"Queen, live in the present, don't dwell on the past or future because neither exists and always remember that women lie about sex to get love and men lie about love to get sex." He bows his head and kisses my hand goodbye.

Big offered his service often and sends cute pictures of his dick dressed up in costumes from time to time. I have seen him at Ground Zero since then and awkwardly catch him staring at my feet. We stay in touch and we meet again later.

# Chapter 23

The party we attended next was at a private home on a lake somewhere Southwest of the Metro. They were having a lot of people out and offered tours of the lake on the pontoon boat. Sex is happening all around us. I never would have imagined sex parties happening in some of the places we went. This lake house was beautiful architecture and landscaped immaculately. This was the place for Nasty Nancy's Gang Bang.

The interior of the house was dated and needed a lot of repairs, obviously a lot of partying going on in this house. Large tablecloths and beach towels were nailed into the window trim to keep nosey neighbors away. The sounds coming from the house were immutable. There were four rooms set up for play. Nasty Nancy was on a bed that was the focal point of the basement level by the bar and walkout to the boat.

I remember walking into the kitchen with fruit and booze and looking around and wanting to clean and organize everything. The point of the party was not to be the ultimate party host, it was to fuck or watch fucking, or go on a boat ride. The second and third were my intention because of having my period. Mother Nature has started messing with my cycle making predictability a variable. At least I won't have it for my trip abroad. I am approached by several guys wanting to play and my excuse holds no water with them. One guy is literally flushed when I tell him I am on the rag like he is ready to erupt with excitement. I stick to my uterus and say no.

I sat on a bar stool and watched Nasty get pounded by five or six guys and got bored. Nasty was trying to be a good little slut and take every cock that came in view. The guys at this party were not Adonis' and many had limp dicks that she couldn't get to come, and it got hard to watch as my cheeks started to hurt for her. Why is it that men having public sex think that they need to make facial expressions like porn stars? It's corny and flashes my mind back to bad porn of the 70's and 80's on VHS.

I slip my clothes back on and walk out back to the boat. The host of the party is getting ready to take a group out for a sunset cruise. I hop on board and share a seat with a surly looking Latino man who introduces himself as he moves to the side to make room for my ass. His name is Jose. We chit chat for the whole ride as I snap pictures of the beautiful pinks, oranges, reds and yellows in the sky. Jose is at the party with his partner Gia. Later, I stumble into a playroom where Gia and Jose are fully engaged in fucking. She is laying on her back and sees me.

"Is this the one you were talking about?" She says to him. "Damn, you have good taste. Why don't you come over here Darling?" She reaches for me with her arm.

"Not playing today. Maybe next time." I respond. I leave the room almost embarrassed for interrupting.

LeFreak has shown up and Voxie and him exchange words. He is told to leave. She is fierce and protects the shit out of me. I appreciate it and I feel overwhelmed by it at the same time. I need to learn how to handle these situations on my own. I am not hers.

After a few more cocktails and watching Nasty fuck another half dozen guys, I'm ready to go. I start looking for my friend and I hear her screaming. She went on the last boat ride of the night and there were too many people on board. The boat started to sink when it slowed to the dock.

The front end was under water and Voxie was holding her camera above her head trying to keep it from getting wet. Jose was on the boat too and carried Voxie into more shallow water. She swooned and fluttered her eyelashes at him, giving him a grateful courtesy. She changes clothes and we leave.

In the morning, Sunday, we go to Market. I buy flowers for her apartment to remind her of me and thank her for her hospitality. After meandering around for a bit, I head back up North and she Ubers home, at least that was the plan.

I head home but Voxie has a detour to Jose's place for a hook up. By the time I got home, 2 hours, Jose was no longer partnered to Gia. He was serving Voxie. She did it again.

Gia had been with Jose for years as his partner. They were both dominant and Gia liked to top men, Jose was a jealous Puerto Rican that expected his woman to heel. Somehow, they had survived everything up to Voxie. It was subtle at first, Jose tried to balance both women. That was not acceptable to my friend and she would constantly lore him away from Gia, especially if she got wind of set plans.

It was game on, challenge accepted, choose me or choose her in an ultimate elimination round. It didn't take very long for the strain of Voxie as a new shiny distraction wedeled away at the foundation that had been shaky at best between Gia and Jose.

Jose and I kissed a few times randomly, he had chosen her, and I was not interested in being a conquest. I treated him like a big brother and he was a perfect gentleman in all aspects. For as much time as we spent together and in very close quarters I figure this wasn't the easiest for him. We often slept together in bed naked and cuddling.

I would have conversations with him while Voxie would orally distract him. He was our escort and protector. He enjoyed his freedom and that was the challenge between these two love birds. Voxie wanted to put him in a cage with a collar and a leash.

I invited them to come Up North for a weekend so that I could be home and packing for my trip and we could work through the plans for the Beehive Party. I was getting very overwhelmed and Voxie was happy to take over. Loki went to spend time with her family for the weekend, this made the house a clothes optional zone.

We used Jose as a cook, a landscaper, and a male model that weekend. We had bubble baths together, nude sunbathed, and relaxed in our skins. What an amazing freedom to just be unclothed and unencumbered. With friends that can touch, hug and kiss you without getting aroused and having to fuck. Like children running around free after a bath, releasing the negativity and constraints of rules and should dos.

Clothes are so symbolic if you think about it. Underwear goes back to leaves in the Garden of Eden, Bras to harness the female breasts that can feed and titillate, and the remaining clothes of righteousness just cover our inner selves one layer at a time. This must be the draw to nudist colonies or communes was my deduction.

The Beehive Party was getting close and vetting needed to be done. I just wanted to have a whopper party but Voxie took over the reins and started turning people down left and right. If they didn't meet her strict obstacle course for entry they were DENIED and blocked. I was open to inviting two hundred people figuring only about thirty to fifty would show. It was a huge commitment for people to chunk out prime summer weekend days to lie to their wives or families and come pitch a tent in my yard. I was irritated with Voxie for stripping down the list to eighty. I gave up and focused on hosting.

I went shopping at Sam's Club alone to give the couple some time alone. I purchased the paper products and the meat for food. I also bought bulk toiletries for good hygiene like toothbrushes, deodorant, mints, enemas, and baby wipes. I turned into the Martha Stewart of the Sex Parties. Using my own experience, I wanted to provide a class act event.

I knew I couldn't pull off Eyes Wide Shut type stuff, but I really wanted to. This was my one shot to provide a special party that would be remembered. Next Summer I may not have the freedom to do this, I may find a guy that isn't into it, what if like Cinderella's wish I "poof" back to being vanilla. This is my Summer, it's now or never.

I meet up with a fellow from Duluth that I have been chatting with casually. His name is Joe and he is home from the service. A member of the National Guard, I was reluctant to play with him until this day. I had been sexually teased and taunted by Jose and Voxie all weekend. I reached out to him with a booty call which was empowering as hell.

We met, he got in my car and drove to a dead-end road in the woods. Joe must have used this spot before based on his knowledge of where to go, I only let that thought in my head for a second and remembered that I called him for a hook-up. I was horny and going to take what I wanted.

Joe noticed how pent up I was and had a look of excited challenge in his eyes. He was a military man, so I expected stamina, which he delivered. If I had premeditated my actions my wardrobe selection would have been very different.

I had gotten a Ford Escape after the engine blew in my Mustang on a trip to visit Gwen. In a pinch and in an upside-down loan I got something that was more practical yet zippy. Joe and I test drove that cars interior and suspension.

Starting in the front seat fondling each other while I essentially ate his face was the warm up. His seat went back to free his bulging cock from his jeans. I was frenzied and had to have this glorious specimen in my mouth while I rubbed his abs. He was big, tall and wide, veins exposing his level of excitement. We decide to move to the back seat and pull the front seats up as far as possible for space.

I sigh as I am typing this because it was so good. He sat in the middle of the bench seat and I straddled him. Using the oh shit handles above the windows, I was spread. The back of the car bounced and rocked, and he thrusted. We came in multiplicity. There was so much sweat, juice and cum that I had to use my socks to clean up, one for me and one for him. It was my Ford Sexcape from that day forward. I choose to leave it there and never contact him again. I am a player.

My company leaves. Loki returns to the house and I catch her up on all that she has missed while we laugh over wine and whiskey. I grumble about the money I spent, and she pipes up with "you'll never be too broke for mascara." She's right. We prioritize what we want, don't we? Another Loki quote that I love, "A dick a day, keeps the Dr. away." Words to live by. She is a wealth of wisdom, always an encouraging word. It's no wonder she was placed in my life strategically. We realize that my international travel is merely a week away and I start packing with her help.

I am not a light packer. I understand now, that backpacking across a country or continent would be a huge challenge for me, like everything else if I set my mind to it I would learn to hike like Reese Witherspoon's character in the movie Wild. Her character learned to acquire only what she needed and to shed or leave behind things that she didn't need any longer to make her load to carry easier. What an amazing concept.

My need to be the consummate Girl Scout and be prepared for anything had already been shaken through the divorce and all my experiences after. I am wanting to knock the socks off Alex in public and behind closed doors, my practical thinking loses this battle. Between packing for every weather possibility and every play scenario I could imagine my suitcase was filling fast. My black paten leather 6" heels made space management difficult, but I wasn't leaving them home since they were the perfect accessory for my legs and ass. I stuffed the pockets of air through the shape of the shoe with bra and panty sets. Viola! Quite pleased with myself, I am ready to go with exception of toiletries and electronics.

I started put my passport in my backpack and remember why I even had one. On my 40th birthday my Mom asked me a big question. It hadn't been a great year for me. My suicide attempt in June and running away to my Sister's afterward had landed me in a treatment center. I subsequently got committed because I didn't want to go home to my douchebag husband and wouldn't follow instructions. After three months of institutionalization and threatening me with electro-shock therapy, I quickly pulled in line. Three days later, I was deemed sane enough to be discharged into my Mom's care for outpatient therapy.

How does someone go from crazy to functional in three days? I wasn't crazy, that's how. I was trying to get out of an abusive situation with no help. I think my Mom felt responsible for my happiness which is honorable but not truth. She asked me what was on my Bucket List that I really wanted to do. I told her I always wanted to go on a cruise. She mailed me a card and copies of a cruise itinerary, she and I were going together. I needed to get my passport.

I think my brain has my Mom's age stuck in her 40's to this day. That is when she seemed the most vital and happy. She had fallen into caregiver mode as my Grandma reached the end of her life and it aged my Mom dramatically. She was recovering from a double knee replacement and her modality was affecting her zest for life. It was a physical push for her to do that trip and I appreciated that she wanted to help me achieve a huge life dream.

I remember the trip as being enlightening about how different we were. I wanted to cut loose and dance, hike, sail, swim, and do everything. She was looking for quality girl time and relaxing by the pool, the sand was too hard on her knees. The only way I was able to go on a trip like that while married to Scott, was being chaperoned by my Mom. I didn't want to be babysat.

We did a ziplining excursion together with the help of a transport guide climbing up the mountain. I swam with sea turtles, snorkeled, had little monkeys climb all over me and try to steal my gold earrings, and saw beautiful sites as we traveled the Eastern Caribbean. I took a local boat tour of St. Lucia while we were at port and Mom stayed behind.

There was plenty of rum punch going around being dispensed from an igloo cooler in flimsy disposable plastic cups. The passengers we all paired off and entertained by the comedic relief of the boat captain. I am sure the alcohol helped fuel a split-second decision to spontaneously take a dip. The engine was idled as the captain told us about this beautiful rock arch that had been filmed in the Pirates of the Caribbean movie called The Love Hole. I started taking off my shoes and socks.

I wasn't interested in what he had to say, instead I was interested in doing something I'd never forget. I dove off the boat fully clothed into the splendid green-blue water with a goal of swimming through the arch. I wanted to be loved, maybe swimming through The Love Hole would help. I'd try anything. The guide wouldn't leave me there, that would be bad form.

I come up from under water and hear splash, splash, kerplunk. I started a movement. Other people wanted to do the same thing and wouldn't until I started it. As I approached the arch, I look up and there is a young native boy about seven or eight sitting on a cliff ledge watching us and he carefully climbs down. He gets to the flat platform under the arch, in the shadow from the sun. He is laughing and smiling, totally joyful about our rebellion. Simply aware and present, enjoying folly.

The captain has out his authoritative voice and is calling for us to return to the boat. He uses the cruise itinerary as a threat that he won't leave but the big boat will. I was in the lead, as I had started before everyone else. Once back on board, I was scolded but didn't care, smirking. I made a memory that I can still go back to in my mind as if I were there right now.

I don't remember if I told my Mom about that or not, she's learned a lot by now. That was the only stamp in my passport. I had so many blank pages to fill up. I was getting more and more excited by the day. Voxie and Gwen thought I was foolish. I would champion Alex as a gentleman and an upright citizen of the neighborhood watch in his community. He called me Love all the time, so he must care about me, right?

I was regularly checking in with myself to be sure I could deal with this going badly. I was nervous but in a joyous wonderment kind of way. I had room on a credit card for an emergency. I was educated enough to figure out travel arrangements and everywhere I was going they spoke English. I could always phone a friend, Loki. I'd be fine.

I parked my car at Voxie's and she dropped me at the airport, she gave me her request for fried egg gummies that aren't sold in the USA. A hug and a kiss goodbye and I'm on my adventure alone. I got through TSA and waited for the flight to Amsterdam departing at 8:47am. The flight would be 21 hours long with a layover in Boston. This is what it took to get over the pond. My trip was two weeks long and four of those days were touted as travel and jet lag days.

# Chapter 24

As my row is called I am in awe of the size airplane I will travel on. Hard to believe this huge bullet can fly across and ocean. I think about the risk of crashing into the ocean for a minute and start talking to a lovely couple seated to my right. Midwestern Caucasian, mid-thirties couple on a trip for their anniversary. She loves windmills. I fib a little and say that I am traveling on business, well it is. The seat occupant to my left is putting his carry-on in the overhead compartment.

"I guess I am your neighbor for many hours," this man with a thick German accent says, "I am Brankov."

"Very nice to meet you," I reply as I shuffle in my seat like I was still a hundred pounds overweight, "to Boston or Amsterdam?"

"Amsterdam this time. I travel this flight a lot, I haven't crashed yet" like he knew I was nervous. I laugh like a little girl.

Brankov is an older man, in his seventies. Tall and thin and very sharp facial features that lend themselves to German ancestry. His is an Aerodynamic Engineer for Lockheed-Martin and has been drawing up plans for flying cars for the last thirty years. He has a home in Germany and California and all his children are grown. He is a widower and has put all of energy into his work, doing consulting and trouble shooting for big companies all over the world. I learned all this in the first hour. Our lay over in Boston is short and we continue the long leg of the trip.

The attendants are passing out cocktails and I have white zin. I also took a muscle relaxer to help me sleep. The couple to my right were watching separate movies with headphones in. I decided to listen to my eBook, relax and day dream about how Alex would take me to a hotel room and not let me touch him at first. I imagine him blindfolding me and sensually teasing me with sensory deprivation until I can't take it anymore. He'd put cuffs on me and tie me down, and he would have his way with me. The element of fear and power exchange was a huge turn on.

I can smell my pheromones releasing as I daydream. Brankov must have smelled them too. My head is back, my eyes are closed, I feel a hand on my knee rubbing and caressing me. I look to my right and Betty Crocker has fallen asleep. I chuckled to myself, atta boy Grandpa. This would be interesting. I wore a maxi dress, so I would feel like I had a blanket over me for sleeping. Keeping my head back like I am unaware, I slowly shift my hips and uncross my knees giving access.

Brankov accepted my invitation and starts to inch up my skirt hem. Once he found my skin under the cotton fabric, his hand found my knee and gently rolled inward. Every now and again he would grab my inner thigh and shake the skin and vibrate my labia. I peek again at the couple to the right and they are both passed out. I tilt my hips forward so Brankov has full admittance to my sex.

He used his aerodynamic knowledge to take the path of least resistance and get directly to the point. I am very wet already due to my fantasizing about Alex and this was hot in a weird #metoo situation. I didn't ask for this, at no time did I tell him anything that should have been perceived as sexual except maybe that I was traveling alone.

I saw him as harmless and that I was doing a good deed for mankind. Karma is a thing. He was relentless. It was all I could do to not moan outwardly in pleasure and to contain my writhing. My eighteen-inch seat width and invisible air wall between Betty Crocker's personal space and mine was close to violation a couple times. Brankov was enjoying playing with my lady bits and showed no signs of stopping even after shooing him away for a reprieve.

I excused myself to go to the bathroom and he followed me. I scooted into the tiny washroom where I gave my pussy a needed rest. I took my time with no regard for Brankov's desire to join the Mile-High Club. It wasn't happening. I passed him on my way back to the seat and his erection was like a pup tent and I tell him he should take care of that and continue.

Returning to the seat, Betty Crocker and Mr. Clean have come awake and are chatting up a storm. The attendant is coming around frequently for drinks, collecting trash, etc. Brankov is having another drink. I am not. I open a physical book in my lap over my crotch, with my legs crossed. It is finished, I hope he gets the message. Before too long, we are preparing for landing in Amsterdam.

Brankov gives me his name and phone number on an airline napkin. I feel awkwardly pressed to reciprocate so I give him a business card, not my personal number.

I am amused at my first escapade within my adventure. Onto Ireland, where I meet Sir. He will be waiting for me at baggage claim. I hope he isn't disappointed in my appearance in person. I continue doubt my worth and value which is an underlying theme still in my thought life. Will it ever end? Maybe, if I find the right Dom that values me as a prize possession I will see myself as good enough, but doubtful. I know Alex isn't Him, this is a transient affair at best, but I can learn from him.

I step off the tram to Baggage Claim and there he is, Sir. He stands confidently with his legs planted firmly below his shoulders, hands in pockets of his jeans. His crisp button up shirt is a pink plaid, real men wear pink, right? It looks fantastic against his olive toned skin. He is my height, I usually like taller men. This was a feature I never even considered since I never saw a full-length picture of him. He gives me a kiss on the cheek and reaches for my hand. We briskly follow the swarm of people to the carousel for my bag.

I spotted my bag coming down the ramp and we position ourselves to grab it. We had a short lay over until our joint flight to Ireland. I don't share about Brankov. I became immediately shy and feel small in his presence, a feeling I do not reject but put away for later consideration. Right then, I was overwhelmed that I had really done it. If nothing else went right, I had traveled over 3,500 miles to meet a man that I wanted to spank me.

Give me a gold star or put me back in an institution, I did it. I found great joy and satisfaction from the fact that like swimming through The Love Hole, this was an experience no one could ever take away from me. Things, even people, jobs, come and go but I would have my memories for as long as Alzheimer's stayed at bay.

The trip with Alex was unremarkable. He was flabbergasted that I came. He had to work very long days. I spent a whole lot of time alone. The alone time was boring at times, but good. As an American Tourist I went to the Zoo, because animals in Ireland are so different, not.

I visited the Irish Museum of Modern Art and saw some fucked up art renderings of Passion According to Carol Rama. She did a unique blend of sexual and psychological art outside the rules of societal norms. She used bicycle innertubes, animal hair and taxidermy eyeballs and eyelashes to complete watercolor and oil paintings. Wild and weird but fascinating.

I visited the Cliffs of Moher and Galloway on a bus company tour for a day. Everything outside the city looked just like the postcards. Gray skies, grassy hills, rock walls and sheep, that about sums it up.

I am directionally challenged so there were many times that I got lost and had to use my walking GPS on my phone to get me back to the hotel. I learned that in the old days the Gregorian bold colored doors were used by the drunk men on foggy nights to find their way home by counting doors or stumbling upon a specific color. I employed a similar tactic to get acquainted with the paths I frequently traveled and how to know I was close to home base.

I hated the food in Ireland and I don't drink beer, not super appealing. The World Cup was happening, and the Irish were in it, so the orange, white and green pendent flags were draped from building to building all over. The busy bar time was at lunch and after work, dead at night. We were there a week and I was done with Ireland after 3 days.

I wish it had been reversed and I had been in London longer than Ireland. I loved the hustle and bustle of the Tube. I had so many options of places to go and things to see. While I was there, I visited the Palace and the flag was flying signifying Her Majesty's presence. It was her birthday.

I bought two 100% wool sweaters from a shop that still smelled like sheep and Turkish Apple Tea from the Twinnings store. I saw the Eye in The Sky and Big Ben. I loved the architecture and the old feel of the buildings. Inside most were completely gutted and modernized but from the outside it was a snap shot in time. The shopping was fabulous, I found food I would eat, and the energy was sparkling everywhere except in our room.

The oddest part of the time with Alex was that he couldn't play with me. He wanted to but wouldn't. He claimed he didn't want to hurt me, I was too special. I wonder if he felt guilt, because I did in fact, fly over the pond and see him. Maybe he was all talk from the beginning and hid behind the screen of his computer. Maybe he didn't want to lead me on any more than he had? Maybe he was getting feelings and it scared him? Who the fuck knows.

I got to cuddle with a man while I visited some places I never would have gone otherwise. My hotel and room service were paid for. It wasn't so terrible. My ego was bruised because I let myself be disappointed. Men are fuckers and talkers. This is a new belief.

We parted in London for the trip home. He cried when he said goodbye to me. I wasn't sure what to make of it all. I had spent a lot of money to meet him and I was no closer to feeling fulfilled. I knew this was an ending. I didn't like how I felt but it was clear when I was honest with myself that I had no more time for this man.

When I returned to Minneapolis and retrieved my car my feet were raw from wearing cute pumps through the airport. I rummaged through my luggage for my sneakers and for the life of me couldn't find any socks. I grab the dry crusty cum, sweat and fishy juice covered socks from the backseat of my car and rubbed them on my body. I slipped them on and thought about how fitting it was that I am wearing them now. I just marked over any trace of Alex with another man's essence as an act of closure. It was weird but felt right, I needed to do something. It didn't matter who it belonged to, I didn't belong to Alex anymore. I was done.

We continued talking for about two weeks and then I started cutting the cord nicely. I continued to be just friends with him, which I think was weak on my part because I didn't want to be mean. He had been there from the beginning of my journey, he had built up my self-esteem by simply calling and genuinely wanting to talk to me. I needed more than talk now. It was time to throw away the crutches and start walking on my own.

I had my plan, my experiment, my limits all that was ahead now was time. My vision for myself was getting clearer. My tolerance was waning for foolishness. It was time to get serious. A party to attend and a party to throw now were my focus forward, and Alex was in the rearview window.

There is little talk of Alex after my trip from Loki or Voxie, Gwen is quite outspoken with I told you so. I lick my wounds and hit the red carpet at RubberBall eyes wide open and free again. Voxie and I have arranged to do wardrobe changes half way through again like we did at Lady K and Jim's event. It causes confusion and makes people do a double take when they've seen you dressed one way and then BAMMO! You look totally different. It gives us a full on second once over by all the ladies and men that appreciate our feminine wilds.

We run into familiar faces and see celebrities in the kink world. We mingle and saunter around making new friends with people based on their costumes. Leather hoods and masks, crafted pup and pony heads, horns and tails are just some of the accessories that set people apart. Our early outfits were more glamorous dresses that had cut outs and slits. The half-time show revealed us in barely any clothing and mostly glitter.

My favorite character was the Baby. A 6'4" man, wearing a blonde wig in ponytails, white tights, and a pink baby doll dress that had sear sucker and white rose buds across the top. He was wearing a bonnet and had a pacifier around his neck while holding a beat-up teddy close to him. He was accompanied by his wife who is also his Mommy. She threatens to put him in the corner if he doesn't behave. This charming couple have three children at home and they live out this fantasy whenever they can without the children knowing.

It was a fabulous night at the ball and then we went out on the town, with slightly more clothes and the vote is tacos. I thought I had fun people watching at the ball. La Hacienda Taco Heaven was the place to be at 3am. I don't think they ever close. It was theatrical eye candy of the Rhinestone Cowboy kind. I was not in the mood for Mexican, so I go find a table. There is a line that snakes through the restaurant wrapping around the tables.

All you would see were the huge cowboy hats black and white, did they represent good and evil I wonder. The fancier the clothes, the fancier the hair on the Chickas. Mohawks and rat tails are on any man without a hat. It looks like a giant cock fight is going to erupt at any minute. The girls are all very petite and wearing form fitting, short, dresses that are about two sizes too small. I don't know what to look at the bedazzled cowboy boots or the stripper heels. I don't know that I have ever seen this much diversity in all of Minneapolis. I am already on to the next event in my mind, my event.

# Chapter 25

I was working on making sure every detail is covered. Voxie was still vetting people and assures me it is going to be great. I typed up an information sheet of all the things going on for people to do during the day, where the closest Walmart was, and House Rules. Simple things like no one was allowed upstairs without expressed permission from me or Voxie, clean up after yourself, do not have sex in my daughter's room, etc.

The party was for the whole weekend. The idea was that people could attend when it suited them. We would have a fire every night and people could camp on the front lawn. Clothing had to be worn outside and no fucking outside during business hours. I thought we covered everything. We waited for people to arrive.

I had food for a hundred, fourteen people showed up. The fact was that my house was an awesome place for a party, but my location was not. I was tense and didn't play because I was worried about everybody having a good time or being available if someone showed up. Moderators from the group were supposed to be there to help and they didn't show up either. It was another disappointment.

Now if I had advertised it as a Gang Bang there would have been a lot more people because it would be a sure thing that a guy would get to stick his dick in something. When it is just a party and it is sex positive there is only a chance someone will hook up. It wasn't marketed in a way that attracted a swarm to the hive.

Voxie sensed that I was disappointed and put an ad on Craigslist to see if she could get some new blood. We had some interesting people show up and then leave because we weren't what they were into. Then there was Thrasher, a local politician, pretty boy face, 30 something that was open to anything. Voxie and Jose were arguing because Jose wanted to fuck Gwen and Voxie was newly distracted by Thrasher.

He had a different name when he came. Voxie got her grips into this naïve openminded little boy and he has never been the same. While Jose had a threesome with Gwen and Clara in a tent in the yard, Voxie took Thrasher upstairs where we tied him to my king-sized bed. I had installed O-ring brackets to the four corners for just such a need. Once secured we blindfolded him and tortured him with tickling. He hated it but was laughing the whole time.

Once he sufficiently learned how to address us as Mistress or Queen, we stopped tickling and started with clothespins. Wooden clothespins still have bite, the plastic ones give too much. First his nipples, then his ear lobes as we emasculated him further by putting lipstick on him and writing possessive phrases on his chest in sharpie marker. He was a good little whore boy. Clothespins around his balls and up his shaft that we would jostle to cause increased sensation. We wouldn't let him cum, we wouldn't let him touch us. He was sent to bed alone on an air mattress with just a pillow and a blanket and one of my old dog collars around his neck. I liked it.

When I directed our pet to an air mattress I heard a loud moaning coming from one of the bedrooms. I did a quick inventory of attendees and the only two missing were Raj and Loki. It was Loki howling in sexual pleasure. I noise I never knew existed. She was having fun and I was happy for her. We collectively giggled as she proceeded to come over and over, and over again. When one of them emerged from the room it was for water or condoms and they would be back at it.

Sunday morning and Thrasher was still at the house. Voxie and I donned matching houndstooth and pink frill aprons and nothing else to cook breakfast for everyone. While sitting at the table, I turned my head to see who was coming in the door and instead see an 8" flaccid cock laying on my table like a Genoa Salami attached to a man named Rio.

Rio was incredible with dick jokes and innuendos. Not one opportunity would get by him. He brought his play partner along who he had been with for sixteen years, a longstanding swinging non-committal friendship. Rio was a gem and kept everything light hearted and was happy to help so long as he could be nude and swinging his bat and balls around.

After breakfast is when Thrasher officially got his name. Voxie ordered him upstairs. She had been educating him on implement play and I had all the implements a gal could want. We tried a bunch and I got to practice using a few that I had hoped would have been used on me by now. The one that earned him his name was my wooden paddle.

A paddle made of oak, like they decorate for the fraternities and sororities is what I had ordered from Amazon. I had left it home when I brought toys to other's houses because it was heavy and cracked hard when you hit something with it. It scared me. I drilled holes in it myself and there were some splinters sticking up still even after sanding it. This was what made him thrash. I got used to the weight in my hand and the angle to hold it at that supported my wrist. I had full control, it's all about the follow through I reminded myself from being a bowling instructor at nineteen.

I started light and he would chuckle almost goading me to swing harder. I slowly escalated to a full-on swing batter, batter, batter. I knocked it out of the park a couple times. His ass was a nice shade of red and he started to perspire. With each lick of the board he would dance around, thrashing. His pride was getting the best of him but Voxie and I knew what to look for and he always had his safe word “Beehive” to call out when he had enough.

A few more well-placed cracks and we decided that was enough for our newbie, but he was hooked on the pleasure and the pain. It didn’t hurt that two dominant women were making him their play thing, which is a fantasy for many men.

The party ended, and the cleanup began. So much work. I wouldn’t need paper plates, napkins, solo cups, toothbrushes or tissues for years literally. We froze the taco meat and the big box of wieners were treats for the dogs. Loki tried to use the fruits and vegetables, a lot went in the trash. My kids were coming home in a couple days, so I had to deflate all the air mattresses and sweep up all the glitter and pretend like it never happened. It was a lot of work for other people’s pleasure. I checked another thing off my list.

Little did I know that my daughter, who I asked to not come that weekend had figured out what was going on and told her father, sisters and brother. Apparently, my sex party was scuttle butt all over town. I could do nothing here without judgment and consequences and my family was the root of it all. I wasn’t trying to hurt them, I wasn’t involving them, I took measures to protect them. My happiness was not a concern for anyone, just my misery. Some would say, serves you right. I say, bullshit.

Voxie calls and says I have got to come down right away. There was a model call for an artist and we need to go. Art? I had always loved art.

I was taught that the body in art form was beautiful and to be admired and respected. This would be in my wheelhouse. My selfies were all from my point of view, would a real artist view me as art? I'll leave it to the artist to accept or reject me and combine the trip with picking the kids up from the airport.

Voxie and I get to the Soapbox Factory and meet Blake. He has a vision, he is a dancer and photographer, and it is a live naked exhibit. Whoa, looking for exit. It is for two nights, first night is closed for photography and practice, second night is open to the public. We all sign releases. There is a wide variety of people present, all body shapes and sizes.

Voxie is there, it is ok. I can do this too. I go behind a faux wall and remove my clothes, nervous and awkward at first, liberated and fearless once I understand and own my part. I am beautiful just the way I am. I am a beautiful piece of art that will hang on people's walls. I am a model undressed from expectations and rules. No sexpectations.

Day one was hard, day two is easy. I feel like I am moving underwater. Every motion is very slow and deliberate, so the photographer and visitors of the exhibit can appreciate the form of the body attached to it, my body every inch exposed. It has been a stretch for me to accept my body since I was a child.

The exhibit is called Rock.Skin.Bone. Between sex parties, fetish balls selfies and live exhibition art, I no longer fear man and judgment, and I embraced the skin I'm in. Voxie and I rolled in dirt and got twigs in our hair, posed in piles of bodies, together and alone. Stretching up and over, left then right, tight into a ball and sprawled out, elongating my exploration, changing my beliefs, bravely being me. I found my value here.

Finding my worth changed everything. I always knew I didn't want to be disposable. I always knew that I wasn't into the idea of giving myself away. I always had a burning query going in my head that looked like the scales of justice. I was over having to do and provide more than my part. I liked the idea of being a Goddess. My attitude shifted from that experience on there was no alter ego, I was Queen Bee.

# Chapter 26

My weekend employee forwards me a message from the business that she says she can't understand. It is Brankov. He wants to meet me when he is in Minneapolis. I deciphered the message because I was used to his cadence and accent from the flight. I ignore it.

The next day, he calls the office again and I answer. The way he says my name sounds beautiful, here we go with the accent again. He is coming back to town next weekend and he is staying at The Grand downtown. He wants to take me to dinner and he has a gift for me.

This was different. I enjoyed his company on the plane. I was going to be in the city anyway. I could do dinner. I was excited about the idea of him giving me a gift. Gifts are my love language, I learned that a long time ago. He was lonely, and I felt sorry for him.

My kids were busy enjoying their Summer with friends they had missed for a month while they were away. The social calendar was slowing down. I was re-evaluating my cash flow and spending after the trip, the ball, and the party. It would be nice for someone to spoil me for a change.

I spend the night at Voxie's place and she pouts when I leave. I chose not to tell her who I was seeing because I wanted to figure this one out by myself. I wore a dress and did my hair like I was going out on a date. It was a date, with a much older man.

I was sick of the men that had nothing to offer a queen. If nothing else, this man was intelligent, and I could talk to him about things other than sex. Brankov only knew that I was writing a book, oddly I hadn't shared what it was about. He had no idea what he was getting into.

He meets me in the reception area and invites me up to his room, so he can get the gift before we proceed to the hotel restaurant for our reservation. I was skeptical but followed him. I knew I didn't have to go to his room. I knew I could have said no. I had enjoyed our encounter on the plane. I was not afraid, no regrets, and I wanted a nice steak dinner.

He goes in his room, I wait inside the door. He grabs a gift and hands it to me. I opened it and there were beautiful truffles inside with a white envelope. I am confused, and he is smiling. In the envelope is five crisp one hundred-dollar bills.

"I don't know a whole lot about you, so I thought I would let you pick out something you really want." He said.

"I don't know what to say Brankov." I reply quizzically.

"I am so thankful you agreed to spend time with me. I don't get to be in the company of a beautiful, intelligent woman like you. Let's go eat and you can tell me what you will buy with it." His thick German accent explains.

We leave the room. I am still in awe. Is this really happening? Are there more men out there like this? This feels like I am doing a good deed. Is it wrong for me to take it without "doing something" for it? Wait, does he think I am a prostitute?

I am eating my steak, looking across the table at this gentle, fragile, smart man. I wait for the shoe to drop, it doesn't. He enjoys my companionship. I thank him for dinner with a peck on the cheek and leave. I give him my cell number so the employees don't get in the middle.

On my way home, I receive a text thanking me for being such wonderful company and making him feel like a man again. I am touched and reply. He will be back in two weeks and he wants to know if I'd like to establish an arrangement.

What does that mean? I tell Voxie what I have been up to and she exclaims "He wants you to be his Sugar Baby!!!"

"Have you ever been a Sugar Baby?" I ask Voxie over tea and a banana one morning.

"Why do you ask?" She replies with a grin that says, but of course you silly woman.

“Well, I think I need to start looking at how I can find a way to stay kinky in my own mind and make some cash in the real world, like to pay bills while I’m having fun.” Said in my best business proposal speak.

What the heck does that mean? Aren’t Sugar Babies usually twenty-year-old’s with smoking bods and perky tits? What does a Sugar Baby do? Is that really what he wants? Thank God for Goggle. I spend the rest of the night researching the Sugar Bowl. It’s not football ladies.

I had always wondered how Voxie had endless money to do things. She has a man that helps her with airfare, another that has her Lyft account on his credit card, and another that randomly buys her extravagant gifts. These men don’t expect sex, just attention. These men are starved for female interaction. Most are married and love their wives but are missing affection and respect.

“It’s a role, just like in scenes. No emotional involvement, just an exchange of your time for a donation. The more mysterious you are the more intrigued they become. Like a character in your book.” She explains. “The pool of men will be mainly vanilla and just want to take care of someone, to feel purposeful. I’ll show you where to go but I don’t want you to be disappointed. It is fierce competition out there. The different and exotic are not in demand.” She loves teaching me and being the expert." I wonder what else she has done for money.

Voxie, once again, is a wealth of information. I ask her how she knows all this stuff and she says she has her ways. The questions get turned back on me, "where do you think I get ...?", "How do you think I afford that ...?", "Who do you think paid for our RubberBall tickets?"

She helps me to respond to Brankov. I need the cash at this point. My year of exploration has cost me a lot and it was worth every penny. I plan to see him again and now I know what this is. I am Queen Bee and I'm gonna make some honey. Brankov was the test and I passed.

I decide that I am not going to limit myself to just the traveling finger fucker. I find a high-end site online and start a profile. This was now part of my exploration. I had moved past did I have any value to what exactly is my value? And more importantly was my value only attached to sex? Money was a good metric.

"Rule 1. Never discuss money in the beginning, landing a meeting is your goal." Instructs Voxie. I am relieved there are rules.

"Rule 2. Interview them. Don't be too eager." She stares into my eyes and knew this is a weakness for me.

This was enough to get me started. I started pouring all my attention into Sugar instead of Fet. I would still go to the cities and go to the clubs but with no agenda of exploring because I was in my next phase. Exploring my worth, what could I get for my brand. I looked at my budget and was looking to make 5K a month or more to supplement my ledger. Brankov was a small fish in a big pond. I was going fishing for Tuna.

I started chatting with a few men and found that I didn't want to give myself away. I felt guilty for about a minute and got over it. The idea of making men pay for my time made me feel incredibly powerful. I was a lot more mature and sexually charged than these little girls that didn't even know what made them appealing. My background in customer service bode well for these blokes because they were going to get their money's worth.

I was a wildcard to this cast of characters. I was confident that I could rock their world and keep them paying. I was older but so were they. I was a Sugar Baby that they could take out places and introduce to family without judgment. I genuinely appreciated attention and I loved to shop. What an awesome part-time job?

I had checked off a lot of my curiosities about sex and now I was going to use my maturity, femininity and smarts to get what I needed...cash. I was getting myself off with my vibrator, orgasms were not a need at this point. I was going to be picky from here on out with my pussy. I had done my exploring alone, now I wanted to explore with a partner. Having a new gig helped me be more selective about what I was participating in. Should I go watch someone on their back or make some green backs? The answer was easy for me.

In Sugar, there are unspoken rules of engagement. Certain ways to entice, the order of conversation verses negotiation, setting your limits, etc. I felt like an actress being paid to play the part Joe Schmoe's girlfriend. Only it wasn't just Joe, there was Mark, and ND Marc, and Danny, and The Cranberry Farmer, and more.

My trips to the cities were now for my process of deciding which man's money I wanted to take. Who could I stand to be with? Who had super compelling reasons for cheating on their wives? How creative was their justification for paying me to be their friend? I would schedule Three-A-Days. Usually located at a Caribou Coffee or Starbucks, I had interviews morning, noon and night.

Most of my suitors were from the cities which meant that I could negotiate more money for my travel time and expenses. I had three hooked for a monthly date, I could manage more if they were closer. Then I got a message from a man in Duluth. We met at Caribou on The Hill and we hit it off.

The Captain was a very affluent man that lived on the North Shore of Lake Superior. He was divorced and had two college aged girls that lived away at school. He had a social circle but didn't want the pressure of dating at this point. He just wanted someone to talk to and cook for.

He liked me, and I enjoyed every minute we spent together.

I could picture myself living in his house. I loved watching the sailboats glide by the huge glass floor to ceiling windows while he fucked me from behind. He loved my sexual freedom and that I was so vocal and orgasmic. He paid my mortgage payment for three dates a month.

This made sense to me. I am sure that it sounds absurd or disgusting even to some people. My work ethic, plus my love of sex, and my natural desire to be feminine were the perfect storm. If I felt yucky about a companion, I thought about how I was making him feel. I really didn't care about the long-term effect of anything. I was making men happy with my company, if sex happened it was on my terms.

I think back to one day after leaving a beautiful date with The Captain. I stopped at Holiday to gas up ad grab coffee. I was chuckling as Roxanne by Sting was playing on the radio. "You don't have to turn on your red light…Roxanne." Roxanne, listen…men are fuckers, turn on that light and own your power.

Relationships are arrangements. I arranged to be treated like a lady, respected, prized, fussed over, spoiled, and fucked if I desired, and all I had to do was be nice. It got boring after a little while. It didn't take long until my part-time job felt like work. I was still interviewing to fill some gaps and be ultra-efficient with my travel and expenses.

On a day the Universe decided, I had an unplanned add on to my trip. I had two interviews scheduled and was planning to be home for dinner. A fellow I had been chatting with asked if I was available to get together for dinner and he was accommodating with location. I agreed.

I pulled up to Zuppa's in Maple Grove. As I walked toward the door, I texted him that I had arrived. He responded that he knew, he was watching me from his Cadillac. "I see you, and you are so beautiful." I look around the parking lot and he is emerging from his flashy red car. He was older than his profile picture had portrayed, silver hair, and dark round glasses that made him look very studious.

We exchanged pleasantries and proceeded inside. We ordered a light meal and carried our trays out onto the patio and watched the sun go down as we talked for over two hours. I knew that night. We parted ways with plans to speak more later. I called Loki and told her I found THE ONE!

Until next book…

Patricia

.

## About the Author

Patricia Engelking is a complex woman that has a heart for living with purpose. Her creative wilds make her life colorful and rich. She will never go back. The river referred to in the title of the book was symbolic of the work that needed to be done to find her true self. Trudging across a river is dangerous and challenging, slippery and you get wet. Being a person that learns best through experiences, Patricia dives into her coaching, topics, projects and life lessons with enthusiasm and wonder. Her authentic delivery and openness make her speaking engagements life changing.

She currently lives in Minnesota with her husband, read book two, and her dog Cantankerous Risotto or "Tank" for short. She enjoys reading, meditation, nature and monogamous, amazing, kinky sex with her partner all while being a happy accomplished woman. She devotes time to her relationship, empowerment coaching, public speaking, and writing as her responsibilities and all other adventures are icing on the cake. In her free time, she is working on her PhD.

Her next book will be about entering and navigating life acknowledging her choice of Power Exchange with a partner.

She loves mail so send messages directly to her through her website ThePowerExchange.co.

Made in the USA
Columbia, SC
20 January 2019